HELL CAN'T WAIT

Satan's
One Hundred-Year Master Plan

By Robert Cybulski Jr.

Hell Can't Wait
Robert Cybulski Jr.

Glowing Light Incorporated
Leola, PA

Library of Congress Control Number: 2016914878

Copyright © 2017 Robert Cybulski Jr.

ISBN: 978-1-944187-18-7

All Scripture quotations designated (NASB) are taken from the NEW AMERICAN STANDARD BIBLE®, Copyright © 1960,1962,1963,1968,1971 ,1972,1973,1975,1977,1995 by The Lockman Foundation. Used by permission.

Matthew 5:29-30 (NASB)

"If your right eye makes you stumble, tear it out and throw it from you; for it is better for you to lose one of the parts of your body, than for your whole body to be thrown into hell. If your right hand makes you stumble, cut it off and throw it from you; for it is better for you to lose one of the parts of your body, than for your whole body to go into hell."

Dedication

Thanks to God for the inspiration.

Thanks to my wonderful family for the patience.

Foreword

"Free My People"

For many, many years, while praying, I would constantly hear the same request. Over and over, *FREE MY PEOPLE* would appear in my head. Year after year, I would look up with despair and asked, "What does this mean? God, please tell me what this means." After searching for countless years, the message finally connected. God wanted me to expose Satan's grasp on his people through this book, *Hell Can't Wait*.

As an information technology professional, I often wondered, "How am I going to do that?" I decided that although I am not yet an author, I can be God's messenger and His message is clear. As I began to write *Hell Can't Wait*, the "free my people" message crystallized. My role in this message began to make some sense.

While writing this book, I began to understand that many of us, frankly, don't know what to believe anymore. We seem to be less and less worried about sin while the world seems to be more and more worried about a short-lived world. We as a people have lost touch with the reality of the consequences of sin.

To bring further clarity, consider for a moment that hell could be real, as referenced in the Bible:

Matthew 25:31-47 (NASB), The Judgment

But when the Son of Man comes in His glory, and all the angels with Him, then He will sit on His glorious throne. All the nations will be gathered before Him; and He will separate them from one another, as the shepherd separates the sheep from the goats; and He will put the sheep on His right, and the goats on the left.

"Then the King will say to those on His right, 'Come, you who are blessed of My Father, inherit the kingdom prepared for you from the foundation of the world. For I was hungry, and you gave Me something to eat; I was thirsty, and you gave Me something to drink; I was a stranger, and you invited Me in; naked, and you clothed Me; I was sick, and you visited Me; I was in prison, and you came to Me.' Then the righteous will answer Him, 'Lord, when did we see You hungry, and feed You, or thirsty, and give You something to drink? And when did we see You a stranger, and invite You in, or naked, and clothe You? When did we see You sick, or in prison, and come to You?' The King will answer and say to them, 'Truly I say to you, to the extent that you did it to one of these brothers of Mine, even the least of them, you did it to Me.'

Then He will also say to those on His left, 'Depart from Me, accursed ones, into the eternal fire which has been prepared for the devil and his angels; for I was hungry, and you gave Me nothing to eat; I was thirsty, and you gave Me nothing to drink; I was a stranger, and you did not invite Me in; naked, and you did not clothe Me; sick, and in prison, and you did not visit Me.' Then they themselves also will answer, 'Lord, when did we see You hungry, or thirsty, or a stranger, or naked, or sick, or in prison, and did not take care of You?' Then He will answer them, 'Truly I say to you, to the extent that you did not do it to one of the least of these, you did not do it to Me.' These will go away into eternal punishment, but the righteous into eternal life."

In light of this, "free my people," and the book *Hell Can't Wait* begin to produce an overwhelming and compelling concern. If hell is real and some of us could actually end up there someday, what does existence look like in such a place?

Hell Can't Wait is an exhilarating tour through the struggles of hell. These struggles manifest themselves in the power the Joint Chiefs seek, in the agony of disobeying Satan during banishment to the place known as solitary refinement, and in the inability to build relationships with humans who were once our fellow men and women.

As you devour the book or the book devours you, I hope the knowledge of hell will prayerfully save you from sin and the path to ultimate demise.

This book will free YOU!

Prologue

CNN Update—Year 2015

It's dinnertime in the city that never sleeps. The sun is low on the horizon, ready to depart from the day. Olivia and John fill their plates with the gourmet spread Olivia has prepared, another delectable result of her chef training. As they sit down for dinner, they turn on the TV and choose CNN to catch up on the news. The broadcaster, Sally Richards, catches their attention for a brief moment. *"We now go live to our reporter in New York City, Orlando Rodriquez. Orlando, what's happening at the top of the Empire State Building?"*

Orlando is standing at the base of the Empire State Building, one of the world's premier landmarks. Tonight, there is more than the typical New York City hustle and bustle as a number of helicopters clip just above him adding to the din.

Orlando responded to Sally, *"Thanks Sally. We are not quite sure what's happening at the moment; however, here is what we know so far. About an hour ago, a woman ascended to the top of the Empire State Building. She seems to be very distraught and suicidal. That's why you see the New York Fire Department trucks behind me just in case she jumps. She has been frantically waving a blue folder and yelling something about reading. The police have made it to the roof and are attempting to dialogue with her—"*

"Do we know who she is or what the folder is?" Sally interjected.

Orlando paused before responding, *"Sally, we don't know much more yet, but we're hoping that within the next thirty minutes, we might know more."*

Sally looked up and replied, *"OK, we will check in with you soon."*

Olivia peeked at John. "What do you think that's all about?"

"Probably just some cult or crazy. So, how was work today?"

Olivia looked up from her plate, which held a generous serving of bow-tie pasta with a chunky vegetable red sauce and a side salad, which she had lightly tossed with a balsamic vinaigrette dressing.

"Work is work. I'm getting a little frustrated with Jimmy, but whatever."

"What about Jimmy?" John asked, his curiosity piqued.

Olivia really didn't want to talk about Jimmy's regular advances, so she was relieved when she saw Orlando pop back on the television, drawing John's attention away from the discussion.

"Thanks Sally," Orlando replied, standing in the spotlight. *"As promised, we have talked to the local branch of New York's finest, and they believe they have identified the young woman at the top of the Empire State Building as Julie Ratelle."*

As a picture of Julie Ratelle and information about her flashed on her TV screen, Olivia dropped her fork. Her chin almost hit her plate. She immediately recognized the woman as her friend Julie.

Speaking in the background, Orlando continued, *"Apparently, Julie was a model student at MIT and has been working for a large computer chip manufacturer, although she recently joined some sort of religious cult. The cult seems to be into satanic worship."*

Olivia glared at the television and carefully read the information about the woman. It was close to her friend Julie's background, but with slight differences.

Sally climbed back into the breaking news story. *"Poor young woman. Do we know what is in the blue folder she is waving yet?"*

Orlando donned his best sarcastic look and replied, *"The authorities think she has some message to Satan. Oh well, it looks as though they will have her in custody soon."*

Sally, with an equally sarcastic look, said with slight sadness, *"Thanks, Orlando. We hope the authorities can help this young woman. Now we'll hear from Jeana. How's the weather around the nation, Jeana?"*

The weather forecast started blaring on the TV. Olivia found the remote and muted the sound. She looked over at John who was chowing down on his dinner. Finally, she said, *"Did you see Jules on top of the Empire State Building?"*

In his own world of multitasking, John was texting a friend about getting together to play golf the next day.

"Can't say that I did," he replied.

Somewhat upset, Olivia said, "John, how could you not watch? Julie is one of my best friends!"

John raised his eyebrows. "So, what's that to me?"

Upset now, Olivia grabbed his smartphone.

"Johnny, Julie looks like she needs help. I don't understand CNN commenting that she joined a cult. Shouldn't we try to contact her?"

Equally upset, John yelled back, "Why should we care if she has gone over the edge? Now give me back my phone!"

Olivia smiled as she thought, *At least I have his attention.*

"John," she said, "she did not join a cult. In fact, she just started going back to church again about six months ago. I think they made that part of the story up. I think we should go to try and help her!"

Annoyed, John said, "Please give me my phone back! Look, the TV and the authorities said she is bonkers. Let her be! I can't believe they just made stuff up about her."

Olivia looked at him. "Maybe you're right."

She gave his precious phone back to him and looked away, thinking to herself, *What if we are wrong?*

Someone else was also watching the broadcast, and he knew John was wrong—very wrong.

Chapter 1

Another Day in Hell—Year 1890

Satan stood in his "office" surveying hell through the "window". His concern grew as he analyzed his market reports on the number of souls arriving in hell. The results looked worse than ever, especially after losing the critical battle of slavery in the United States. For years, slavery delivered a steady stream of unexpected souls to his kingdom.

His regime was at a critical juncture at this point in history. If this flat growth in soul acquisition continued, good would reign over evil. He had to do something!

According to the reports, his latest Darwinian attempts to dispute God's existence had a minimal impact. Even with these reports, most of his closest advisors and minions were in favor of continuing the philosophical debate against the existence of God and Jesus. Satan was frustrated. Although the arguments for evolution had grown stronger, Christians were still proving to be the most powerful faction on earth.

Satan glanced at his desk, spying the two strategic plans to boost his soul-a-meter. One plan, the safest choice, recommended continuing with the current strategies—like Darwin's theory of evolution. The other plan, presented by a new addition to hell, Sal, not only had him quite confused, but the old guard of hell despised it. In fact, Satan's chief of staff, Chad, openly cursed the plan. He consulted with Satan and explained that it would be the ruin of hell when it failed to work. Satan shook his head as he contemplated his options. He just wasn't sure what to do, and he didn't have the desire to implement both plans.

He should trust what Chad had to say on the new plan. Chad reviewed the plan for weeks. In his view, the major downside is that it didn't promise any major increases in souls to hell for many, many years. In fact, the biggest increases were seventy to one hundred years away. Sal argued that his plan was a better long term solution with the goal to get more souls over many years, not just next year. Sal had a great marketing resume. During his bitter existence on earth, he was a tremendous advertiser who always broke the rules and challenged societal norms. He won his unfortunate ticket to join Satan's gang because of his unending practice of bending the truth and infidelity to his wife. In the beginning of his tenure in hell, he was a welcome addition. Over time, he upset Chad on multiple occasions. In fact, Chad began to invent sinister new ways to torture him.

Satan read the title of the plan again, "Satan's One Hundred-Year Master Plan." He was aghast! *One hundred years—wow—that's a long time*, he thought to himself. *Why should I wait one hundred years?*

Sal answered that question so many times he was getting exasperated. He contended yet again, "It's simple. The plan's foundation is deception, supported by a series of diabolical inventions. If you start to deceive overnight, everyone will see the trick. The plan's deception will take time to SLOWLY mature, but once the deception is in full effect, I promise you unbelievable and amazing results."

It is difficult for the king of deception to debate a good trick. However, one hundred years is a long time. He decided to take a break and look at the plan in more detail another day.

Chapter 2

Sal is Summoned

About one month later, Satan began grasping for straws after yet another abysmal monthly report. Satan decided to start reading Sal's plan again. He opened it to the introduction and began to read, *"Let the human creature go to church...."* He threw the plan down on his make-shift desk and roared, "No wonder Chad is so upset! This is ridiculous! Don't worry about the humans going to church? That's insane!"

He grabbed the plan again and threw it at the wall, thinking, *Why am I wasting my time reading this trash?*

"Summon Sal and Chad!" He yelled to his secretary.

He would tell Sal he needed to stand down on his ludicrous plan and that they were going back to the strategy of arguing against the existence of God.

About five minutes later, Chad arrived and immediately said, "You called, your majesty? I'm always at your evil service."

"Chad," Satan said, "we need to put this plan to death. I just started reading the introduction and consumed the part about not worrying about humans going to church. I don't get it. Why were we even con-sidering this rubbish?"

"I'm glad to see you are coming back to reality, sir," Chad responded. "I agree the lad's theories are all based upon pure specu-lation, and some of his inventions—you've got to be kidding me! I'm sure that if some of his inventions were possible, the humans would put them to good use and regulate evil out of them."

"I have not read about any of his inventions," Satan intoned. "However, the introduction was pure stupidity! When he gets here, he will be corrected," Satan screeched.

"I can't wait for him to get here!" Chad drooled.

Sal received his summons from Satan and somehow knew it was bad news, especially when he heard that Chad received a similar summons. He put out a call for help from his consultants on the plan— Harold, Barb, and Sam. They had previously agreed to accompany him and help plead his case. Sal had been waiting for this moment for six months. He had prepared his counterarguments for a long time and was now as ready as he could be. He chirped, "If I can prove my theory, I can take Chad's position as number one on the Joint Chiefs of Staff." Sal was never happy to follow anyone, and was not about to start now in this hellhole, *no pun intended.*

He turned to see Barb enter. "What's up, Sal?" she asked.

Sal looked away. "I've been summoned to his office. I'm sure he is going to tell me to stop talking, working, or even thinking about the master plan. He will also have Chad with him. Chad hates this plan and has managed to get the Joint Chiefs to recommend against considering it."

Barb snarled, "How can I help? I've never liked Chad and would love to see him get eliminated."

"I could use your support," Sal replied. "Unfortunately, if we lose, it could get worse for you. You could be placed in something like solitary refinement for eternity."

Barb grinned. "Hmm. Although I don't need more torture, I am sure Satan will support the plan once he understands. I will join you. How can he not implement it? It all but guarantees more souls than Satan can count!"

While they were talking, Harold and Sam entered the space. In Harold's human existence, he was one of the top lawyers in the United States. Using elaborate technicalities, he helped many who were guilty of murder get out of prison. One example was the case where he defended a murderer who had killed six children. He even confessed his guilt to Harold in their first consultation as lawyer and client. Harold contended that the evidence was secured without due process, convincing the jury to find the man innocent. One year after his release, the killer destroyed three more lives prior to his subsequent conviction and capital punishment. Now in hell, the killer greets Harold with evil smirks every time he sees him.

Sam was a top ranking marketing executive for a major alcohol company. He personally helped many get to hell. His marketing campaigns tripled sales at his company, and as a result, the number of alcoholics in the country rose by 18 percent. In his spare time, he ran a gambling organization and solidified his trip to Satan's house with his lust for sex. It didn't matter whether his partner was married or unmarried. He could not and did not abstain. Sam teamed up with Sal on the plan right after he started making it.

Sam and Harold listened intently to the tail end of Barb and Sal's conversation.

"Count us in," they both growled.

An evil grin formed on Sal's face. Since his entry into this horrific place, he had become accustomed to the constant pain of existence. He had thought his arthritis and subsequent cancer were painful, but the daily pain in hell was a hundred times worse. He used to think regularly about escaping. Recently, he concluded that he would be here for eternity. He decided that if he was going to suffer, everyone on earth should join him.

Sal looked at his group and said, "OK, let's go see what damage we can do."

Chapter 3

Satan meets Sal

Satan and Chad had been waiting over thirty minutes for Sal. Neither of them had an ounce of patience. The longer they had to wait, the fiercer the fire burned within them. Finally, after about forty earth minutes, Sal showed up at the office. For some reason, he brought three other junior devils with him. Never mind the others; Satan wanted a piece of Sal. He started right in, saying, "Not only is your plan absurd, but you made me wait for the earth equivalent of over forty minutes. Who do you think you are?"

Before Sal could form a word, several bolts of energy hit him in the head and stomach. Next, he felt several blows to his head. The last punch or kick, he didn't know which, finally put him on the fiery ground. After several moans and a twist of his head, he saw that Chad was standing next to him delivering the overwhelming punishment. This gave Sal yet another reason to take dear Chad out of the number one position.

Sal's anger began to boil. As he crawled to his knees, Barb grabbed his arm. Before he could acknowledge her help, three more fire bolts slammed the two of them. This time, the two junior devils actually flew backward, the force of the blow denting the fire boulder wall that encompassed Satan's royal office. Quite dazed and confused, Sal could barely hear Satan's continued ranting.

"How could you devise a plan that tells humans to go to church?" Satan stormed. "Why don't you just tell them to pray all day? What are you thinking?"

Sal got to his knees and reached out to help Barb when he noticed Chad was about to speak. After listening to Satan's utter disgust and disappointment with Sal's plan, Chad remembered Satan had not read much more than the first sentence of it.

Snickering, Chad said, "Satan, sir, you obviously haven't read much of Sal's silly plan."

Shooting an evil look at Chad, Satan hissed, "Who gave you a speaking part?"

Chad grinned in mock humility before responding, "I simply realized that you had not read the section on Christian prayer. Perhaps Sal would like to explain that part of the plan to you?"

Enraged, Satan turned to look at Sal, who looked as if he wanted to speak. *Now the plan could possibly also include prayer?* His rage soared completely out of control. He hit Sal with five more bolts. Overcome, Sal lost consciousness.

As Satan meted out punishment on Sal, Barb attempted to jump in front of one of the bolts to protect him. Before Satan could respond, Chad delivered several blows to her, leaving her semiconscious. Satan finally relented, but only because he wanted Sal to have the capacity to hear his departing message clearly.

Satan looked at Sal's other two companions and decided to hit them with energy bolts as well. As the smoke cleared, all four of the junior devils lay sprawled on the ground. Satan turned his back to them all and looked out his office window. He would give them a moment to recover prior to delivering the last unfathomable blast.

Sal managed to roll over onto his back. He tried to open his eyes, but regrettably, at least one of them was not functioning. The working eye opened, but only briefly. He could not see much. He couldn't determine if his lack of visual clarity was due to the punishing bolts from Satan or all the smoke that engulfed the room. Sal did not want to move for fear of another lightning strike. He slowly turned his head to the side. He could see Barb lying flat on the floor. She wasn't moving.

Sal wasn't sure what to do next. His first thought was to just lie there, even though every evil bone in his soul told him to attack Chad. His next thought was to wait for Satan to calm down. Unfortunately, he was quite sure this would be his last chance to talk to the prince of evil. Sal knew it was now or never.

Just as he started to move, he heard, "Just listen to Sal for—"

"Chad is correct," Sal interjected. "The plan does not care if Christians pray every day. In fact, they can be encouraged to pray regularly. The premise—"

"Are you serious?" Satan interrupted. He grabbed the plan and threw it at Sal.

"This rubbish also encourages Christian prayer? You have to be kidding me. I will banish you to the holes of hell forever! You must immediately stop all discussion on this plan and the ridiculous ideas contained within it."

Sam started to speak. As soon as Satan saw his mouth move, he hit Sam with fire just as he had done to Sal, then Chad disabled him with a karate chop.

Sal marveled at how evil could stick together. Sal would remember to thank Sam, though "thank you" was not a term to use in hell. He wasn't sure how to thank him, although he knew he would find a way. He thought back to when he first arrived in hell. He remembered Barb thanking him for something, and then somehow, the ground swallowed her! She later recounted her experience in painful detail. She had been taken to a very dark place and physically abused in unimaginable ways. The memory from the experience haunted her regularly.

Just then, Satan spoke again. As he did, Sal turned his head just in time to see Chad's foot approach. He tried to roll over, but it was too late. Sal blacked out.

When Sal awoke, he thought he heard Chad say, "Shall we send them to solitary refinement, sir?" He saw Satan glare at his senior advisor before saying, "Yes, then we won't have to listen to anymore trash about a one hundred-year plan. As for that woman devil, I would like to visit with her. She has a lot of spunk." Chad knew the wishes of his master.

Chapter 4

Satan Encounters Barb

Once Chad sent Sal to solitary refinement, he carried Barb to a chamber. He thought about his own ambitions but decided to leave her for the master rather than risk crossing him. Reluctantly, he left her behind.

Barb slowly regained consciousness. She wondered what had hit her. She felt pain, but in hell, there is always pain. The pain centered in her lower abdomen and was as intense as labor and delivery. She yelped, howled, and began to cry. As she rolled over, she noticed that she was not in her normal habitat. She was on some sort of exotic looking bed.

Overcome, Barb rolled around in agony. When she attempted to stand, she fell to her knees. When she looked up through teary eyes, she thought she saw some sort of being hovering over her. She fell and cried out. She was forced to roll over onto her back, still in excruciating pain.

Barb thought she recognized the figure, but regrettably, before she could confirm the image, it was on top of her. Her pain intensified and she tried to get it off her. After several minutes of intense struggle and screaming, she realized she was under its control. She surrendered to it and eventually passed out.

Chapter 5

Solitary Refinement

As Sal awoke on the floor in solitary, his first reaction was relief. It was the first time in his existence in hell that he did not see or hear anyone. The ever-present crowd was one of the challenges of hell that grated on its inhabitants. There was never any alone time, and you were always being watched. Devils moved about, attacked, or screeched constantly. He shuddered to think more about this world that he now called home.

As Sal lay there looking up into the dark, he thought, *Wow, there is peace in hell!* He sat up and strained to look around, trying to remember if he had ever experienced an environment so dark. He remembered a trip to the countryside in a deep valley in the United States. On that trip, it was quite cloudy and neither he nor his fellow travelers brought a lantern. Sal remembered he could barely see to walk, even after hours of allowing his eyes to adjust to the deep darkness.

He raised his hand directly in front of his face. To his surprise, he could not see any part of his hand. *Peace and dark; they're almost as good as peace and quiet!* he thought. The quiet gave Sal a few moments to reflect on his meeting in Satan's office.

"Chad!" he cried out. "You will pay! I will be avenged."

To Sal's surprise, something seemed to respond to his outburst.

"Sal, what are you doing?" a voice asked.

"Who wants to know?" he responded.

"Sal, watch out," the voice cautioned.

"Watch out for what? Who are you?" Sal screeched with extra irritation in his voice.

"Sal, what are you doing? Sal, watch out!" the voice repeated.

Sal had been in situations like this in hell. He knew the last trait you wanted to show in hell was fear. The other devils drew energy from fear.

"Show yourself!" he shouted.

"Sal, what are you doing? Sal, watch out!" the voice repeated.

Sal decided that a direct attack was better than waiting for the unknown to attack him. He ran full speed in the direction of the voice. *Thud!* He hit a wall. The blow stunned him for a moment and the voice continued.

"Sal, what are you doing? Sal, watch out!"

Sal made a couple additional runs at the sound of the voice. Each time, he hit a wall. He decided that yelling at the voice was more productive.

"Leave me alone! Leave me alone!" he bellowed.

"Sal, what are you doing? Sal watch out!"

Sal's agitation level was high.

"Sto-o-o-o-p! Show yourself! I will kill you!"

"Sal, what are you doing? Sal, watch out!"

As Sal became more and more agitated, he felt little twinges on his skin. He swatted at them.

"Sal, what are you doing? Sal, watch out!"

As he swatted, the twinges turned to something that felt like little legs crawling across his body. They started crawling up his arm. He attempted to brush them off. It didn't matter because they kept crawling. He could not determine the size of the "crawlies." They seemed to be either giant spiders or mice. The more he brushed off, the more crawlies came. They moved to his chest and his back, and then onto his head. As he brushed uncontrollably, the crawlies decided to burrow under his skin. They crawled down his spine, across his ribs, then up through his esophagus, and ultimately, ended up under his face. Instead of brushing now, he tried to squeeze them out, but regrettably, he could not catch them. The more he tried to catch them, the more they multiplied.

"Sal, what are you doing? Sal, watch out!"

He began to run and brush at the same time. He ran and ran, hitting wall after wall. Finally, after running into walls at full steam well over a hundred times, he lost consciousness.

The next day, Sal returned to a conscious state and thought his experience was simply a nightmare. It was just another dream state to mess with his mind in the land of the weary. He looked into the dark and remembered how real the dream seemed.

"I'm glad that was just a dream," he said aloud, then waited. Nothing. *Great, it was just a dream,* he thought to himself, relieved. He decided to enjoy the dark and peace for a while. Just then, he thought he heard someone speaking. It was the voice. *Not possible!* The day repeated. In fact, every day, it was the same voice, the same walls, the same agitation, and the same godforsaken crawlies.

Over time, Sal's experiences grew more desperate. Once, as he lay squirming on the floor, he began to wish he were dead! Then, he wondered how he could be dead and wish he were dead.

The torture grew worse each day. After what seemed to be many months, Sal learned that if he focused on his plan, he could tolerate the crawlies and the voice for a couple extra moments before the situation overwhelmed him. He forced his mind to think about his master plan to the point that he started to recite the words he could remember from it. Chapter 1 was the introduction, and it helped Sal remember why he wrote the plan in the first place.

Sal's master plan began with no concern for human prayer or church attendance. "Let them pray and go to church every day!" Sal knew these actions would not matter one single bit as long as Satan and his minions were able to distract the humans.

One excerpt early in chapter one of the master plan read, "*Satan's current strategy is centered on convincing the humans that God and all his work does not exist. The concept makes for a great argument, but unfortunately, even Satan the master of evil believes in God, so why continue down a path that cannot be successful? The foundational aspect of the one hundred-year master plan is to distract humans. To accomplish this goal, the plan consists of a set of major innovations that will excel in distracting humans from the mission of Jesus.*

As Sal contemplated his plan, he wished he could get ten minutes alone with Satan. One on one, he was sure he could convincingly sell him on the merits of it. He thought and then screamed—the crawlies were back.

"Go away! Please go away!" he shouted. Nevertheless, the crawlies and the voice intensified. He ran around his room hitting wall after wall. The next thing Sal knew, he was lying on the floor and waking up to the same nightmare all over again.

Sal made many attempts to think of alternate worlds versus his daily torment. One day, Sal's mind wandered back to his life BH (Before Hell). He often thought of his earthly existence as a living hell. Back then, he always seemed to be upset about the world, his significant other, or his colleagues in his workplace. In fact, he could not understand his colleagues' desire to follow ethics and principles when there was money on the table.

He took a second and remembered his last 6-million-dollar deal. He was working to purchase a small enterprise that produced marketing and advertising materials in Massachusetts. The owner of the company was a Christian evangelist, and he did not want to sell his company for fear it would fall into what he called the wrong hands. To gain his trust, Sal even went to church with the man on two occasions. He had done a great job pretending to participate in the services, all while thinking, *What a bunch of hypocrites!* The people exhibited intense love for Jesus in the church service. However, once they left the church, they turned into mini demons. They would participate in gossip and complain about others right there on the walkways outside the church doors. He knew why Satan had so many souls in hell. He started to think of the joy he felt in taking over the poor soul's company and dismantling it piece by piece. With these thoughts of happiness, the crawlies and voices started again, causing Sal to shriek.

A couple days later, Sal lay on the hot floor, staring at nothing. His mind drifted to the witch he had married. When he first married Sally, she was a beautiful young princess who could not be satisfied at any level of their relationship. Unfortunately for Sal, after about three years of marriage, she decided to join a church. Over time, she began to dress more conservatively and developed less of a desire for wealth. It upset Sal. Regrettably, the more he tried to change her back, the more Christian she became.

Sal ultimately fixed the problem after meeting Jasmine, a stunning beauty with an insatiable desire for money and love. As Sal thought again of the great pleasure Jasmine brought him, the crawlies and voice came back with a vengeance. This time, he felt far more crawlies under his skin and the voice was much louder than normal. Again, he was unconscious after he ran into every wall possible.

Chapter 6

Satan Reconsiders

Sal awoke to a voice, though it was not *the* voice. *How can a new one exist?* he thought to himself. He thought he recognized it and tried desperately to place the sound, but could not. He waited for the crawlies, and fortunately, they did not come. Somehow, he knew, or at least thought he knew, he was in a different place.

Satan glared at Sal who was sprawled on the floor of his office. He still wanted to rip the young devil apart, but he was troubled. The Darwinian approach was making progress and showed potential, although, even at its best, the number of new souls coming to hell had leveled off—even dropped in some areas of the world. Satan discussed the situation with Chad and the Joint Chiefs. They believed he should just stay the course and more souls would come, though slowly.

Unfortunately, they gave him that assurance five years ago when he sent Sal and his buddies packing to solitary refinement. The situation did not improve. Just two weeks earlier, Satan read the first two chapters of Sal's master plan and responded the same as Chad. He hated it. It seemed unbelievably ridiculous—even obscene. The distractions and inventions were not even remotely possible!

Imagine getting more souls through inventions, Satan thought to himself. Going back even as far as the time of Nero, none of the great minds he obtained had even thought of such a plan. *Though in hindsight, those great minds of old were not all that great*, he mused. The "kill all Christians" plan wound up failing miserably. Satan still could not believe that such an obvious plan did not work.

Though Jesus and ten of the first twelve apostles met their demise via murder, somehow Christianity not only survived, but it flourished. Eventually, Rome even became the home of Catholicism. Satan marveled that though Rome had been his home and was a city filled with murder, infidelity, war, and every vice, it still became the home of the pope. *How did that happen?*

Back in the day, we killed Christians as fast as we could find them, Satan fondly recalled. *Obviously, we totally underestimated the power of martyrdom. That plan of old was so simple. Through fear and death, wipe Christianity from the face of the earth before it can get roots. Looking back,* he saw clearly that this had not been the best strategy.

Satan thought of how deeply he despised failure and sealed his commitment to discourage it by making those who failed him suffer bitterly. He pondered this for a moment. *Imagine suffering on a higher level than the normal suffering already in hell. What a concept!*

His desire for a new, higher level of suffering gave rise to the idea of solitary refinement. The first victims of solitary refinement were the founders of the "kill all Christians" strategy, implemented after Jesus' crucifixion. Satan never second-guessed his decision to banish them, nor had he ever checked the status of the twenty-two devils that he sentenced to the ultimate hell.

As Sal gradually gained consciousness, he could hear a voice again. He wanted to move, but was concerned that movement would attract the crawlies more quickly. As a result, he lay perfectly still. Every few seconds he would open an eye, only to be blinded by light. Sal thought it was odd to see light. He could not remember the last time he saw fire. *Could it be I'm not in my dark cell any longer?* He wondered.

After evaluating the situation, he concluded this was just another trick, so he remained silent and still. Then, he felt a slight nudge, peeked out, and thought he saw Satan. Fear gripped him as he worried that his situation could get worse. However, after a moment, he reasoned, *Right. As if it could get any worse.*

Sal felt another nudge and heard his name. He slowly rolled over and peeked again. He thought he might be back in Satan's office. *Oh, no,* he quivered, *that would be a completely new level of torture—even worse than the crawlies!* He squinted with both eyes, and indeed, it appeared as though he was in the prince of doom's office.

He turned his head slowly and caught Satan's withering glare. Satan was eager to see the effect of solitary refinement on Sal. He thought of his team's earlier days, over 1700 years before, when Chad had taken over as chief of staff. Chad saved his kingdom from utter destruction due to the fallout from the "kill all Christians" strategy. He had been instrumental in developing the "splinter Christianity" strategy that had been quite successful. Satan was deeply indebted to Chad. However, he had started to wonder about his objectivity since Sal arrived in hell.

Satan came out of his reminiscent trance to notice that Sal started to open his evil eyes. Sal dared to sit up and look around the office.

Satan glared at him, saying, "Sal, you have five minutes to convince me your plan is worth my consideration."

Sal glared at Satan, confused, still unclear why he was there. Satan waited for Sal to explain his plan, but the young devil sat silently, looking dumfounded.

"You have five minutes to explain why I shouldn't send you back to solitary refinement!" Satan threatened.

Sal began to grasp what Satan was saying, finally asking, "How— how—how long have I been in there?"

"You now have four minutes to explain the plan," Satan said.

Sal thought to himself, *This is another great conversation with this concept of a king.* "How long have I been gone?" he asked.

Satan's red eyes nearly cut through Sal. "You now have three minutes, and not that it matters, but you have been in solitary refinement for five years in earth time."

Sal almost collapsed at the thought. He had been in the ultimate hell of hell for five years. He wanted to tear Satan apart. His anger hit such a major boiling point that he decided he would *not* respond. He reasoned that if things had been going well for Satan, he would not be there, so Satan needed him more than he needed Satan. Though Sal wanted nothing to do with solitary refinement or threats from Satan, he would soon find out if he was serious about his ingenious plan or not.

Satan looked at him and roared, "You have one minute left!"

Sal recoiled and yelled back, "Get lost! Find your own plan! Go get a plan from Chad!" Then he turned his back on the prince of doom.

Satan couldn't control himself and fired two lightning bolts that hurled Sal across the office. Satan seethed with rage. "You imbecile! How dare you think you can be non–non–non–insubordinate!"

Satan hit the listless devil with three more lightning bolts until Sal was unconscious. The last bolt nearly split Sal in two and pinned him to the floor.

Satan exploded in rage and launched into the night sky of hell.

Chapter 7

Frankie Believes?

Though Satan's rage was incendiary, he thought long and hard about his decision to send Sal back to solitary refinement. He admired the ambition of the young devil, although he could not tolerate his in-subordination. *I am the king. Chad is the second in command, and that's all there is to it,* Satan thought to himself. *Or, is it?*

Chad was called in to "clean up the mess" in Satan's office. When he arrived, a devilish grin engulfed what remained of his face. Chad was delighted to find Sal buried in the floor of Satan's office.

"How could Satan go back to Sal again?" Chad asked Frankie as he used a pickax-like tool to remove Sal from the floor.

"What was Satan thinking? Sal has no real, workable plan. He is a silly and wasteful fantasy. Don't you agree, Frankie?"

Frankie looked at Chad and picked up the newly dislodged Sal from the floor. Though he liked part of the plan, as Chad's right hand and evil slave for hundreds of years, he was not about to disagree with him.

"Maybe the big guy is getting nervous," Frankie ventured. "Maybe he is worried," he added as he lost his grip and dropped Sal.

Chad shot him a dark look for dropping Sal. Then he said, "Frankie, you have doubts now, too? How could you?" Chad's anger boiled. He contemplated an attack on Frankie. "Tell me Frankie, why do you think the big guy is getting nervous?"

Frankie looked at Chad. He could tell this issue had become personal for him. He decided to ignore Chad's question and contin-ued to clean up the floor.

Chad grabbed what used to be Frankie's arm, which now looked like some sort of wing, full of red scales that resembled their fire red eyes. He looked into Frankie's evil eyes and said, "Why did you not answer my question?"

Frankie felt butterflies in his belly, but he finally decided to answer Chad's question. "Look, Chad, I've served you for a long, long time. We've shared many evil adventures. I've always been at your side. I would never question you. However, I believe Satan is uneasy with the status of hell."

"What does he have to worry about?" Chad shot back.

"Look at the soul meter charts," he said. "The number of new souls coming to hell has declined by about 2 percent per year for the last ten years. I believe he is losing faith in your plan. I really believe that—"

"Come on, Frankie!" Chad interrupted, simultaneously delivering an elbow to Frankie's head. "That's just a minor setback. We're going to bounce back better than ever with our current plan. I have no doubts. I just can't understand Satan doubting our capabilities."

"I hope you are right," Frankie growled back. Then he asked subserviently, "Can you help me with Sal?"

The two devils strained and threw Sal into a wheelbarrow. Frankie began pushing the wheelbarrow and started to wonder whether he could devise a way for Chad to embrace the young devil's plan.

As Sal regained consciousness, he noticed the dark once again. He had an odd sense of remembrance related to his current situation. He looked around. Without the fire, it was quite dark. Resigned, he waited for the voice.

Chapter 8

Barb Finds Out

Barb often wondered what happened to Sal. She hadn't seen him for quite some time. *Could they have killed him? Could there be death after death?* Barb thought to herself. *I must be going crazy! Death after death—seriously?*

The silly thought caused her to remember her time BH (before hell). While on earth, she often wondered about the afterlife. She was a saloon madam in the West with many girls at her disposal. She was personally responsible for helping many men feel good. She loved her girls and her whiskey. She could even remember getting into a heated argument with Hale Johnson, who went on to be a vice presidential candidate for the Prohibition Party. She was an advocate for free liquor! She hated the concept of temperance and would often show up at rallies to defend her beliefs and career! She remembered one of the rallies and felt some pleasure. This slight feeling of pleasure caused her to have a sudden pain in her abdomen. The pain was as strong as being kicked by a horse.

The discomfort was beyond the worst she could imagine as she snapped out of her pleasant daydream. She looked around what she called her abode. It was hard to call it a house. In fact, it was hard to call it anything. It had something that looked like walls, but if you made the mistake of leaning on them, you would fall right through them to the outside! These types of mistakes had left many holes in the illusion of walls. There was no hope of privacy. There wasn't any semblance of furniture. Each day cycle, she would find a spot to curl up and try to rest. Regrettably, the heat from the floor would leave burn marks all over her body.

Today, she longed for a fan or something cool to drink. If she couldn't lie down comfortably, she would settle for a place to sit. Alas, there was no relief of either kind in hell.

She paced around her abode. As she walked to the front, she looked up and saw four huge devils approaching. She knew what this meant. She shuddered. She froze. She cried.

When they loomed in her entryway, she stood motionless. On previous visits from these escorts, Barb had fought and resisted them. In response they increased the escorts from three to four as her feisty reputation preceded her. When they sent three she managed to break away. Regrettably, four were just too much for her. They would pin her and jump on top of her. Resistance would be futile. If she did not resist, they would just pick her up and carry her, although some would surely insist on licking her during her transport.

She tried to close her eyes. Some force would not let her eyes close. She knew her destination. It was time to go back to the exotic bed. Barb had lost count of the number of times she had been to the den. Regrettably, the experience was always the same.

As they dropped her into the lair, Barb was determined that this trip would be different. She would have a discussion with the ultimate evil one.

Barb could sense him approaching as the pain increased.

"Satan," she shouted out, "wherever you are, I'd like a word." Met with silence, Barb managed to get the words out a second time, although with much more strain and pain than the first attempt.

Satan observed her desire to communicate. He remembered the reason he had to have her. He remembered that he had seen few female devils with her determination and boldness. *Imagine, she is even trying to speak to me*, he mused. *She was not asked a question, nor was she presented a problem, and yet she speaks even through the pain*, Satan thought to himself. *Very interesting.*

Satan entered the room. She tried to speak again, but her voice wouldn't work. Her desire to speak intrigued the most evil of all evil. He was so intrigued that he allowed Barb to "dialogue" with him just a little. Satan gave her a hint of the world of solitary refinement and mentioned he was going to show it off to her one day.

Chapter 9

I Must Find Sal!

Barb returned to her abode and made a firm commitment to find Sal. After thinking about her next steps, she left the abode and wandered through hell, eventually stumbling upon the solitary refinement planes of existence. She had to find Sal and release him, though she wasn't sure how to accomplish her mission.

She forced herself to remember her last encounter with Satan and his description of the solitary refinement area. He said that to the individual, each area was dark and desolate. However, to the observer, there was enough firelight to see everything in the cell area. He mentioned that every once in a while, he would watch because the torture areas gave him new ideas for the capture of earthly souls.

Barb broke from her memory trance on solitary refinement just in time to realize that she had nearly fallen into one of the cell areas. She looked into the nearest cell. She was able to see a young female devil surrounded by around twenty devils who were viciously attacking her. Barb cringed. Though the female fought bravely, ten of them were on top of her in a matter of minutes.

Just as the last devil jumped on the young female devil, Barb lost her balance and cried out as she fell over fifty feet to the floor. She hadn't realized solitary refinement was on a hill. As she shook off the sting from the fall, she looked around, hoping her noisy fall had gone unnoticed.

As she looked up, she noticed that solitary seemed to be a giant honeycomb made up of countless cells. She saw many devils flying in and out of the cells. No one had noticed her yet. She crawled away quietly and began to form a plan for finding Sal.

As she crawled back up the hill, she peeked into one of the lower cells. In it, she saw a woman reach out toward a baby in what seemed like an attempt to caress his or her head. Suddenly, a devil appeared and snatched the baby away. The woman jumped on the devil. Her efforts were in vain as other devils forcefully pulled her away. She was still fighting when Barb crawled away.

Just then, one of the flying devils flew toward Barb. With her heart pounding, she rolled onto her back. The devil veered off and entered one of the cells.

She lay on her back and stared at the honeycombs for a few moments before deciding to restart her quest. As she rose to her knees, she saw a somewhat familiar devil fly overhead as fast as the winds of a hurricane. She rolled over to her stomach and realized Chad had just arrived. *Finally*, she thought, *a lead to Sal. Chad could only be here for Sal.* She strained to see where he went.

Chapter 10

Chad Watches

As Chad approached solitary refinement, he looked around, checking to see if he had been observed. He easily discovered Sal's cell and decided to watch a torture cycle before approaching him. He could tell that Sal particularly did not like the crawlies. He thought to himself, *Solitary works amazingly well; it draws upon its captives' utmost fears.*

As Sal started to brush off the crawlies, Chad decided to enter the cell. As he moved toward the cell, a devil hit his wing. Chad spiraled down out of control. Just as he was about to slam into the floor, he managed to regain enough control that only his left foot actually hit the hot lava floor. As he flew upward, he noticed what looked like four devils outside Sal's cell. He decided to fly past the cell rather than draw attention to himself by stopping. As he did, he peered at the four devils and did not recognize any of them. As he flew past the devils, he thought, *So that no one thinks that I'm stalking Sal, I will look into multiple cells.*

As he flew ten cells higher than Sal's, he heard a bloodcurdling shriek. He flew in the direction of the sound, rising above the honeycomb shaped structure. As he veered off to the left of Sal's cell, he heard a louder shriek and thought, *This I've got to see. Anyone that horrified has to be exciting to watch!*

He found the source of the shrieking and peered into the cell. *Oh, my evil one,* he thought, *you have outdone yourself this time.* Chad was good at keeping thoughts of pleasure out of his conscious thought. He devoured the agony from the cell. *The poor victim probably had no idea what hell could actually be like,* he thought. This pain was so creative that Chad was disappointed he had not thought of the idea himself.

After the cycle completed in the cell, Chad looked over at Sal's cell. It remained heavily guarded. He looked down for a place to land and wait when he thought he saw something move on the floor below. He flew toward the lava floor. As he drew closer, he recognized the female devil from Satan's office when Sal attempted to present his plan.

Hmm, how did she get here and what is she trying to do? He thought. *I wonder if she is trying to find Sal. What an opportunity!* He decided to fly out of the solitary area and find a way to observe from afar.

Chapter 11

The Reunification

Barb tried to stay completely still after she noticed Chad. It was close to impossible since the floor temperature felt like it was rising. As she contemplated what to do, she thought back to her time in Satan's office. She wondered what she could have done to avoid her current predicament. If she had never gone with Sal, Satan's Guard would never have come for her. She might never have encountered Satan. She shrieked slightly with disgust for Satan. She went back over recent events in her head, wondering what she could have done differently.

She slowly looked up and noticed Chad swooping down toward her at light speed.

Oh no, not Chad! she thought. She quickly calculated the time to impact. Five seconds, four, three, and a scream rose up in her throat. At the last second, Chad veered off and headed back toward Sal's possible cell location. She lay motionless and watched curiously as Chad stopped at a different chamber.

She began to despair. Perhaps Sal was in a different cell. She wondered what to do. Sluggishly, she fell into a daydream about escaping from hell. *There has to be a way!* she thought. As this thought solidified in her consciousness, she began to feel elevated pain levels across her body. As the thought of escape matured, the pain escalated—specifically in her neck and lower back. The pain was as intense as a sword piercing her body. She jumped to her knees and let out a shriek.

She covered her mouth with her hands and rolled across the floor several times. When she came to a stop, she nearly cried out again. Her outbursts almost guaranteed the guards would find her location.

She tried, unsuccessfully, to push the thought of escaping from hell out of her mind. She desired to leave hell far more than wanting to push her first child out of her womb during the final moments of labor. With her hands still over her mouth, she let out yet another shriek.

Once again, she rolled on the floor, hoping to go unnoticed. No such luck. This time, two of the devils that had been observing Sal's cell looked down toward her location.

She slowly rolled onto her stomach and buried her face and her fiery eyes into the floor. Though the heat on her face was as intense as a hot stove, she could not risk the possibility of capture by crying out. She did her best to control every part of her body. She lay motionless for what seemed like hours, though in truth it was only minutes.

She turned her head upward to see the status of the devils huddled around the cell above her. Her fiery eyes caught sight of only one of them. She wondered where the others had gone. A horrifying thought occurred to her. *They must be on the floor with me.*

She quickly buried her head and eyes again. *What do I do? Do I make a run for it? Do I stay still? I don't want to go to Solitary Refinement.* After changing her mind several times, Barb decided to look around to see if she had company.

First, she raised her head straight up and looked forward. To her relief, no one was there. She turned her head gradually, first left, then right, but still no one. She rolled over onto her back and sat up slowly. Just then, she noticed someone or something just forty feet from her. Fortunately, it appeared the entity had not seen her and it flew away.

She decided to rise to her feet. She rose with such force that she lost her balance and fell backwards. As she fell, she thought she felt something grab her and she let out a shriek. She began to run. She ran as fast as she could remember ever running before. She thought she gained enough speed to attempt flight. When she jumped into the air, her wings caught little wind, and she flew for only a split second before crashing to the floor below. She rolled over and leaped back to her feet. She scanned her surroundings and believed she still escaped detection.

She looked up and tried to find Sal's cell again. She noticed two devils outside one cell and decided to climb up to get a closer look. She climbed two stories when another cell caught her eye. She gasped at what she saw. The poor devil within the cell was running around as if being chased, but Barb couldn't see the pursuers. The captive screamed as it ran, then stopped and engaged in a conversation before exhibiting rabid behavior, rolling around on the floor of the cell. Barb broke her gaze and decided to move on. She'd seen many things in her life, but not many were as concerning as what she just witnessed.

As she continued her climb toward where she thought Sal's cell was, she stopped looking down, and even more importantly, stopped looking into the cells. As she drew closer to what she thought was Sal's guarded cell, the two guard devils exited. *This seems too easy,* she thought to herself. *Why are they letting me get to that cell?*

Her thoughts slowed her down. She frequently looked around for potential danger, just as she used to when walking home after midnight BH. She was growing weak, but had nearly reached the cell.

What's my plan? she wondered. She realized she didn't have a plan and felt slightly panicked.

With trepidation, she peered into the cell. She was surprised and excited to see Sal. Her excitement caused pain to shoot through both legs, which threw her off balance. As she fell, she grabbed the edge of Sal's cell within the massive honeycomb and held on with all her strength.

Surprised she had not fallen, she pulled herself up to the outer edge of the cell. As she peeked in, she saw Sal brushing at his arms and legs. Then he started to run into the walls of the cell at full speed.

She whispered to him, "Sal, it's me. Barb."

He didn't acknowledge her, so she whispered again, "Sal, come on, we are breaking you out of here."

Barb expected Sal to come running to her, not knowing the torture continued for him. She decided she had to go into the cell. As she started to walk into it, she became fearful. How would she get out? If it were easy to get out, Sal would have found a way. She decided to keep one foot near the opening of the cell.

She was about to whisper again when Sal ran toward her. She thought Sal saw her and she would succeed in freeing him. Sadly, he merely hit the wall to Barb's left and fell down, letting out a loud squeal. As he got back up, another round of torture began for him.

Barb had to think fast as there wasn't much time. Either Sal would knock himself out or the guards would return.

"Sal, come here. NOW!" she shouted.

Though, certain that the guard devils would hear her, she yelled again, "Sal!"

Once again, Sal ran toward her at full speed. She needed a quick plan of action before Sal knocked her off the giant honeycomb structure. Barb quickly lay down on her back. As Sal drew closer, she put her feet up. As Sal hit her feet, Barb lifted him over her head. She noticed Sal falling on his face as she completed her somersault move. As she came to her feet, she jumped on Sal's back.

"It's me, Barb," she whispered, "and I'm here to break you out. Let's go!"

Sal pushed her off and started back to the middle of the cell. Barb kept working on remembering the way out of the cell. She grabbed Sal's neck and pulled him down to the floor. She grabbed his hand and pulled him in the direction of the exit. He tried to attack her, but before he could move, Barb ran into him and knocked him backwards. As he tried to get up, she ran into him again.

The last run pushed the two of them to the entrance of the cell and jolted Sal out of his trance. Barb grabbed his hand and motioned that they had to climb down the honeycomb.

"What are you doing?" he mumbled.

"I'm breaking you out of here!" she said. "Look, we have to crawl down across the cells."

The two of them started their descent. Barb almost prayed as she realized they were only two levels from the floor.

She shouted out triumphantly, "We've almost made—"

Chapter 12

Chad Captures Sal

Chad observed Barb's feeble attempt to free Sal. *How silly could these young devils be? How could they possibly think escape is an option?* he nearly said aloud.

He shook his head, marveling at the astonishment so many young devils displayed when they arrived. Even on earth, the documentation is extensive surrounding the torments and horrors of existence in hell. In fact, the anti-Satan discussed the existence of hell during His short time on earth. Fortunately for Satan, most humans do not believe in hell and certainly do not believe in the pain and agony associated with it. Even the Christians who might believe in it didn't seem to believe that a loving God would send humans there. Fortunately for Satan, the concept of hell had to exist for humans to have free will. Without free will, there would be no choice.

Chad continued his reflection. At first, young devils would walk around hell with a "deer in the headlights" look in their new fiery eyes. This gaze could last for months. This was followed with the intense, "I've got to escape" look. *None of those looks or thoughts matter,* he reflected. *There is no escape from hell and never will be. Once banished to everlasting torment, you were done forever.*

As Chad reflected, he kept careful watch on Sal and Barb. He noticed that the two spirited young devils had just about reached the bottom of the solitary refinement facility. He calculated his strike time to limit his possible exposure and decided to inflict two strikes on his unsuspecting victims.

He initiated his flight at top speed. *I've never reached this speed before!* he marveled. As he approached Sal and Barb, he took aim at

Sal's midsection. He hit him with a shoulder to his stomach and a fist to his head. The objective of the abuse was to knock Sal unconscious.

Sal didn't see Chad coming until it was too late. Chad knocked him unconscious. With a scream trapped in her throat, Barb realized she was in a headlock and airborne. Chad motioned for her to be quiet and swooped down over Sal, latching onto his feet as well, before executing a quick turn and zooming away from the solitary refinement facility.

He frequently glanced back over both shoulders checking for pursuers. As he analyzed his maneuvers, he was sure he captured the two devils undetected.

Chapter 13

Satan Intervenes

Satan gazed at the wall that displayed the latest soul acquisition chart delivered by Chad. It showed another .5 percent loss in market share on souls. With disappointment and rising anger, he stared at the chart of new arrivals in hell. Just before ripping the chart off the wall, he received a curious message. He couldn't believe what he read. Chad had captured Sal and Barb and was holding them in his chamber. Both were strapped into large chairs and had strange devices attached to them.

Why are they are so predictable? Satan thought to himself. He knew Barb would make a feeble attempt to find Sal. He had made a bet with himself that Chad would connive a way to capture Barb. He expressed outrage about Satan's frequent visits with the young and devious she-devil and insinuated some sort of nonsense about "fraternizing with the enemy." Satan thought aloud, "Perhaps Chad is starting to lose it." Surprising himself with a verbal comment, he thought quietly, *What would that mean in hell anyway?*

Satan flew out of his office and into the area where Chad held Sal and Barb captive. He landed right behind Chad, who was so focused on the two devils he remained unaware of his arrival.

"You two continue to be a menace!" Chad roared at them in a most diabolical voice. "You should be in hell if you weren't already here." He formed his most evil grin and continued, "And, now I have you. There will be no more master plan, Barb meetings, and no more challenges. I will—"

"You will what, Mr. Chad?" Satan hissed.

Fear that the evil one had found him overcame Chad. He turned. "My evil one, I will eliminate this danger from our world."

Satan glared at him and Chad continued, "Satan, you must focus our attention on our plan, not this rubbish. I insist that you—" suddenly stopping midsentence before becoming a victim of fire and brimstone from the almighty one. He looked down in disgust, then turned to continue his work on Sal and Barb.

"Enough!" Satan commanded.

Chad did not respond or stop his evil work.

"ENOUGH!" Satan roared, his words echoing throughout hell.

As if out of nowhere, multiple devils landed. They quickly sealed off the perimeter.

Members of Satan's Guard always materialized quickly when Satan had an issue. This elite group had the authority to use force on any being in hell at the slightest whisper from Satan.

In spite of the Guard's presence, Chad was obsessed with his prisoners and determined to continue. As he began his work on Sal, the Guard approached him. Chad attempted to stare them down. Sadly, he soon realized he had lost. He decided to stand down.

Satan signaled for the Guard to take Sal and Barb back to his office. He looked at Chad with narrowed eyes. "We will discuss this later!" Then he turned his back and flew away.

Chad looked around and reclined in the chair that had contained Sal seconds before. He didn't know what to do next. He did know that whatever he was going to do, he had to do it quickly. He decided to summon the Joint Chiefs.

Chapter 14

The First Invention

Sal found himself in the unfriendly confines of Satan's office yet again. His previous visits had been horrific and quite painful. He and Barb both stood, though she could barely stand, as Satan paced around the two of them. Sal wasn't quite sure why Barb had sought him out, though he felt fortunate to be out of solitary refinement and away from Chad, even if reduction in torment was short-lived. He managed an evil grin. Regrettably, Satan noticed.

"Oh Sal, Sal, Sal," Satan shouted, his voice echoing. "You think this is amusing in some way?"

Over time, Sal learned to speak only when Satan requested his commentary. Otherwise, he would have responded immediately. Instead, he merely held his breath.

"What am I to do with the two of you?" Satan continued. "We have not had this much extra drama in hell for a long time!"

Sal kept holding his breath and braced himself for more jolts from Satan's bolts. He could tell they were coming from the wrinkle of Satan's brow, though he wasn't sure that what he was looking at was actually a face. Sal began to duck.

Satan noticed Sal was bracing for incoming energy. He agreed with Sal's assessment of what was going to happen and prepared to unleash his fury on him, when another chart on the wall caught his eye. He froze and went into a daze. *If I banish these two again*, he thought, *what am I going to do about the future of hell?*

"Why did you decide to find him and try to escape?" he asked Barb.

Barb felt the familiar pain again and then mustered enough energy to respond. "Satan, you need to review this plan." She winced. "You don't have any other plan and you are losing the battle." Glancing toward the wall, she felt another shot of pain and collapsed to her knees.

Satan wanted to hit her with energy but refrained himself. He turned to Sal.

"OK Sal, I'm guessing this is your last chance." He pointed to the chair. "Sit! What's in your plan that is so magical that I should spend a second listening to you?"

Barb crawled into one of the hot seats while Sal stood his ground. Satan shot a bone-chilling glare at him. Sal chirped, "I will sit, only under MY conditions."

Satan had enough. Lightning shot at Sal and the junior devil went flying! Barb knew better than to move or say anything.

Satan flew over to Sal. "How can you continue to be rebellious? What are you thinking? I'm ready to give you back to Chad!" Satan was about to hit him again when Barb spoke very softly.

"Sal, stop!" she said through her discomfort, releasing every ounce of her energy.

"What did you say?" Satan growled as he flew back to her and stared into her eyes. Suddenly, his desires caught fire and he licked her face.

"Sal, stop," she managed to whisper from her position on the floor, on her back with her knees pulled up to her chest.

"You want to talk to that worthless devil?" Satan snarled as he pointed to Sal and shot an energy bolt into his belly for emphasis. Then he pounced on her and slowly licked her multiple times.

Barb was unable to speak and nodded her head in affirmation. Satan jumped off her and pointed to Sal again, hitting him with another bolt. This time, the jolt hit him in the leg. Sal fell face-first onto the hot lavalike floor. The heat scorched his face and tongue.

Barb took Satan's pointing as a signal to go to Sal. She ran over to him and flipped him onto his back. Even though Sal was nearly unconscious, he still recognized her.

For a second, Sal thought they had escaped again. Regrettably, he soon realized that he was back in Satan's office. He attempted to speak, however, Barb signaled for him to be quiet.

For the moment, her pain levels were lower, so she spoke some-what easily, "Sal, stop this battle with Satan. Stop trying to get your way. You cannot win!" She thought of all her failed attempts to resist Satan's regular visits and knew firsthand it was futile. "I want you to sit there and explain the master plan to him!" she added.

Sal looked at her. He was trying to figure out what was in it for her if he did this. While attempting their escape, she had begun to explain her frequent meetings with the king of evil. *Perhaps she's trying to have him stop meeting with her, or perhaps she wants to continue meeting with him*, he thought. Either way, he sensed she was right. He nodded to her and she helped him up.

Barb looked at Satan, fearing he might send more energy their way. As he was set to strike, she said, "Wait. Just listen for five minutes."

Sal and Barb sat down in chairs. Satan decided to remain standing. He turned to Sal.

"You have five minutes to explain your mystical future."

No way! Sal nearly blurted out, but Barb grabbed his hand and slapped him. She yelled, "For the last time, explain the plan!"

Sal yelled, "OK!" He glared at Barb and started to talk. "The plan is based on pure deception. The deception will occur through new inventions that will take many years to develop. However, upon their development—"

"This is the one hundred-year lunacy?" Satan interrupted.

Sal was struck with abdominal pain, although he managed to nod in affirmation. Satan signaled for him to continue.

Sal continued to glare at Barb. "Once developed, these inventions will guarantee an increased stream of souls to our God forsaken world."

Satan noticed that Sal said "our" and immediately thought, *This devil wants power. No wonder Chad is worried about him!*

Sal stopped and wondered, *Is he actually listening?* Satan looked at him and said, "Tell me about one of the inventions."

Sal thought about which invention to disclose first. He looked at Barb. She shot him the "go for broke" look. He decided to start with the wildest idea. He wondered how to describe it. His lengthy pause displeased Satan.

"Come on already," he hissed.

Sal grinned from sudden clarity. "Imagine every home on earth with a machine. Through this machine, you could appear to everyone on earth at any time. Imagine—"

"What madness!" Satan sounded off. "What craziness! What are you talking about? Neither the humans nor God would allow me in their homes every day. You are not a threat to hell or Chad, you are a certifiable lunatic!"

As Satan spoke, Sal was set to argue with him, but decided to wait. He looked at Satan, and for some reason, Satan motioned for Sal to continue. Sal felt a slight twinge of excitement.

"OK," he continued, "the key function of the machine is to display your messages nonstop. People will find them entertaining and pleasing!"

Satan failed to understand. "Let me get this straight. I'm going to show up in homes on earth and they are going to enjoy listening to me?" Satan would have laughed if he permitted laughing in hell. "Sal, if I showed up on a machine—which I don't understand—every Bible in the world would be open and prayers would ring out to heaven. I'm not sure what Chad was worried about. We don't need to stifle you!" He pointed to his door. "Go ahead and walk around out there, talking about this idea. The residents of hell will help us to correct you." His voice lowered. "Imagine. Huh! You have one wild and stupid imagination—"

"The machine will work, and the number of souls coming to you will be endless. Religion will not matter," Sal countered, searching for new words, fearing bolts might come his way.

Satan was about to energize him, although he stopped when he heard, "religion will not matter."

"Yes, but the first part of your plan urges us not to worry about church and prayer."

Sal guessed that, minimally, Satan was intrigued, so he looked at Barb and continued.

"That's the point! We will turn them into hypocrites. For example, we have all heard of the Ten Commandments?" They both nodded.

"The machine will show images of people breaking those sacred commandments every hour of every day."

"So this viewing machine does not show me. So, how will it show—"

A loud bang on the wall interrupted Sal. Satan had not summoned anyone to his office, so he yelled to his secretary.

"I am not to be interrupted!"

"But sir, it's Chad with the Joint Chiefs."

"Chad again," he said only to those in the room. "He is really stuck on this plan or these devils. I'm not sure which."

"Show them in," he ordered his secretary.

The ten Joint Chiefs filed into the room and formed a tight circle around Sal and Barb. Chad approached Satan.

"Is there something here that we can help you with, your evilness?"

Satan was intrigued. Though Sal's plan was clearly ridiculous, the Joint Chiefs seemed intrigued by the amount of attention given it by Chad. This only piqued his interest in hearing more about the plan, though he was fairly certain the first invention could not possibly work. He noticed Chad glaring at him.

"I don't remember asking for any help here, Chad. You can leave."

At that point, one of the Joint Chiefs, Envy, spoke up.

"Sir, at the risk of your just anger, I believe we should stay or help remove these two despicable devils from your confines."

Satan raised his hand, ready to launch an energy bolt, when Chad grabbed his wing.

"Wait. If you are to strike someone, it should be me, not him!"

Satan swung his wing and sent Chad flying through the air. Then he flew over to him. He didn't speak, but thrust his own face squarely into Chad's face. Both of them knew that Chad had overstepped his bounds. Satan picked him up. For a moment, he considered inflicting great pain upon him. Instead, he simply dropped him and returned to the circle. *Should I banish Chad forever? How dare he touch me? What was he thinking?* he fumed silently.

"OUT! OUT! All of you, OUT!" he roared louder than they had ever heard before.

None of the Joint Chiefs protested. They quickly made their way out. One of them, Lust, grabbed Chad on his way out.

Sal and Barb began to realize the pure desperation of an existence in hell. They darted for the door at the same time. For his part, Sal thought, *I've got to get out of here! What a mess!* Just before they reached the door, Satan landed in front of them.

"You two stay here. Go back and sit down."

After Barb and Sal sat down, Satan continued, "Look at what you caused. I order you to stop spouting your lunacy! All hell is breaking loose!" Sal looked at Satan and decided to take a chance.

"Your evilness, how do you plan to get more souls to hell? You are losing. Look at your disappointing charts. Chad knows that my plan will work or he would not be trying to stop it!" Frustrated, Sal got up to leave.

At this, Satan's anger boiled over. He wanted to destroy something. He howled and screamed. All of hell surely heard his rants and growls. He was ready to dismiss the two junior delinquents when he looked at the miserable chart again. It was really ticking him off. As much as he hated to admit it, Sal was correct. He needed a new idea, just not Sal's idea.

He howled again and said, "I give you five more minutes, go."

A twinge of pain shot through Sal's body at the last howl. *How do I explain this in five minutes?* he wondered. He wasn't sure what to do, then he felt a solid blow across his head. He thought Chad had returned, until he noticed it was Barb. She was on her knees in tears.

"Sal," she cried out, "stop messing around. Explain it!"

"OK," Sal continued, "before we were rudely interrupted by Chad, I was saying that the viewing machine would show people breaking the Ten Commandments around the clock. For example, the first commandment, 'Thou shalt not kill,' will be on the machine all day."

Satan envisioned watching murder all the time. He could not imagine humans, and especially Christians, watching this regularly in their homes, however, he allowed Sal to continue.

Sal was getting used to Satan's lack of full concentration on the idea. He guessed the concept was eluding Satan's grasp.

"The viewing machine would not show real murder, at least, not at first. It would show simulations of them as through plays like *Romeo and Juliet*. Such plays allow us to show murder and suicide without outrage from the humans. In fact, the human creatures love it! The problem is that currently, socioeconomic status and geography limit the audience for such plays. As a result, most humans do not have access to them. With the machine in homes, murder and other sins would be available to everyone all the time."

"So, why one hundred years?" Satan queried, the Romeo and Juliet example having helped him put the pieces of the puzzle together.

"Great question!" Sal responded, earning a glare from Satan.

"One hundred years, sir," Sal said humbly, "are needed to gradually introduce the concept and the other complementary inventions. We cannot start by showing murders and suicides every day on the machine. The human creature would throw away the machine in a second. So, it must start as entertainment and evolve to utter decadence and depravity."

Satan's head was spinning. He wondered if he needed to check himself. He was actually listening to what he had originally considered lunacy. Had he become so desperate that he was considering inventions and imagination versus reality? He bolted Sal and Barb as they departed, then he sat back in his chair and stared at the soul charts.

Chapter 15

The Joint Chiefs

After their dismissal from Satan's office, the Joint Chiefs paired up for post meeting commentary. Joint Chiefs Lust, Wrath, and Envy gathered in a small circle.

"What in the world is going on with Chad?" Lust questioned. "He seems to be willing to challenge even Satan over this Sal devil."

"Yup," Wrath agreed. "I've never seen Chad so vulnerable and distracted. Look at him. He is still standing there, frothing with anger. What does he have to worry about?"

"Have any of you seen this magical plan?" asked Envy.

"I have not seen the plan," said Lust, leaning in closer as if about to share a special secret. "I've heard that the plan calls for us to not worry about Christians going to church."

Envy seemed surprised. "So Chad is worried about a plan that says something about letting Christians go to church? There must be more to the plan if Chad is willing to openly disagree with the almighty evil one."

Wrath was about to concur when Envy flew over to Chad.

Wrath looked at Lust and said, "Nothing good can come of this encounter!"

Lust nodded his head and leaned back to watch the fireworks.

As Envy approached Chad, he said, "What was that about?"

Chad didn't acknowledge Envy was anywhere near him. Envy maneuvered so he could make direct eye contact with Chad, but still he would not acknowledge him. He looked intently at Chad, giving every sign he wanted to have a conversation with him. Chad simply ignored him. He drew closer, and still received no acknowledgment.

Chad looked right through him. Envy looked back at Lust and Wrath, shrugged his shoulders, and decided he would have to push Chad. Just then, he felt a crushing chop between his shoulder blades, which was immediately followed by an elbow to his head.

Envy found himself on the ground looking up at Chad. He managed to roll over and kick Chad's feet out from under him, which caused Chad's next punch to miss horribly. He jumped to his feet and gave Chad a knee to the stomach. Then both devils exchanged punches to the head. Chad was about to kick Envy when they were interrupted by a thunderous, "ENOUGH!"

Immediately, Satan and his Guard landed and surrounded them. The Guard grabbed the feuding devils and threw them to the floor. Three guards wound up on top of Envy and three others on Chad. Satan pushed the devils off Chad and grabbed his neck. Satan didn't say a word. He simply glared at Chad, then led him away.

Chapter 16

Barb and Sal Reunited

As Barb and Sal left Satan's office, they hastened their pace past where the leaders of hell would soon brawl. Their futile attempt to slip by unnoticed failed. Joint Chief Lust flew in and landed squarely in front of them. Lust was the most peculiar devil Sal had seen in hell.

Most devils were hideous or on their way to hideous. Even Sal looked more like a creature than a human. Existing in hell, exposed to the unbelievable heat and the burning lavalike floor, left the outer shell of the devils looking burned and scarred. Lust, on the other hand, was unique. Half of his appearance was a hideous and burned creature and the other half was like one of those lenticular prints that looks like one image, but changes to something entirely different the longer you look at it.

Sal peeked at Barb. It was growing more difficult for him to recall she was once an attractive woman. He couldn't imagine what she would look like in another five years.

Sal could not help but stare at Lust. He started to notice that the second half of Lust's outer shell had the appearance of both a naked woman and a naked man. As the image became more distinct, pain surged through both his eyes. Sal dropped to his knees and grabbed his head. He did not dare to look up at Lust again.

"Where are you two going?" Lust inquired.

Barb saw that Sal was unable to answer. She motioned in the direction behind Lust. "We are going that way."

Lust turned to look in the direction she pointed. At that moment, she grabbed Sal and took off. She was sure Lust would be in pursuit. When she looked back, she noticed instead that the Guard was landing outside Satan's office. She assumed that Satan now detained Lust. Nonetheless, she continued to sprint.

After running for what seemed like hours, Barb stopped and looked at Sal. The pain in his eyes started to subside.

"Did you take a good look at Lust?"

Barb nodded affirmatively and said, "Yes. What's the big deal?"

"Did you not see the naked humans on him?" he blurted. "They were perfect in every way! As soon as I saw them, my eyes all but exploded!"

Barb looked at him and thought he must be delirious. "What are you talking about? Lust looked like all ancient devils—downright hideous!"

"No," Sal insisted, "he was different, very different!"

Unsure of what to say next, Barb mustered, "Well, I guess if he is Lust, then causing lust with pain in hell actually makes sense."

Sal shook his head. He thought he had seen it all in hell, but Lust showed him he still did not understand the land of everlasting torment. He looked at Barb with a "now what?" look.

"I'm not sure where to go," she replied.

Sal looked at her and blurted out, "Go to hell!"

Glaring into his eyes, she said, "What is your problem? We are in hell and you are yelling—"

Something or someone slammed into Sal, causing him to hit his head hard on the floor. He was totally unconscious, once again. Barb shrieked when the thing that attacked Sal landed full force on his stomach and delivered an elbow to his head.

The beast grabbed Sal's limp body and moved to fly away. Barb gasped at how fast Sal was gone again. Her instincts said, *RUN.* As she started to sprint, the Guard immediately surrounded her. *No, no, no,* she thought, *not again.* She wanted to fight. Rather, she found her strength depleting rapidly to the point that she passed out!

Chapter 17

The Viewing Machine

Sal slowly regained consciousness. His first thought was amazement at how well traveled he was in hell. He had been to Satan's office, his living quarters or "abode", solitary refinement, and Chad's torture chamber. *How can there be so many horrible places to go?* he thought to himself. As he began to understand his current location, he noticed he was face down on the ground or floor somewhere. Of course, it was hot. Of course, he felt pain. He winced from a sharp pain in his stomach. He must have been kicked in the stomach—so hard he was now on his back.

He looked up to identify his attacker. He expected it to be Chad again. He really despised him. To think, if not for him, Sal would be the Chief of Staff now, or at least one of the more favored devils.

Just then, he was kicked again and he heard someone say, "Get up! Get up, you no good bum!" He looked up to see an incredibly tall hideous devil looking down upon him. As he looked past him, he noticed he was in an area with string, metal, and glass. The tall devil was readying another blow when Sal sprang to his feet and landed in a karate position.

The weird devil slapped Sal in the head and growled, "Your name is Sal, correct?"

Sal nodded affirmatively, staring curiously at his captor.

"You will be visited by Satan in the next few moments. He intends to discuss some sort of invention with you."

Just as he finished speaking, Satan and Chad landed behind him. Their landing was so intense that it sent Sal flying. He wound up with another burn mark on his face.

Part of the operation of hell was that, over time, one's human form transforms into a devil. He thought of the devils he had seen that had been in hell for a while, and they all had several characteristics in common. The features that caught his attention in particular were the hideous bright red eyes, the wings that became more mature over time and enabled flight, the black scales, tails, and webbed hands and feet. Over time, all their faces amassed scars that ultimately made them unrecognizable as former humans. The burn marks on his face were just the beginning of his grotesque transformation. He figured after another hundred or so crashes to the floor, he would not be able to recognize his BH self. In a moment of sarcasm, he thought, *Let's see, one hundred more crashes would probably take another couple hours with these two torturing me.* Suddenly, a pain shot through his stomach, flipping him over. He noticed the one inflicting the suffering was not the tall devil. Unbelievably, it was Chad!

Sal was about to protest when Chad grabbed his arm and threw him toward a rocklike chair. Sal landed five feet away and was once again face down! Before he could protest, he felt another shot to his stomach—another kick from Chad that rolled him over again. *This is getting old rather quickly*, Sal thought.

He looked up, expecting another batch of torture from some-where and noticed that Satan gestured for him to sit down. Sal slowly scrambled to his knees. Out of the corner of his eye, he caught Chad in flight. Sal jumped up and landed in the chair just as Chad landed.

Satan glared at Sal. He spoke in a deeply urgent voice, "Sal, Chad and I have discussed your plan." He slowed his tone even more. "We have decided to learn more about the viewing machine idea and want to know why you need one hundred years. You are in our Innovation Center. The center is where we come up with new and creative ways to get human souls. We demand that you start your explanation with your reasoning behind requiring one hundred years to accomplish your plan."

Sal gave Satan an equivalent glare and pointed to Chad. "What is he doing here?"

Chad immediately delivered a thunderous shot to the back of Sal's head. He hit his head on a table and bounced to the floor. Sal felt like he had 500 pounds hoisted upon him. He realized that Chad had pinned him down and was ready to deliver more agony.

"Enough!" Satan roared. Chad froze.

Just as in Chad's torture chamber, a squadron of devils surrounded the three of them. Chad rolled off Sal. Sal looked around and slowly gathered himself back into the rock chair.

Satan looked at him with utter disgust, hissing, "As you know, patience is not my best virtue. We are not going to tolerate another outburst from you. Do you understand?"

Sal was about to provide his terms for the discussion when he remembered Barb's comments at the last meeting and froze.

"You got it?" said Satan.

Sal gave up and nodded yes. With a devilish grin Satan said, "OK, why one hundred years?"

Sal thought for a moment. Satan and Chad were poised to attack if he took another second. Sal noticed their uneasiness and thought back through this whole nightmare, from the first encounter with Satan in his office to two trips to solitary refinement to that attack from Chad.

Just as Satan prepared to strike, Sal gasped as pain shot up his back and squeaked out, "Incrementality!"

Satan looked at Chad and thought to himself, *This young devil is a lunatic.* Chad returned the same look. Satan decided he needed some sport, so he spit out, "Continue."

Sal decided to start his journey of explaining the viewing machine with the first Christian commandment, "Thou shall not kill."

"When people first get my amazing viewing machine in their homes," he began, "we won't be able to show people killing others all day and night." Turning to Satan he said, "If we did this, there would be millions upon millions of Bibles opened on our wondrous debut. Rather, we must start slowly."

Sal noticed that Satan and Chad were actually listening to him—somewhat. He smirked for a quarter second and immediately a searing pain shot through his head like a twelve-inch needle. He banged his head on the desk three times to find some relief. The misery subsided for a moment and he decided he would no longer make any gestures, though he knew that was probably impossible for him.

Satan nodded for Sal to continue. He restarted his thought process, although his head was killing him!

"In the beginning, we must respect death in the viewing machine," he began. "The implementation plan for murder and showing people breaking the first commandment will be broken down into specific phases. In the first phase, we will not show an actual murder or killing on the viewing machine. Rather, we will show the anger and let the observer guess that murder has occurred. For example, let's say we create a show about two people who are angry at each other. In the scene before the murder, we would show the murder weapon and the intent to kill, but the machine would switch off to something else right before the actual killing. Then, the actors would express remorse and concern over the murder, which would culminate in a funeral. The funeral would be sad and full of Christian overtures."

Sal looked at Satan, who seemed to be getting upset. Before Sal could say another word, an energy bolt shot past his ear.

"Do not use blasphemies down here!" Satan raged. "The next bolt will hit you between the eyes."

Sal looked at Satan and Chad and pondered, *How will I talk about Christians without mentioning the word Christians? How does hell stay in existence with these morons running it? It's amazing it hasn't gone to hell in a hand basket, no pun intended.*

As Sal continued to think, Chad and Satan moved twenty or so paces away.

"Chad, what do you think about this first phase thing?" he asked.

Chad looked intently at Satan. He wanted to tell his master to banish Sal to oblivion, though he himself tried that strategy and failed miserably.

"I continue to think this guy has NO credence," Chad replied. "However, since we've come this far, a few more moments will not kill us," he said, frowning doubtfully, all the while plotting Sal's destruction.

"Agreed," Satan said, matching Chad's gaze. He would have preferred his right-hand devil be interested in Sal's idea, although he gave up on that idea long ago. He still needed Chad, at least for now.

They returned to the table. Satan looked at Sal and simply said, "Continue."

Pain shot through Sal's leg, causing him to kick Chad in reflex. The kick nearly knocked Chad out of his chair. Chad returned the volley with a blow to the back of Sal's head. Sal hit his head on the table again, then he shook it and glared at Chad. He decided to remain motionless rather than have another altercation with Chad.

"OK, OK," said Sal, remembering the secret sauce to this idea was incremental implementation. "In the first phase, breaking the first commandment, we will show anger and disagreement, but not actual murder. In the second phase, we will show the actors dueling—perhaps in a sword or knife fight. We will then show a couple cuts on each actor, with blood."

At the thought of blood, both Chad and Satan leaned forward in their chairs. Sal thought, *Ah, they are not unlike their victims on earth. This is why the plan will work!*

Sal felt energized!

"In this second phase, we will still not show the actual murder. However, unlike the first phase, viewers will hear the murder. The person using the viewing machine will hear the suffering and last gasp of breath and will still have to imagine the actual killing. Again, there will be a funeral and remorse for the dead. The users of the viewing machine will be attached to the machine, watching with excitement and intrigue. They will love the adventure and mystery," Sal said, noticing both Satan and Chad leaning further into the discussion and venturing, "just like you are at this moment."

Satan caught himself becoming fully engrossed in Sal's plan, though he thought that insanity was the cause of continued consideration. However, he noticed his adrenaline was pumping. He wanted to kill something! He snuck a quick look at Chad. His right-hand devil was staring out into space and totally not listening. Satan knew that Chad continued to hate this plan and the entire concept. Before he knew it, Sal was sharing the third phase.

"In the third phase, we would show the actual killing and murders on the screen, but only the 'bad guys' would be killed—"

"No, we must kill the good guys!" Satan interrupted. "Good guys must die!" For emphasis, he peered at Sal and asked, "Do you understand?"

Sal thought, *What is wrong with this guy?* Of course, that thought caused more pain—one pain shot through his head and the other through his chest cavity.

Straining to speak, Sal said, his voice rising with each word, "Yes, the good guys will eventually be killed, but remember incrementality. You see, in the third phase, we will only show the bad guys being killed and there will be cheering. The viewing machine users will be excited to watch the killing because of the righteousness of revenge. The good guys always win!" he continued, now standing and finally yelling, "That is the ultimate trick!"

Sal was so taken with his oratory that he didn't notice Satan was also out of his seat.

"That's the trick?" Satan bellowed. "That's outlandish! The good guys win?" he continued, looking over at Chad who rolled what used to be his eyes.

"Sal, we are leaving!" he said as Chad exposed a most evil grin.

In a moment of pure desperation, Sal protested, "Wait! The good guys will die too, but not until a later phase. You two have heard almost the entire plan for the first commandment. In just a few more moments, I'll be done."

Sal knew he was taking a risk. He expected a few more bolts and a trip to solitary refinement. Instead, Satan got right up into his face and bellowed, "You have wasted much of my time. This idea is preposterous. However, since you said that the good guys eventually die, I will give you another minute." He motioned for Chad to have a seat.

With much less excitement, Sal reviewed, "In the first phase, we will let the viewing machine user guess that a murder occurred and show a funeral for the victim. In the next phase, we will expose them to the sound of the murder. In the third phase, we will show killing, but only of the 'bad guys.' As I noted, the viewing machine watchers will cheer the death of the bad guys and there will be no funerals for the dead."

"In my next phase, we will focus the machine on action and adventure that exhibit real life events, like war or robbery. We will show scenes from a war like the American Civil War. We will show battles and many people dying. Again, the humans will be fooled into thinking it is OK to murder, as long as it is right!" Sal felt renewed energy. "Once again, we won't have any funerals or recognition of the lives left behind by the dead. Moreover, once again, the humans will cheer at the destruction of the enemies. We will show bullets piercing heads, hearts, and legs. We will show bayonets ripping through the stomachs of their victims. We will show cannonballs ripping apart body parts that will fly across the screen of the viewing machine. The humans will love the adventure, the intrigue, and the victory!"

Sal was no longer looking at Satan or Chad as he spoke. He did not want to know if more suffering or energy bolts were coming. He wanted to display his unparalleled passion for this concept. However, he did decide to sneak a quick peek at Satan and saw he was drooling. The concept of utter destruction of humans had him excited, particularly the possibility of new souls coming to his kingdom of doom. Sal decided to continue.

"After many years and phases—maybe one hundred years—the viewing machine can show anyone being killed. It will be a normal, everyday activity on the machine. No one will question the showing of the murder because everyone will consider the show to be mere fiction. However, and most importantly, they will become OK with murder and death. It won't hurt; there will be no remorse. This deception will have them—"

"Will have them what?" Satan interrupted impatiently. "You believe that if we could invent this machine, which I doubt, we would be able to show murder all day without protests, without prayer, without—"

"Not only all day, but all night," Sal interrupted. "In fact, I predict those humans will actually pay to watch! They will pay to watch people sin! They will fall in love with the action, the adventure, and the mystery. Murder and death will have no emotion; they will become statistics."

"Absurd!" Chad shouted, deciding this was his moment.

"Agreed. Absurd!" Satan agreed, nodding at Chad. He then hit Sal with an energy bolt for interrupting him, knocking him out of his chair.

As Sal contemplated getting up, he noticed that Satan and Chad were talking. He wished he could hear their discussion, though he was sure it wouldn't matter. He knew he was doomed again.

Satan looked over at Sal and said, "At least his disobedience is waning. I think we've learned enough about this viewing machine and his one hundred-year theory."

Chad nodded and flew off. Satan moved over to the large devil that ran the Innovation Center.

"Doug, I'm not sure this guy's idea has merit. However, I want you to learn about the viewing machine. I'll be back."

At that, Satan flew away.

Sal felt another stinging shot to his stomach.

Chapter 18

Frankie and Chad

Chad left the Innovation Center and flew back to his office. His office was one of the few in hell. He had a desk constructed out of lava rock. His chair was a boulder with a makeshift back to keep him from falling off, and there were pictures on his walls of his greatest hits. As he stared at those pictures of crusades, he remembered the good old days.

Just as the memory appeared, a shot of pain ran up his spine. He fell to his knees and felt a sharp pain in the back of his head. He fell to the floor and rolled over. He jumped up and remembered that all inhabitants of hell feel torment regularly. However, Satan allowed his staff a minimal amount of pain because he needed them to work and think. Nevertheless, good thoughts always caused additional pain for anyone in hell.

Chad's mind quickly turned to Sal's destruction. During his time on earth, Chad's notoriety was based upon his ability to take advantage of friends or foes as long as it benefited him. He was the king of politics. He could maneuver through any situation and couldn't believe he was still struggling with Sal. He really wanted to rip him apart. He was pacing when Frankie entered the office.

"How did it go?" he asked.

"Horrible. Crazy. Stupid," Chad snarled. "I can't believe his plan still lives! It sounds like the big guy is going to continue considering this plan—it keeps living. He even has Sal at the Innovation Center as we speak!"

Chad looked over at Frankie, his laser red eyes piercing Frankie's brow. Then he inched closer and leaned in toward Frankie before saying, "I sense you favor this plan."

Frankie attempted to look away.

"What do you see in this plan?" Chad growled. "It cannot work! Even if it could, we won't know for so long, I will be displaced as chief of staff!"

Frankie mustered the strength to look into Chad's eyes. He knew he should not answer Chad's raves. He decided to look down again. Before he could get a view of the floor, he saw Chad approach. Chad grabbed Frankie and raised him above his head. "How could even you betray me?" Chad yelled as he threw Frankie across the room.

Frankie got up and made no move that could be mistaken as aggression. He had been through this with Chad on other occasions. He continued to look down at the floor.

"How could you betray me?" Chad complained again, flying over to Frankie and peering into the smaller devil's eyes. Frankie managed to look back. He saw the unparalleled anger in his devilish eyes. He decided it was better not to answer.

"Answer me!" Chad bellowed as he grabbed Frankie again. He was ready to throw him when Frankie screamed out.

"All right already!"

Chad dropped him to the hot floor.

Frankie rolled over, popped up, and spouted, "You want to know why I like this plan, eh? I will tell you why. Because it might—"

"Might what?" Chad screamed as he grabbed Frankie. "You should choose your words very carefully."

Frankie was preparing to respond when Chad received a note. Satan called a meeting of the Joint Chiefs, and he needed to leave right away. He looked over at Frankie.

"We'll finish this later!"

Frankie decided he wouldn't respond and just looked at the floor. He thought to himself, *How do I get out of this? Maybe instead of telling him what I like about the plan, I will give him ideas for fighting the plan, but I like the plan. Fortunately, I have some time to think.*

Chapter 19

The Joint Chiefs and the Viewing Machine

The Joint Chiefs assembled in the conference room. Two of them were experiencing pain on the level of a recent accident victim falling off his horse. The other three were having a side discussion about the theory of evolution. The remainder of the leaders were sitting at a makeshift table, glaring at Satan's chair as they awaited his arrival.

"Human creatures can be very proud of their religion," said Pride. "This evolution concept challenge is gaining traction."

"Agreed," intoned Envy. "When religion gets challenged, the human almost becomes patriotic about his or her beliefs, which causes Christians in particular to divide rather than unite!"

Just as Wrath was about to speak, Chad entered the room. Instead of continuing his conversation with Envy and Pride, he flew over to Chad.

After gaining Chad's attention, Wrath smirked and said, "Are you still fighting and losing to that pitiful new devil, Sal?"

Chad grabbed Wrath and threw him. After the initial surprise, Wrath gathered his senses and flew into Chad. The two rolled like a giant bowling ball, right into Satan as he entered the room. Satan grabbed a devil in each hand and flung them both. Chad and Wrath lay on the floor for a couple minutes, then they sprang to their feet.

Satan positioned himself between the two of them and snarled, "Time for the meeting to start. Settle your issue another time." He opened the meeting with a review of the most recent market share soul data. He looked at Gluttony for an update.

Gluttony reported, "Once again, we lost market share. The number of souls to hell dropped not just in the previous month, but also in the previous quarter and even the previous year, compared to previous years." As Gluttony reported, fire steamed from all parts of Satan.

"Didn't you say that you were going to fix this problem?" Satan growled to Chad. "Should I go back and talk to Sal?"

Without thinking, Chad immediately growled back, "The plan is working and you would notice that if you were smart enough to actually read the report!"

Satan immediately hit Chad with multiple energy bolts that were much more intense than those that hit Sal. The bolts drove him back several yards and knocked him unconscious. Satan simply turned away from him and continued the meeting.

"When this meeting is over," Satan turned to Gluttony and Envy while pointing at Chad, "you two grab him and go over those numbers again." Then he pounded his desk. "I want action! I want it now!" Gluttony and Envy nodded their heads in agreement.

The next topic on the meeting's agenda was a discussion of the Gold Rush Recession. Greed provided an update that even though the broad impact of the recession had been great and most humans suffered, the effects of this recession were winding down. He concluded his update with, "As the recession ends, it will impact our soul meter negatively."

Finally, it came time for an update on Sal's hundred-year master plan. Satan let his evil team know that Chad and he listened to Sal share his concept of a viewing machine. He mentioned that Sal was working with the idea in the Innovation Center. He did not spend much time on the topic and closed with the fact that he still thought the idea was crazy. He ended the meeting and left.

Chapter 20

Barb Looks for the Innovation Center

Barb was in her abode, daydreaming or dreaming, she wasn't quite sure which. She began to feel remorse over being in hell when the sharpest pain ever struck in both her stomach and back.

After what seemed like a half hour, Barb got up and looked out her window. She saw four of Satan's guards approaching again. She shrieked and started to run. Regrettably, another stab of pain hit her in the head, which caused her to trip and fall. She tried and tried to get up and run. She only managed to rise to her feet before being surrounded by the foursome. *Not again*, she thought to herself. *I have to find a way to stop this!* Unfortunately, she knew that if she talked to Satan or resisted, she would wind up in solitary refinement, the horrors of which she had seen firsthand! Although, when she was with him, she could hardly speak, let alone resist.

She closed her eyes and almost thought of praying, but focused on communicating instead. She shrieked. One of the guards turned their attention toward her and started to lick her face. She constricted every muscle in her body and froze.

After what seemed like forever, he stopped paying attention to her. She decided that if she ever had a position of authority in hell, these four would wind up in solitary refinement. Just as this thought occurred, she saw the devil that licked her grimace and fall to his knees. She turned her head to look at him and just as she did, the ground swallowed him up. *How did that happen?* she wondered as she was tossed into Satan's room just as he entered.

She tried to speak, but found she could not talk as she fell to her knees. She could sense him coming toward her.

"Sal!" she managed to eke out. Even in the midst of this, she was determined to find Sal again.

Satan gave her an evil grin as he pounced on her. *Innovation Center,* he thought to her. Barb thought she heard Satan speak. Before she could totally comprehend the moment, she blacked out.

Chapter 21

Sal and the Innovation Center

Sal had trouble keeping track of time in hell. There was no sun and no moon, so day and night were impossible to determine. There were just periods of consciousness and unconsciousness. He tried to guess how long he had been in the Innovation Center. Sadly, he really had no clue, although he guessed that it was probably about two weeks. Much of his time centered on trying to sway giant Doug to the reality of the invention of a viewing machine. Sal realized he had to get Doug on his side or he would be returning to solitary refinement in the near future!

Sal learned much about Doug. In his existence BH, Doug had invented military weapons. He enjoyed destroying humans and was most content when discovering ways to destroy body parts or increase bleeding to extend suffering before death. Unfortunately for Sal, he brought this passion to hell, so he had to stay clear of becoming a dynamite test dummy for Doug.

Besides ducking from Doug's destructive testing, Sal's other problem with him was that he had no time for the concept of intellectual inventions. Doug wanted to destroy humans, not trick them. Every time they interacted, Sal struggled to get Doug to listen for more than five minutes. Doug would rush to end each session with, "When do we destroy?" Sal decided he would try a new approach in his next discussion.

Just then, Doug approached Sal, who expected some sort of confrontation. He was relieved when Doug merely grabbed his shoulder and said, "Ready to test today?"

"Test?" Sal grimaced. "Test what?"

"Glad you asked! I have this new delayed explosive device. It will destroy! I'd like your help in testing it."

"How about before we test, we talk about the viewing machine one last time?"

Doug looked at him curiously, thinking, *Satan was right about one thing, Sal does not give up easily.* "We've talked about this machine a bunch of times. Let's test this time."

Sal jumped up. "One more time, Doug." Though Doug tried to interrupt, Sal continued, "What if we were able to show your destruction on the machine?"

"What?"

Sal pounced on the opportunity, sensing Doug was considering listening to him. Of course, even the thought of excitement and pleasure caused the pain modifiers to elevate. He grimaced and said very slowly, "Doug, imagine that you could create all kinds of destruction on the machine. You could show humans being blown up all the time in ways constrained only by your imagination."

"What?" Doug said after simply staring at him.

Frustrated, Sal said, "Look, you big dummy, you could."

At "dummy," Sal felt a shot to his head. *Oops.* Sal went flying.

Doug grabbed him and said, "Now we test and you are the dummy. What were you thinking?"

Sal made a number of objections. All his concerns fell on deaf ears. He soon found himself attached to one of Doug's latest explosive devices, the countdown already started. For whatever reason, Doug started at sixty instead of ten. At first, Sal thought that Doug was only trying to prove he could count. However, when reality set in, he began trying to think of ways to escape.

"Forty-five...forty-four...."

He tried to loosen himself by using his still immature fangs. Sadly, chewing at the ropes failed.

"Thirty...twenty-nine...."

He wondered what happened if he was killed. After all, he was already dead. He wasn't sure, although he was sure he did not want to find out.

"Fifteen...fourteen...."

After his efforts to escape failed, Sal resolved himself that total destruction was in his near future. There was no way out.

"Ten...nine...."

Sal decided to join in the countdown, thinking, *What the heck? Why not? It doesn't seem to matter.* He was about to find out if his existence would be totally wiped out. He lowered his head and closed his eyes tight.

"Four...three...two...one...."

Hold on, Sal thought, *where's the boom? Did Doug's invention not work? He would be so surprised and maybe disappointed.*

As he slowly opened his eyes, he was shocked!

Chapter 22

The Joint Chiefs After Staff Meeting

As the meeting broke up, Gluttony and Envy stared blankly at each other. Gluttony was not interested in any discussion, so he flew from the meeting room to find Frankie.

"You must remove a devil from the main meeting room. By the way, you will need a wheelbarrow."

Hearing "wheelbarrow," Frankie asked, "Sal again?" His question went unanswered as Gluttony was already gone.

Frankie retrieved a wheelbarrow and headed to the meeting room. As he plowed through hell, he thought of his time BH when he had been a police officer. He remembered that early in his career he enjoyed fighting evil. Regrettably, as soon as he had this slightly pleasurable thought of time BH, a severe pain shot through both his legs. He tried hard to keep remembering the days when he dismantled major crime families in the Big Apple, but the discomfort was too intense and his knees buckled.

As he fell, the wheelbarrow tipped backward and slammed into his forehead, causing him to perform multiple reverse flips. As he landed on his belly, the wheelbarrow tumbled toward him and landed on his back. Frankie kicked the wheelbarrow off his back, rolled over, and continued his BH thoughts.

His thoughts turned to darker times BH. He remembered his wife. After he discovered that his wife was cheating on him, he wound up murdering the two of them in a park in New York City. He had been deeply in love with Lucille for seven years. He recalled the day they first met in Central Park. It was on one of the biggest snow days in New York's history. As he walked his beat that day, she fell into the snow and could not get up. Frankie had come to her rescue. As he helped her to her feet, his eyes locked with hers and he fell head over heels for her.

The discovery that she could even look at another man caused brokenness so deep in his heart that after the murder of Lucille and her partner, he turned against the world and his badge. As Rocco, his best friend and partner, attempted to solve the double homicide, Frankie turned to taking bribes from crime families.

As Rocco watched his partner and best friend fall into a tailspin, he vowed to kill Lucille's murderer with his bare hands. Rocco would not rest until he discovered and destroyed the perpetrator. Rocco turned over every stone he could to find the murderer of Frankie's precious Lucille.

A year after her death, Rocco made a disturbing discovery. Lucille had been cheating on Frankie. Rocco wasn't sure how to break the news to Frankie. He had to share because he thought the information would help in determining a primary suspect. Rocco invited Frankie to the house for dinner with his wife and they enjoyed her scrumptious pasta with gravy.

After dinner, Rocco and Frankie went downstairs. Rocco pointedly raised the issue of Frankie's connection with the crime family. Frankie looked at him with an evil glare and said, "Rocco, what's it to you? The world is messed up. Evil wins! Look at Lucille. She was murdered in cold blood."

"Frankie, I can't know what you are going through," Rocco said haltingly. "We desperately need you to come back to the fight on our side!"

"Is this why you invited me to dinner?" Frankie said as he smiled and grabbed his coat. "Well, tell the Missus thanks. It was delicious. I've got to go."

"Wait," Rocco insisted, grabbing his arm. "I did invite you to dinner, but not to discuss your situation with the crime family. I invited you over to discuss Lucille's murder."

Frankie pulled away and headed for the front door.

"Did you know she was cheating on you?" Rocco shouted behind him.

Fear froze Frankie, leaving him without a quick response. He wasn't sure how Rocco found out but dread filled him as he wondered what else he figured out. He went on the offensive, ran back to Rocco, and hit him on the side of the head with a left cross, yelling, "How could you say such a thing about my Lucille?"

Rocco had fallen back and ended up sprawled out on the floor. Frankie turned his back on Rocco and headed to the front door.

Rocco apparently decided enough was enough. After all, he was three inches taller and forty pounds heavier than Frankie. He jumped to his feet and sprinted toward Frankie. Before he could even turn to see what was coming, Frankie found himself face down on the floor with Rocco on top of him. Rocco delivered a forearm slam to Frankie's head.

Although the hit was painful and made Frankie dizzy, he remained conscious.

"Look, I don't like delivering this news to you, of all people," Rocco sounded off. "Undoubtedly, I know that she was dating the guy who was killed with her in the park."

Frankie's attempts to rise against Rocco's weight were futile. He struggled for words.

"OK, I don't want to believe you, but how about you get off me so we can discuss this like adults?" he said.

After about ten seconds, Rocco released him, allowing him to get up.

"How do you know this?" Frankie asked.

"You know that any of my sources are always anonymous."

"Well, how did your source know anything about the murder?"

Silence engulfed the two of them for several moments, then he said, "The source, in this case, knows that she was cheating on you because they witnessed Lucille with this man many times. In fact, the source also thinks they know the identity of the actual murderer. When they told me, I told them that their theory was impossible!"

Frankie panicked, fearing Rocco knew what he had done. He was able to calm himself and decided to continue playing dumb. "Who might this mystery killer be?"

Rocco looked deep into his eyes and said, "Frankie, the source said they knew the killer of Lucille and her lover personally. When he told me this information, I drew my gun and almost killed him on the spot. With my gun pointed at his head, he swore on his mother's grave that...you did it. You, Frankie. In ten years, this source has never been wrong."

"Do you think I could have killed my Lucille, Rocco? Really?"

"Frankie, I've already told you, I threatened to kill my source at that crazy thought, although you did have means and motive."

Frankie reached for his gun, but before he could draw it from its holster, Rocco had his gun out and placed the barrel against Frankie's temple.

"So Frankie, you are hanging out with criminals and murderers. Have you become one, too? Did you kill them? DID YOU?"

Lightning fast, Frankie drew his gun, raised it to Rocco's chest, and squeezed the trigger, firing a bullet into Rocco's heart. Instinctively, Rocco also fired his weapon.

Both of them died instantly.

Frankie's next memory was the escorts coming for both of them. Regrettably, Frankie's escorts were devils in Satan's army. The escorts for his friend were angelic and bright white.

Frankie crawled to his knees and found the wheelbarrow. He started back on his route to the meeting room. As he trudged, he thought of contacting Chad to let him know he had another cleanup for Sal. Then he remembered his last encounter with Chad had been quite distasteful, so he decided to take care of Sal on his own.

On the last leg of his journey to the meeting room, he saw Satan.

"When he's awake, tell him I want to see him," Satan hissed.

Frankie nodded in acknowledgement.

As he turned to enter the meeting room, he wondered why Satan would want to see Sal. He looked at the wall and gasped in shock. Chad was unconscious and embedded in the wall. He quickly moved the wheelbarrow over to the wall and slowly removed Chad and placed him in his crude form of transportation.

He strained to move the wheelbarrow with his new cargo. As he transported Chad, he grew concerned. *What could Chad have possibly done to be blasted like that by the evil master?* He decided he would find a way to help Chad. Frankie did not want to lose the special "reduced pain" status Chad granted him. Yet, even as these thoughts materialized in his head, a searing pain shot through his stomach. As he doubled over and gasped for air, he looked at the wheelbarrow and, amazingly, it was still steady and Chad had not fallen out. This was fortunate because Frankie was sure he would not have been able to place him back in the wheelbarrow.

Chapter 23

The Joint Chief's Decision

After Gluttony left, Envy flew over to Lust. He attempted to under-stand what had just happened at the staff meeting. Startled, Envy had watched Satan's reaction to Chad with surprise. *Was Chad really blasted or was he imagining things?* Envy almost thought aloud. *There is no way Satan would nail Chad unless something was wrong—really wrong! Is this my chance?* He was careful with this thought. If he made a move and it was wrong, he would end up in solitary refinement for all of eternity. Envy had noticed that many of Chad's challengers disappeared, and had heard rumors of the amazing tortures Chad inflicted on his foes.

In deep thought, Envy didn't realize Lust had been talking to him, perhaps for minutes. Lust was blabbering about something to do with brothels. Envy didn't have a clue what Lust was rambling about.

Envy looked up and asked, "What do you think?"

Lust looked puzzled. "What do you mean, what do I think? I was the one talking. What are you talking about, 'What do I think?'"

Envy felt a surge of anger. He soon noticed Wrath approaching from behind him and decided to remain calm.

"What did you think of Satan and Chad?"

"That was perfect!" Wrath responded. "I haven't seen those types of bolts in a long time!"

Envy looked at Wrath. "Not the bolts, you idiot. What about Chad?"

Wrath was about to strike on "idiot." Fortunately, Lust signaled for him to stand down. This gave Lust an opportunity to jump into the conversation.

"That was quite odd. This worthless master plan really has Chad in quite a dither. He must really hate this plan—either the plan or that Sal guy—to cross and question the evil one as he did."

Envy listened intently to Lust's comments and noticed Wrath had lost interest in the conversation and had flown away.

"I wonder if this plan is really a hoax?" Lust continued. "It must be provocative enough that it could displace even Chad or he wouldn't be so concerned. By the way, what's a viewing machine anyway? Sounds like an unrealistic thought—" Lust kept on rambling.

When he finally took a breath, Envy responded, "Hmm."

Puzzled again, Lust responded, "'Hmm?' After everything we've been discussing, all you can say is 'Hmm?' What is wrong with you? Have you hurt your feeble semblance of a brain, or do you even have a brain?" Lust expected some sort of rebuttal. All he got was another "Hmm" from Envy, who then flew away.

Lust contemplated what to do about his exchange with Envy. Should he report it to Satan or Chad or sit on it? He thought about approaching the evil one and decided nothing good would come of that discussion. Then he thought about talking to Chad. What could he possibly tell that poor excuse for Satan's number one? "Envy was distant when we discussed the master plan?" Perhaps he could make something up, like, "Envy is going to work on this master plan to over-throw you as the head of the Joint Chiefs."

Lust liked the second idea. It would be great sport and might cause some excitement in the land of never ending agony. Of course, as soon as he thought of the pleasure of telling that story, pain hit his lower back.

As the suffering subsided, Lust knew his next move.

Chapter 24

It's Unbelievable

Sal did a double take and still could not believe his eyes. Somehow, it happened again. Barb rescued him from yet another level of torture. Moreover, now she was speaking with Doug. Doug nodded to her and moved away from his explosive device. Sal couldn't tell what they were saying. He was even more surprised when the countdown stopped.

"Zero!" Sal yelled out. The comment caused both Doug and Barb to look at him. Then they approached him.

"Sal! Yo, Sal," Doug yelled. "Barb here has come from Satan. She needs a word with you. I'm going to find someone else to help me test," he concluded before walking away.

Sal looked at Barb. She gave him a "What am I going to do with you?" look, but said nothing. She moved behind his back and started to unbind him. Once free, he wanted to hug her, though he knew the punishment for a hug would be horrible for both of them. Instead, he shouted, "Why are you here again?"

"I'm not sure why I keep seeking you out," she stormed back.

"Me neither," he fired back.

Doug had been watching this exchange. Though he couldn't hear the exchange, he decided this Sal devil had gotten into trouble again. He went back to his testing procedure.

Once Sal and Barb noticed Doug was no longer interested in Sal, they walked to the other side of the Innovation Center and began a quiet discussion.

"How did you find me?"

"I have my sources," she said, looking at him intently.

She wanted to share that Satan continued to take her, but knew this fact would rouse his anger. Though Sal thought she gave him a strange answer, he didn't probe further.

"Look at the progress I'm making," he said with an evil grin. "I'm working with Doug there and we're going to invent the viewing machine."

Confused, Barb said, "Progress? If I was a few minutes later, you would have been blown into many pieces. I can tell you, Doug had you right where he wanted you."

Sal had a wise guy answer but kept it to himself. After all, Barb was right. He had been seconds away from discovering what happens when you die when you are already dead. He decided to catch her up on the progress he had made since they last saw each other.

Barb tried to listen intently as Sal described his meeting with Satan and Chad, but she kept getting distracted. She attempted to discern Satan's intrigue with the plan because he still did not accept it. *What is it with Satan? Why does he not just leave the plan alone— and leave Sal alone? He must be really alarmed*, she thought. *Sal was right. He had a unique opportunity and an innovative plan. The tough question in her mind was, Is Sal the right guy to make the plan a reality?*

"Barb! Yoo-hoo, Barb! You in there?" Sal asked, noting she seemed zoned out.

He tried to draw her out from what appeared to be a trance.

"Barb! Wake up!"

"Oops!" she said, startled. "I was processing your comments. I believe you have made progress, but you're still stuck. How are you going to get the plan to work, Sal? You've been trying for years, and sadly, you still don't have acceptance. In fact, you have single-handedly caused dissension at the highest levels of hell!"

Sal shook his head. "I'm close to making progress, and I think I can convince Doug—"

"But even if you convince Doug, then what?"

"If Doug can convince Satan, the plan will make it!"

Sal looked up at Barb and saw Doug returning. Barb looked at Sal.

"Let's get him!" she growled.

Chapter 25

Chad Learns of More Betrayal

Chad slowly came out of his prolonged unconscious state. He noticed his pain modifier was elevated. He guessed he had been out for a week or two. He rolled over to his back and realized he was in his abode. Slowly, he started to rise, but regrettably, he found he couldn't bear the pain and fell back. His back and head burned like fire. After several attempts, he finally rose to his feet. *How did I get here?* he wondered.

He looked over his shoulder and noticed Frankie approaching.

"How did I get here? Did you help me?"

Frankie nodded. "I got you back here via my classic transport." Frankie knew Chad could not and would not thank him.

"So, what happened?"

Frankie looked at him with sadness. "I'm not sure, boss. All I know is Gluttony came to me and said I had a pickup in the meeting room. I assumed it was Sal. I was horrified to see that it was you. What happened?"

Chad thought for a second. His memory was definitely foggy. He could remember Satan's anger and unprecedented pain! However, he couldn't remember what caused the misery. All he could see was an image of Sal. He then screeched at a decibel level Frankie was certain all of hell could hear. As Chad took his next breath, Frankie ducked.

"SAL!" Chad roared.

At that moment, Frankie knew Chad would spend every moment he could hunting Sal. He wasn't sure what Chad would do, but he knew it would not be pretty!

Frankie decided to speak prior to another outlandish scream.

"What has Sal done now?"

Chad's memory was returning. "He —he—ahh, he got me bolted! He will feel my wrath!"

Frankie avoided eye contact with Chad.

"Where is that menace?"

"Before—before—before—"

"Spit it out!" Chad roared.

Frankie tried to continue. "Before you go find Sal, you might need to see, you might need to see Satan."

Chad looked at Frankie, wanting to pounce on him. However, he knew Frankie was just the messenger. Instead, he flew off with unbelievable speed.

Frankie watched and wondered what he could do to help, and more importantly, where Chad was going.

Chapter 26

Lust Catches Chad

Chad guessed Sal would be in the Innovation Center. He decided to take care of him once and for all. He flew faster than ever. His anger boiled over to the point that it was going to be either Sal or him. He would tear that young threat limb from limb. He didn't care about the repercussions. After all this time in hell, Satan actually bolted him. Never, ever, in his wildest imagination did Chad think he would be bolted!

Since this Sal moron arrived, he fumed silently, *I have been humiliated to the point of utter disgust. I have brought doubt to the master about my loyalty. I have caused hell to wonder about my leadership, and now Satan has bolted me!* Chad couldn't believe this was happening to him—*him*—the right hand man for the ultimate evil one. *How can this be happening? How is this even possible?*

As he started to think more about what he was going to do to Sal, he noticed someone was flying at the same light speed next to him. Without thinking, Chad swerved to hit him. As he flew to his left, he kicked out his foot. The kick missed the mystery flier, who suddenly disappeared and then reappeared a moment later to his right. Chad tried to punch him and missed yet again, and the flier disappeared. Chad looked left and right but saw no one. Just as he decided the flier was a figment of his imagination, he saw something headed toward him from below his left wing. The unknown flier clipped one of Chad's wings just enough to send him into a spin. As he completed the spin, something grabbed him from behind.

Chad's anger swelled. He gave the attacker a backwards head butt and spun around with a punch to its stomach. Chad was about to hit with an uppercut when he noticed the unknown flier was not resisting and looked like one of the Joint Chiefs. He grabbed his assailant in a headlock and exerted a reasonable amount of pressure on his neck.

"What do you want? Where do you get off following me?" he shouted.

Lust attempted to speak, but the grip on his neck was too strong. He motioned for Chad to let him go. As Chad released him, he gave him the formerly withheld uppercut, which sent Lust spinning.

"What do you want?"

Lust struggled to recover from the punch. "I want to help you," he said in a deep and serious voice. "I witnessed your bolting at staff meeting and was concerned for you, and I have some advice for you."

Chad gawked at him. *Lust wants to help me? Yeah right! I wonder what he is really up to?* Chad decided to play along with Lust while not trusting him for even half a second.

Lust had never seen Chad so far off his game, so he took the opportunity to work on him, becoming very serious again.

"Well, Cha-a-a-d? If I were you—"

Before he could finish his statement, he felt shots to his head and stomach and heard Chad growl, "You are *not* me, nor will you *ever* be *me!*" He gave Lust another kick and sped off.

Lust thought for a second and realized this would be more interesting than he ever dreamed possible. He decided to follow Chad. As Chad drew closer to the Innovation Center, he slowed down. The slowdown gave Lust an opportunity to fly beneath Chad. As they neared the landing zone at the Innovation Center, Lust flew straight up, delivering a mighty shot to Chad's stomach before delivering an uppercut that sent Chad spinning out of control. Through Chad's disorientation, Lust placed him in a headlock. This time, it was Lust's turn to speak.

"Now Cha-a-a-d, you listen to me! I am only trying to help. Nothing more. I witnessed Satan's fury and anger that he directed to you! I would recommend that before you have your rendezvous with your intimidating little friend, Sal, that you go see the evil one. In addition, Cha-a-a-d, you should be watching Envy!"

Lust delivered a karate chop to Chad's neck and tried to take off again. Before he could accelerate, something grabbed his ankle.

Chad did an amazing aerial wrestling move and put Lust in a half nelson before he could figure out what happened. Chad the Warrior leaned in to Lust's ear and whispered, "If you ever interfere with me again, it will be the last thing you do."

He flipped Lust again and grabbed his ankle. He spun Lust in the air many times, and then flung him into the front wall of the Innovation Center, knocking him unconscious.

Chad took a moment to gather his thoughts. Just as he approached the entrance to the center, he saw what looked like another Joint Chief land and attempt to waken Lust, and decided to make a hasty exit instead.

Chapter 27

Does Doug get it?

Sal and Barb didn't have any time to develop a strategy for a discussion with Doug. Barb only wished Sal would use some of the brilliance he used in preparing the master plan to convince others of its value.

Doug came over. "Did you guys see the result of my test? Did you see it? It was amazing!"

Sal looked at Doug. "No, we did not see it. However, from your excitement, I'm guessing it worked perfectly?"

"Perfect," Doug shared excitedly.

When Doug felt even that small twinge of contentment, he fell to the ground in pain as if an arrow pierced through his heart. Doug moved the image of contentment out of his brain and slowly got up to leave. Just then, Barb grabbed him.

"Dougy, we need to talk to you about Sal's idea." She paused and waited. When Doug seemed disinterested, Barb followed with, "I really w-a-a-a-n-t you to listen and I'm a personal friend of Satan!" Sal looked at her and thought, *What did she just say?*

Doug was sure she was lying, but was curious about her intentions. He decided it wouldn't hurt to spend a few moments with the two of them. Although, if this Sal guy insulted him like he did in the last discussion, Doug decided he would blow him up. He was just waiting for Sal to speak when he heard Barb talking.

"Look Dougy, this is a great idea for you. You will be able to cause more violence than you ever thought possible." Barb rubbed up against him. "C'mon Dougy, just listen for a few minutes, for me?"

Doug was unmoved. *Why should I listen to these two?* he thought. *Ever since they got here, this place has been getting way too much attention!*

Doug pulled his arm away and growled, "Leave me alone!" Then he turned as Sal yelled something he couldn't quite hear. He was too distracted by the tall figure walking toward them.

Chapter 28

Chad Reminisces

As Chad flew away from the Innovation Center, he didn't quite know where to go. He had no desire to go to Satan's office. Clearly, for the first time in his hellish existence, he was lost. He decided to fly back to his abode.

After landing just outside his abode, he proceeded to kick everything he could find on the molten floor. Then he sat down behind his desk. He looked at the tasks piled up on his desk.

He read one of them and the subsequent description, "New devil orientation. Go to the initial meeting place, inflict first introductory anguish, and then teach them about their goal in hell." Chad glared at the task description. He remembered the day he invented this set of training processes. The goals of the processes were to standardize and ultimately perfect Satan's vision of dominance. It still amazed him to watch new inductee devils arrive in hell. Chad watched hundreds of millions of souls arrive, all of them still in utter disbelief that hell actually existed. Most of them were astounded and unpleasantly surprised on their first day. Once they got over the initial shock, Chad's process mandated that suffering engulf the new resident in everlasting torment. Many of them fell into a state of shock as a result.

In addition to all the well-executed processes, Chad remembered one of hell's greatest innovations, hell mansion. Constructed almost two hundred years ago, the mansion took about ten earth years to complete. They decided to locate the mansion at the entry point to hell.

Upon entry into the mansion, new arrivals entered a three-story foyer painted perfectly white. They would ascend a grand staircase where fifty perfectly decorated bedrooms awaited them. The bedrooms each had a wonderful personal touch including the new guest's name posted on the door. After they entered their assigned bedroom, the door closed behind them.

Chad recalled the reaction of one of the first new recruits as she entered into her very own room. Her name was Sally. As she looked around her room with a perfect smile, she had a sense of relief. Then, she jumped onto her bed and pumped her arms in the air exultantly, exclaiming, "After all that I did, I still made it to heav—" Just then, Chad and his team cut her off by inflicting her first introductory pain upon her, collapsing the floor of her room and causing her to fall onto the hot molten floor of hell. Her bloodcurdling screams of "No! No! No!" went on for hours, such music to his ears.

Satan was quite pleased with Chad's innovation. Hell mansion caused Satan to agree to the introduction of the Innovation Center. He wanted to find similar innovative ways to influence humans on earth as they did in hell. The goal of the Innovation Center was to harness the unlimited creative power of all the evil in hell, and then unleash it on earth.

Chad slowly fell into a trance. In his mind, he continued to remember his history in hell. He remembered his rise to number two when he proposed the plan to stop the Christian persecution shortly after the death of the anti-Satan. Hell's old guard leadership focused on Christian elimination through persecution.

Chad countered with an alternative strategy focused on splintering the church of the anti-Satan. Chad's plan was not popular, so he pushed his agenda hard. He pushed so hard that banishment would be the result if his plan failed!

Just then, two surprise visitors broke his daydream. He recognized the first one, while the second visitor was unknown to him.

Chapter 29

The Viewing Machine Captures Envy

Doug looked up with surprise and dismay. *Ever since Sal came to the center, Satan, the head of the Joint Chiefs, and now this guy, have visited me,* he thought. *When does this end?*

Envy walked up to Doug. "Where's this menace called Sal?"

"Menace indeed," Doug replied. "Would you like me to blow him up?"

"No, Doug," Envy replied, "I will take care of him! Where is he?"

Doug pointed to where Sal and Barb stood talking. Envy did not bother to acknowledge Doug and flew in the direction of Sal and Barb. Doug shrugged his shoulders and moved on.

Envy flew full speed at Sal and struck him with such great force that he crumpled to the floor. As Sal tried to get up, Envy landed on him and delivered an elbow to his nose, immediately rendering him unconscious. Envy looked at the broken younger devil and thought, *That was easy!* He threw Sal over his shoulder and began to fly away. Barb gasped and attempted to jump on Envy, but she was too late.

After landing with Envy, Sal slowly began to wake. He heard a voice and fear encompassed him. *No way!* he thought. *I can't be back in solitary!* He didn't recognize the voice but knew it wasn't Satan or Chad speaking. It did not sound like the voice from solitary, either. He attempted to sit up. Unfortunately, his movement was constrained by what felt like a heavy object on his chest. The more he tried to move, the heavier the object became.

As his vision cleared, he could see the heavy object was no object at all. It was a giant foot. He tried to move the foot, but to no avail.

"Lie still! Don't try to move," Sal heard the voice say.

Sal decided to listen to the voice and eventually spoke. "Who are you, and what do you want?"

Envy looked at the pitiful devil and wondered how Chad could possibly fear this pitiful weakling. Envy's instructions were simple.

"Who I am does not matter to you! What I want matters greatly! I want your plan."

"What part of it do you want to hear?" Sal responded with a twinge of gratitude that *someone* seemed to want to hear the plan.

Envy didn't care for the answer, so he doubled the pressure on Sal's chest. "I want it all," he replied coolly, "but start with the first invention."

"Can you remove your foot from my chest?"

Envy shouted, "You are not asking the questions!" He moved his foot from Sal's chest to his throat, although, when he saw that Sal was about to lose consciousness, he decided to move it back to his chest. "Tell me about the first invention!" he screeched.

Sal was too busy catching his breath to respond, so Envy applied more pressure on his chest. Sal managed to place his index finger in the air, indicating that he needed him to wait a minute.

Envy looked at dismal Sal and released some of the pressure on his chest, though he was starting to think that he was wasting his time with this devil. Sal showed no strength and seemed unworthy of respect. Envy started to believe Sal was entirely worthless.

At that moment, in a scratchy voice, Sal managed to say, "I will explain the first invention if you give me a second to catch my breath."

Envy rolled his evil fiery red eyes and released some of the pressure on Sal. Then he waited for him to talk.

Sal looked at the giant devil who clearly wanted to tear him apart. He couldn't figure out the attacker's motive. Did Chad, Satan, or Barb send him here, or had he come of his own devices? He wanted to know, though he had no desire to ask the massive devil another question. He decided to try explaining the viewing machine.

"The first invention is known as a viewing machine. It will allow Satan and us to show up in anyone's house at any time of day."

Envy gave him a quizzical look. "Stop screwing around! Tell me about the first invention!!!"

Sal responded, "I don't make a habit of chiding beings that are standing on me."

Envy delivered a kick to Sal's head, jumped off him, and prepared to fly away.

"Wait!" Sal said as he charged Envy and knocked him over. Envy was surprised to look up and see Sal standing on him. Regrettably for Sal, his victory lasted just a few moments. With a quick twist and two flips, Envy was standing on Sal's throat again.

"If you ever try that again," Envy threatened, "you will think Chad was a heavenly angel. What were you thinking?"

Sal seemed to be trying to say something, so Envy eased up on the throat pressure.

"You obviously came here for a reason," Sal whispered. "Why don't you listen to the idea for a couple minutes before storming off?"

Envy thought quickly and decided he had nothing to lose by listening. He grabbed Sal and threw him in the direction of a sitting area. Sal rose slowly and climbed into something that resembled a chair.

Sal started to explain the viewing machine in the same way he had explained it to Satan and Chad.

"Imagine you could show humans images of other humans breaking the Ten Commandments all day, every day. The humans will love it! They will be enthralled with the machine. They will get their information and news from the machine. The machine will rule." Envy could sense Sal's passion. However, he was bewildered with the absurdity of the invention.

"Imagine," Sal began, "human theater in all homes. Imagine—"

"What if," Envy jumped in, "you could build this machine? How do we prevent Christians from using the machine for their agenda?"

Sal almost smiled, though he knew better. "That could—and probably will—happen. Christians will find many uses for the machine, but it just won't matter. Their message will be boring and we will outfox them by far in the usage of the machine. The hum—"

Before Sal could finish his sentence, Envy flew at him, leading with an elbow, knocking Sal unconscious again. Envy returned to the center and looked for Doug. Once he found him, they left the center together.

Chapter 30

Barb's Twist of Hope

Barb watched in amazement as the enormous devil basically destroyed Sal. It happened so fast, she only had a small chance to protest or protect him. She wondered, *Should I start working on Doug, or should I just give up and let Sal figure it out by himself?*

As she tried to untangle her thoughts, a four-devil escort landed and surrounded her. She was in no mood for these leeches or Satan, but she felt absolutely helpless. She allowed them to grab her and lick her. It was as vile and disgusting as ever. She wondered what she could have done differently on earth to avoid this fate. Sadly, before she could answer her own question, she was back in the land of Satan's bedroom.

She burst into tears. As the tears flowed, so did the pain. The first pain shot through both legs and she fell to her knees. The next streaks of anguish struck her head and stomach simultaneously. These pains put her flat on her back. She tried to fight. She did not want to give up again, but the pain was so intense she couldn't move.

She tried to focus and form a plan. *Somehow, I need to communicate with Satan and tell him that evolution will not work and that I know Sal's plan will work! I know it will work!* At the last thought, the level of suffering began to decrease.

She slowly opened one eye and realized her fear. There he was again, hovering over her. She tried to get up and run away. She wanted to run far away. She tried and tried to move. She tried to roll over. She tried to raise a hand or make a fist, all to no avail.

This experience was eerily similar to her worst dreams on earth in her BH life. She would scream in her dreams, but no sound would come out. Regrettably, this was not a dream!

Chapter 31

Chad's Next Move

Chad looked at Frankie. "Why did you bring him?"

Frankie looked away, knowing he didn't want to further anger Chad. "I brought him to help you, sir. I believe his knowledge of humans and hell can be an asset for you."

Chad's immediate reaction was anger. Instead, he decided to hold his tongue and motioned to Frankie to continue. However, Frankie wasn't sure what to say. He didn't really have a plan other than to get Chad and Frankie's guest to dialogue about Chad's situation and his struggles with Sal.

"Chad, sir," Frankie began, "I've explained your interactions with Sal and Satan to our guest. I've shared the concept of Sal's viewing machine with him."

Frankie knew he had made a mistake. At the mention of Sal's name, Chad flew into Frankie, knocking him into a large stone. Chad was about to strike again when he realized that his victim was Frankie and not Sal. He stood down.

Turning to the guest, he said, "So you think you can help me? And if so, why would you want to help me?"

"He can, he can absolutely help," Frankie interjected, standing up as he spoke. "Hear him out!"

Chad turned to the guest. "The floor is yours for about one minute."

The guest glared at Chad, making him uneasy—a rare thing. He held the stare until Chad finally ended it with, "Time's up." Then he looked at Frankie. "You brought me a mute devil to help? Looks like your guest can't even speak, let alone help."

At the last comment, the guest erupted, spewing out unintelligible sounds. Frankie ducked down in fear. Chad didn't move or respond, he just looked at the guest and said, "OK, so you are not mute."

The guest screeched again, looked at Frankie, and gave him an, "I'm wasting my time" look. At this, Frankie jumped up and said, "No, please stay. You two need each other."

Chad and the guest were now nose-to-nose.

"Chad, please listen!" Frankie implored again.

Chad nodded. The guest looked at Chad and began to share his simple plan for him. Chad was about to respond when more company arrived.

It was Satan.

Satan looked at the three devils and wondered, *Now what? Why were Chad and this devil together?* He was not overly concerned. However, he still exclaimed, "Leave him." At his command, the guest and Frankie quickly moved away.

Satan looked at Chad and immediately hit him with an energy bolt. Chad flew through the air and Satan followed, landing on top of him. "Didn't I tell you to come see me? Did you not get the message?"

Chad attempted to respond, but before the words came out, he received an elbow to his head. Satan growled, "I will not tolerate your insubordination—you out of all devils!" as Satan hit him again.

"You need to pull it together, Chad. Your behavior is unacceptable. I want you back to your number one position in the organization. NOW!"

Chad attempted to speak again and another bolt greeted his speech. Satan got up, hit him with another energy bolt, and departed.

Chapter 32

Can Prayer Be the Answer?

Sal awoke and found himself on a hot lava floor. He was unsure of where he was and glad he didn't hear a voice. As he shook the cobwebs from his head, he knew he had been unconscious and beaten, due to the pain that seemed to consume his entire body.

He reflected on his time in hell. He had been zapped by Satan, tortured by Satan's number one, almost blown up by an Innovation Center leader, banished to solitary refinement a couple times, and was now being abused by some unknown devil. Sal decided he wanted out of hell. He had enough!

At this thought, pain penetrated through his hands, feet, and head simultaneously, rivaling the mental pain of solitary refinement. He let out a shriek and then curled up into a ball. As he used every ounce of mental energy he had left to fight the pain, a thought popped into his head that he had not had since childhood. He actually attempted to put his hands together and pray. Regrettably, the thought of a prayer caused a seizure that sent his body flopping across the floor. He wanted to scream out. He wanted to yell. All attempts were unsuccessful when he realized that his vocal cords were no longer functioning.

The seizure seemed to last for days, though in reality, it was only a couple hours. In the midst of it, he heard a new voice—a deeply distressed voice. It actually sounded as if it were crying. Sal felt relief and concern at the same time. His relief was selfish. He was not zapped or abused again. The concern was that someone else was being tortured at the same time, which could mean that it would be his turn for more torture yet again.

As his seizure began to subside, he rolled onto his side and tried looking at the source of the voice, a sobbing devil sitting on a rock about ten feet from him. The ordeal blurred his mind and vision, so much he could not recognize the distraught devil.

He managed to get to his hands and knees and slowly crawl toward the devil. As he drew closer, the other devil began to scream and sobbed louder. When he was within three feet of the devil, he finally recognized it was Barb. He would have liked to console her, but he knew what would happen to him if he attempted to help her. In fact, the initial nudge toward consolation caused his pain level to elevate noticeably.

Barb started shrieking, eventually so loudly that she passed out and rolled onto the floor. Sal climbed up on the rock she previously occupied and gazed at her lying listlessly on the floor. He knew what he would have done with Barb had he been on earth, but in hell, he just stared at her.

Chapter 33

Lust's Fun Time

Lust stood outside Chad's abode for a couple of earth hours. He was amazed at the traffic that passed through Chad's world. As Lust pondered what the mystery visitor wanted with Chad, he saw Satan join them. He was astounded to see Chad bolted again. As he continued to piece together the logic of these visits, he saw Satan fly off in a hurry. He wasn't sure what was happening, although he decided Chad had to be vulnerable.

Lust entered Chad's abode and found him semiconscious on the floor. *How could this warrior just give up his number one slot in Satan's organization?* he thought to himself. *Chad is weak,* he concluded.

Suddenly, Lust found himself flat on his back with Chad standing on him.

"What do you want, and why are you here?"

Caught off guard, Lust stammered, "M-m-my dear Chad, I just wanted to help you again. We departed on such rough terms at our last encounter."

"You can help me by getting out of here!" Chad growled as he grabbed Lust and threw him.

As Lust gathered his senses, he yelled, "OK, have it your way!" and got up to leave. As he started to fly, he spouted, "Good thing you don't know what's going on!" Then he launched himself into the air.

Something grabbed Lust's wing, threw him twenty feet, and proceeded to pounce on him. Chad wasn't thinking, only reacting at this point.

"What did you say?" he hissed.

Lust tried to speak. He noticed that Chad's position on him had a slight weakness, so he grabbed Chad's foot. As Chad lost his balance, Lust sprang up, grabbed Chad's wing, and threw him. Lust wound up on top of Chad.

"Forget you, Chad. I try to help you and you attack. Watch Envy!" He then hit Chad with an elbow that clearly dazed him. Lust bolted off into the air.

As Lust took off, Frankie caught sight of him and decided to visit with Chad. As he entered the abode, he noticed Chad on the floor. Frankie crawled over to help him. As he approached, something slammed him to the floor. Frankie looked up just in time to see an elbow about to strike his head. Fortunately, he ducked in time to miss most of the blow.

"Chad, what are you doing?" he managed to shout out.

Chad was about to strike again and fortunately noticed that it wasn't Lust, but Frankie. He grabbed Frankie and threw him.

"What are you doing here? You could get yourself hurt!"

"I noticed that Lust flew out of your abode," Frankie replied, "so I decided to check in on you. That's all."

Chad looked at him and remembered his encounter with Lust.

Chapter 34

Now What?

After his encounter with Sal, Envy returned to his lair. He went into a trancelike state. *How could Chad and Satan be enthralled with Sal's idea? It is plain stupid! Why are there any discussions about it? A viewing machine? You've got to be kidding me!*

Envy considered the invention to be a crazy idea. He could not imagine the possibility of such a machine and the potential usage of it seemed even more outlandish.

Envy's thoughts turned to Chad. For the longest time, Envy had coveted the number one slot in hell. He remembered when Chad ascended to the position. Envy crafted a wonderful plan for knocking out the Chief of Staff. Before he could put the plan in motion, Chad launched his plan, which seemed absurd at the time. Envy decided to lay low, figuring the fight between Chad and the existing number one would leave him with a breakthrough opportunity when both of them failed. Unfortunately, Chad's plan was wildly successful.

Chad's ascension to power was merciless. In hell, you don't have to be nice to those on the way up because you don't meet them on the way down. Chad was as ruthless as Envy had ever seen anyone BH.

Fortunately, Chad never heard about Envy's plan. As a result, Envy maintained his position as one of the Joint Chiefs. Since that day, he waited for a break between Satan and Chad. Now his dream had come true. He began to pace. The moment he had been waiting for had arrived, though it certainly had not come on a silver platter! Envy thought long and hard. *Sal is crazy because his invention is not possible. Chad is crazy for even worrying for a second about this invention. Satan is bonkers for listening to both of them. If Chad is so concerned, there just might be something about this innovation, but it is just not possible! Or is it?* As he finished this thought, he turned and trembled at the sight of the visitor ascending to his abode.

Chapter 35

Lust as The Instigator

If they had not been in hell, Lust would have enjoyed the fray between Chad and Sal that might now involve Envy. The role of instigator suited Lust perfectly. He began to ponder another visit to the frazzled Chad. Lust had known Chad for quite some time and had never seen him so far off his game. He formed an evil smirk at the thought. He considered visiting Envy again. Then, he considered visiting the Innovation Center, or perhaps, even visiting the big guy. He started to pace. *So many options and choices, what is an evil devil to do?* he thought.

As he paced, he reminisced about the past. He pondered his ascension to Joint Chief in hell. It was about three hundred years ago when Lust started to become more important in hell. As he started to demonstrate the weakness of the male human for desires of the flesh, his dominance on the staff grew significantly. Satan was only interested in more souls. He was not interested in rhetoric or the promise of more souls. He wanted more and more souls to devour.

Initially, it was difficult to demonstrate the weakness of the male species. This all changed when Lust discovered the concept of pornography. He began to step up man's desire for loose clothing on women. Lust's initial idea was only to show the parts of a woman's body that had traditionally been covered from head to toe. Lust discovered that even the most holy men could not resist a picture of a beautiful woman with some clothing loose or missing.

Lust elevated his agenda to the point that Satan could observe a clear increase in souls due to marriage infidelity and premarital activity. He also saw prostitution grow during the same period.

Lust knew he had a chance to dethrone Chad, but decided not to try, at least for now. He didn't always want the number one position, but gravitated to the intense specialization of his current role. He was an expert in causing others to lust for each other. He had an uncanny ability to provide nearly irresistible temptations within beings, causing them to be obsessed with desire for others or their things—things to which they were not entitled. The passion Lust could generate for desires of the body topped a mountain of unfilled ecstasy.

His daydream continued to the point that he began making up a new way to seduce men and women, when a sudden image of solitary refinement popped into his head. The image sent chills up his spine. "I never want to return to that forsaken place!" he blurted out, surprising himself.

Lust paced and finally selected the next move in his masterful game. His only hope was that the game would never end!

Chapter 36

Wrath's Next Move

Wrath had witnessed things he thought he would never see in hell. He was trying to understand and figure out the current state of affairs. He clearly did not understand what was happening in hell. It looked as though Chad was crumbling, but how could that be? *Chad was the Warrior! No one crossed Chad and remembered to tell of the exploit,* he thought. *Why is the "Warrior" so concerned about this viewing machine? What's that about?* he wondered. *Why would the Warrior care about this simpleminded new devil, Sal? Why? Why? Why? Was it possible the viewing machine could, indeed, knock Chad out of his number one slot?* Wrath shook his head in disbelief. *No way this Sal thing has a chance against the Warrior!*

Then he began to think of Lust. *What is Lust up to? He is performing his magic by fueling the flames, causing Sal to lust for the number one position. He is causing Chad to act just as he once said, "When a man wants something—I mean really wants something—he will stop at nothing to get it. The trick from hell to earth is to make the person really want something."* Wrath remembered Lust's speech advertising lust! He remembered it quite well.

The order of hell worked. It was efficient. It could not fail! Wrath's anger began to boil. *Our goal is souls! Although,* he wondered, *is there an opportunity for me to ascend? No, the Warrior is too dominant! Hell is efficient. Our goal is souls!*

He continued his thought, *Should I make an allegiance with one of the Joint Chiefs? No, the Warrior is too dominant!*

"Hell is efficient. Our goal is souls! Our goal is souls!" Wrath found himself chanting.

He knew his next destination.

Chapter 37

The Escape

As Sal ran from the listless Barb, he ran as fast as he could for what seemed like days. The pain in his chest grew to what he remembered from his BH heart attack. He wanted to rest, but had only one thought on his mind and that was to *find a way out!* The thought of another day in hell helped him overcome his chest ache. In fact, he found a way to accelerate his running.

As he ran, he thought back to Barb. He wanted to help her. Sadly, the moment that thought came to him, he tripped. After hitting the ground, he rolled and landed on his knees. He begged for mercy. He felt excruciating agony in his head, as if a molten sword was splitting his head in two. He fell down to the ground force. As he hit the floor, he lost consciousness.

Satan's Guard had been searching for Chad. At the Sal sighting, two guards broke away to let the king of evil know Sal had been found, while the remainder encircled him. Sal slowly regained consciousness and then rolled over, shaking his head as the pain enveloped him. The pain was similar to a hangover, he reminisced. He stood up and set out on his quest for an exit from hell. After a few steps, he hit what felt like a wall and staggered back. He moved forward cautiously, probing for a way around the obstruction. Wherever he touched, he hit the obstruction repeatedly, until finally, the wall grabbed him.

He heard a voice. "Stand down and await orders."

"Huh, what does it mean to stand down and await orders?" he asked aloud.

He directed himself toward a sharp, angled trajectory and ran full speed, hoping to break through, but only hit the obstruction again. The wall grabbed him again, this time throwing him into another wall.

"Stand down," a voice said.

"By whose authority?" he retorted. Sal sensed that he was surrounded by what was likely a blockade of devils.

"Stand down and await orders," the voice responded.

Sal pondered his next move. Just then, something huge and fast flew by him. As he turned to see the flyby, he became aware of the sound of someone crying. He started to walk toward the crying. As he drew closer, he recognized Barb's sobs.

Every part of his miserable being wanted to help her, but sadly, he did not know how. He could not hug her and tell her it was going to be OK. Not only would the embrace cause enormous agony, but even the desire to console her would also cause pain. He could not even cry with her. He could not tell her to run away with him. His emotions were gone. They were trapped.

As he approached her, he fell to his knees. He crawled over to her and whispered, "We must escape."

She looked at him and tried to scream. Just as in her most frightening earthly dreams, nothing came out. She tried again without success. She tried to merely speak, but could not. Eventually, she threw herself on the floor and cried inconsolably.

Sal decided it was time to try another escape. *Maybe Barb served as a distraction to the blocking devils*, he thought. After one more look at the sobbing devil on the floor, Sal jumped to his feet and bolted at an even sharper angle than his previous attempt.

Sal was correct. Barb distracted the Guard and he had broken free and was running at full speed. As he looked up, he thought he saw something he had never seen in hell, so he ran toward it with all his remaining being, thinking, *I can escape! I will escape!*

Just then, two guards flew into him, knocking him down hard. He did several flips and came to rest on his back. He quickly rolled over to his side. He could still see his destination. He attempted to get on his knees. As soon as he rose, both guards dropkicked him. This time he hit the ground so hard the guards thought they had broken his skull. Sal lay still on the burning floor.

Barb watched the attempted escape in horror. She knew there was no escape. She had also seen two guards drop Sal within fifteen feet of her location. She crawled over to him. She wanted to console him, but knew better. She kept crying. Suddenly, she was lifted into the air and was moving. She looked and saw that Sal's limp body was also airborne and that Satan's Guard was escorting them.

Now what? she wondered. *Where could they be taking us?* She was sure that solitary refinement was their destination. She strained to hear what they were saying. She thought she heard one of the guards mentioning "orders" that seemed to have come in during Sal's feeble attempt at escape, but she could not make out what they were saying.

As she was dragged through the air, she could see pockets of hell. One area caught her eye for a split second. She saw a row of burning crosses—and they appeared to be occupied. She heard a chant rise from the crowd around the crosses that appeared to number in the millions. Just when she thought she understood the chant, the Guard began to descend to their ordered location.

Barb looked at her destination and cried. This time, sound came out.

Chapter 38

Chad's Dilemma

Chad's encounter with Lust was still annoying him when Frankie spoke up.

"Chad what are you going to do? Banishment will be your punishment if you aren't careful in your actions. I would suggest—"

"Where do you get off making suggestions to me?" Chad raged, bristling at even the thought of Frankie making a suggestion. "I am the leader of this domain of evil! I am the Warrior!" he roared.

Undaunted, Frankie looked him in the eyes and hissed, "Then I suggest you start acting like the leader!"

Chad's rage burned greater and he threw Frankie. Frankie immediately jumped to his feet.

"Go ahead. Hit me again. It won't change that you aren't king! Come on! Bring it on!"

Chad flew hard at Frankie and then stopped dead in his tracks.

Chad turned away and began to pace, thinking to himself, *How did this happen? How could this happen? Is Frankie right? Am I not acting like the Warrior? Has Sal made me weak?* This thought created a pain that he had never experienced before.

Frankie watched Chad roll around on the molten floor. Frankie wasn't sure what was happening to Chad. It resembled an epileptic seizure he once observed as a police officer in his BH life. Frankie wanted to reach out, but he had been in hell much too long to be that stupid. He decided to leave and return later.

Chad caught Frankie's departure out of the corner of his eye. He attempted to get to his feet to stop Frankie, but his suffering increased. He continued to roll on the floor uncontrollably.

As one of the designers of the pain behavior modifiers, Chad should have known the best ways to beat the suffering. Unfortunately, this pain was too intense. He tried focusing his thoughts on something else—another place or time. He chose the time when they invented the pain modifiers.

At that time, Satan was concerned that even the worst souls to arrive in hell had a good side to them. In fact, one of the many passages in the anti-Satan book that upset Satan was the one about loving one's enemies. The anti-Satan said even evil people love evil people, but that his disciples were to go further and love their enemies. Regrettably, they had to admit the anti-Satan was correct. Even evil people loved at least someone in their family.

Back then, Satan decided he needed a method to enforce his ten commandments. Some of the commandments were: "Thou shalt not love," "Thou shalt not care for others," and, "Thou shalt not show thanks." Since these were basic human instincts—as humans were made in the image of the anti-Satan—he knew they needed to be broken, so he implemented the system of pain behavior modifiers. Whenever a thought or action occurred that broke Satan's commandments, pain would hit the offending devil.

Chad had overseen implementation of the modifiers. Every new devil that arrived in hell quickly learned the anti-Satan's ten commandments were dead. These devils never realized the importance of those commandments in their human existence, hence, they were damned for all eternity. They soon realized the emptiness they felt when forced to live within Satan's commandments.

Chad reflected on one of the first devils to experience the behavior modifiers. *What was his name? Alfred?* he wondered. Alfred was sentenced to an eternity of agony due to his issues with the anti-Satan's commandments, particularly in regard to adultery and stealing. However, though Alfred was evil, he loved his children and would do anything for them. Chad knew he would have to be broken.

On his third day in hell, Alfred met a female devil, Beth, who was also relatively new to hell. As they had been in the process of "getting to know" one another, the ground opened up, and Beth disappeared. As Alfred dove to help her, pain hit him across his back, head, and neck.

As his distress subsided, he saw Beth return. She looked shocked. He asked her what happened. She tried to explain the horrors of the physical abuse she had suffered and started to cry as her modifiers caused her pain. The pain that engulfed her head caused her to lose her balance. Alfred ran over to help, but his modifiers took both of his knees out and he hit the lava floor with a great force that shook the ground.

As his despair increased, Alfred tried to do something no one in hell should ever attempt. He tried to pray to the anti-Satan for mercy. Alfred's entire essence seemed to explode with his attempt. He felt anguish in so many places he thought he had died of a stroke all over again.

After observing Alfred and the other early victims of the behavior modifiers, Chad and Satan knew they were capable of breaking in even the most stubborn devil. Pain served two purposes in hell. The obvious purpose of physical discomfort was the just reward for those fallen to an everlasting life of torment. The less obvious purpose was control. Satan required control over all inhabitants of hell. The pain from endless fruitless battles and the modifiers kept each devil in hell under the control of the almighty evil one. There would be no such things as caring or comfort in Satan's world.

Ironically, now Chad was feeling the torture from his own design. The more he had inappropriate thoughts, the more he felt the pain. Finally, he realized that to stop this pain endeavor, he needed to reverse his thoughts.

I am number one in the land of evil. I am the dictator for this existence. I will cause destruction across hell. I am the Warrior. He repeated these thoughts, causing reductions in his modifiers. Soon, his level of suffering was back to the regular threshold.

He decided to go to Frankie's abode because he needed to discuss the "plan" with him. As Chad flew above hell, he noticed Satan's Guard pass by. He ignored his curiosity and stayed focused on his current task.

As he landed in Frankie's abode, the meeting Frankie was already conducting surprised him.

Chapter 39

Lust's Next Move

Lust heard several loud screeches. He looked up through where the ceiling would be in a normal house and saw Satan's Guard flying overhead. He stood at attention to see if the king of evil was with the Guard. He did not see him.

Lust admired the formations the Guard could maintain while flying. It was a perfect circle, containing a flying V. He decided to follow the Guard. Within seconds, he was airborne.

This did not go unnoticed. Just after he took flight, two guard members in the rear of the flying formation broke off to investigate the new flier. As they neared Lust, they must have recognized him because they veered off and went back to their points on the circle.

Lust watched as the Guard landed. To avoid attracting further attention, he flew past the landing area before finally landing a reasonable distance away. Success! He avoided detection.

He watched the Guard encircle their transport. He couldn't make out what they were saying, so he inched closer. A sudden hurricane force wind knocked him down. As he arose, he looked at the circled Guard and noticed Satan had joined the party.

He crept still closer in an attempt to hear what they were saying. He got close enough to recognize Sal and moved closer still. The sound of his approach caught the attention of the Guard. Two of them immediately took off, canvassing the grounds to see what caused the stir. Lust dove to the floor and hid behind an enormous rock. The Guard was only about fifteen feet away, so he thought detection was inevitable. He froze. The two guards broke off their search and hurried back to the circle.

As they left, he thought for sure that they would find him. He formulated answers for the impending questioning because of his obvious new spying habit.

As he inched forward, he heard the two guards that had just performed the search defending their actions.

"We heard a noise, so we wanted to make—"

Before they could finish, their leader cut them off and they both ended up on their backs. Then they sprang back to their feet and stood at attention. They offered no additional explanation.

Lust strained to listen as Satan spoke, but without getting closer, he couldn't hear much. Lust decided to move away slowly. As he moved away, he thought about his next destination. Regrettably, he tripped and fell. As he got up and started to walk, he found himself airborne. Though he was thinking of flying, he had not yet begun. He looked back and gulped.

Chapter 40

Make it So!

Barb's screech pulled Sal out of his stupor. As he shook his head, he struggled to remember the last thing he saw prior to passing out. He remembered the vision. The memories made him want to get up and run again. He attempted to get up before he realized he was not on the ground. He was flying without moving his wings although his escort felt familiar. As he turned to look, the Guard let him go.

Sal fell about fifteen feet. The crash broke his left leg. A kick to his left leg greeted his attempt to roll over. He cried out. As he grabbed his leg, another guard delivered a kick to his chest. Just as another guard seemed set to deliver more punishment to Sal, he stopped. Sal kept rolling around in intense agony. As he rolled, he caught a glimpse of Satan. *Just when I thought it couldn't get any worse,* he winced.

Satan saw one of his guards kick Sal. Just as another was about to kick him, Satan hit both of them with a bolt that sent them flying. He landed about five feet from Sal and shouted, "Stop it!" as he glared at the remaining guards. They snapped to attention and dared not make eye contact with their leader. Though Satan had just admonished his Guard, he was pleased with their subservient nature.

He yelled again, "It is my job to dispense suffering!" At that, he hit Sal with a bolt that sent him into convulsions. He figured he would allow Sal to internalize his latest pain. After a minute or two, Satan bent over and grabbed the bellowing Sal by the neck. "So, you wanted to escape? How did it feel to get s-o-o-o close?" At the end of Satan's rant, he dropped Sal and proceeded to step on him. Satan shouted at him, "Make it so!"

Satan prepared to fly away. Just then, he noticed Barb and approached her. As he drew closer, Barb fell to her knees in unbelievable agony. Satan slowly licked her face and said, "Help him!"

As he departed, he grabbed one of the guards he had zapped and said, "Bring her."

As Satan flew away, Barb shuddered. She was at her wit's end. She wanted to cry, but her tears failed her again. She tried to wail, but again, to no avail. Barb remembered her first days in hell, and her early time with Sal. Just as the memories began to materialize, she saw the Guard approaching her. She shouted, "Wait! Satan told me to help Sal. You can't take me! No!" she shrieked.

She attempted to run, but the Guard was ready for her escape attempt. They grabbed her and proceeded to lick her. Desperate, she thought, *Please God, make them go away. Please God.* The Guard heard the sirens go off and knew immediately that she said a prayer. Without any more warning, the ground swallowed Barb.

Sal caught a glimpse of what was happening to Barb. He watched them lick her. Although Sal wanted to get up to help her, he was sure that his leg was still broken and pretty sure his ribs were cracked. Since moving wasn't possible, he blurted out, "Let her be." Just as the sirens wailed, he thought she looked at him and then she disappeared.

He managed to get to one knee when the guards approached him. He could not run. He could not help Barb. He could not escape. As they drew closer to him, one of them dropkicked Sal in the head, knocking him unconscious. The guard that kicked Sal muttered under his voice, "Get *me* in trouble with Satan? Who does he think he is?"

Doug observed Sal's welcoming committee from afar. Once the Guard departed, he went over to Sal and looked at his limp body. Sal reminded Doug of Slim Marino from his time in the military BH. Slim questioned every move from the commanding officers. Because of that, he was regularly hazed and dazed. Regardless of the punishment, he kept being a jerk. Over time, Doug developed a reasonable relationship with Slim. However, that was BH. Now there were no such things as relationships.

He grabbed Sal with one hand and dragged him into the Innovation Center.

Chapter 41

The Catch

Envy looked at the visitor. He decided to query the reason for the visit, but for some reason, he could not speak. He waited for the visitor to speak.

The visitor crept slowly toward Envy. As he approached, Envy could see the scarred face. The visitor must have been in hell for a long time. Very little of the human remained. The visitor got nose to nose with Envy and quickly hit him with a knee to his lower stomach. As Envy bent over, another knee struck him in the nose and knocked him flat on his back.

Envy was about to speak, however, the visitor had his foot on his head. The more Envy resisted or attempted to speak, the more pressure the visitor applied to his head. Envy ceased resisting.

The visitor eventually reduced the pressure on Envy, looking around Envy's dwelling. It looked somewhat familiar to him. He could not place the familiarity.

He spoke slowly. "You will help Sal."

Envy looked at the visitor. "Sal? Why should I help Sal?"

The visitor was not pleased with the question. The ensuing rage matched that of Satan. Envy bounced off several walls. At the end of the tirade, the visitor wound up back on top of Envy.

The visitor whispered, "Now, will you help Sal?"

Envy wasn't sure what to do. He was worried that if he agreed to help Sal, he would have to deal with Chad—at a minimum. If he did not agree to help Sal, it was clear this devil would inflict as much distress as needed to make his point. Envy searched his memory but couldn't determine the name of the visitor. He asked the visitor to identify himself.

The visitor was only interested in an affirmative answer to assist Sal. He had no interest in questions. He increased the pressure on Envy's throat significantly.

"Will you help Sal?"

Envy noticed a slight weakness in the visitor's left knee. He managed to kick out the knee. The devil fell forward to the floor. Envy sprang up, attempting to catch his breath. He grabbed the visitor's arms and twisted them behind him as he lay face down.

Envy retorted, "Now I am asking the questions. Who are you?"

"Who I am should not concern you. What I am should have you running from here."

Envy delivered a shot to the back of the visitor's head.

"Once again, who *are* you?"

The visitor attempted to break free. Envy delivered another hit to the back of his head.

"Who are you?"

The visitor refused to answer. Just as Envy was about to deliver another jab, more visitors arrived. Envy could identify these visitors— Satan's Guard. At sight of the Guard, the visitor flipped Envy off his back and took flight. The Guard followed him.

Envy grabbed one of the guards. The guard blew his whistle. The whistle caused two guards to break formation and return to Envy's lair. The two slammed into the back of Envy. As Envy fell, he asked, "Who was that?"

The guards kicked Envy and returned to their pursuit of the visitor.

Chapter 42

Wrath Vows Vengeance!

Wrath found himself waiting outside Satan's office for quite some time. He remembered his flight to the evil one's headquarters. The Guard almost crashed into him in flight. They were obviously in hot pursuit of someone. Wrath attempted to follow them for a few minutes, but then decided he should focus on his mission. He was already confused enough.

Wrath decided to go into the office. He looked at the soul chart.

Wow, Chad's evolution theory is really not working, he thought as he noticed the slight decline in souls over the preceding ten years. *Does this mean the Warrior is vulnerable?* Chad had been arguing the evolution concept for probably the equivalent of fifty earth years. How could it be that it wasn't working?

Wrath paced for quite some time, stopping to stare at the chart frequently. *Should I make a move on the Warrior? No! Hell is efficient. Our goal is souls!* he found himself chanting as he paced more quickly.

He was just about to stop and determine his plan when an astounding wind encircled him. As Wrath turned, he was hit with something he had never experienced. The bolt knocked him over. The pain in his chest matched the pain he felt from the massive heart attack he experienced BH, only much worse. As he grabbed his chest, another lightning strike hit him. This blow was aimed at his left knee and just as sharp as the pain in his chest. Wrath found himself on the molten floor in Satan's office, attempting to grab his chest and knee simultaneously.

"Wrath, what is your business here?" his assailant asked.

Wrath attempted to look up. The return for this effort was another heat force that exploded on his left cheek.

He came to the realization that the evil one was bolting him! In his now semiconscious state, Wrath decided to neither move nor talk.

"Wrath," he hissed, "stay out of this affair!"

As the word "affair" rang in his ear, Wrath's stomach burst into a new level of suffering. He reeled in misery, rolling from side to side. After a failed attempt to screech, he opened his eyes to see the evil one moving further into his office. Wrath attempted to make his anger boil, but the pain overwhelmed him. He continued to roll side to side.

On each roll, he glanced at the soul chart. The chart's clear documentation of a lack of performance caused his anger to dominate his suffering. Crawling away, he thought, *I will avenge this attack!*

Chapter 43

Chad and Frankie Together Again

As Chad landed, Frankie thought he looked almost apologetic. Frankie knew better than to think that Chad cared about anyone other than himself, though. Another of Satan's ten commandments, "Thou shalt not show sorrow or forgiveness," destroyed the concept of "sorry."

Frankie quickly determined the best way to get his visitor into a real discussion with Chad. The visitor wasn't going to be patient with him much longer. Frankie thought of potential ideas. *If he said the visitor could help Chad, he would react with anger to the suggestion he needed help. If he said the visitor had an idea, Chad would throw him for inviting the visitor. If he—* Before he could complete his idea, Chad jumped over toward him.

"So, why were you still meeting with him?" Chad queried.

Frankie initially stuttered and then blurted out, "Master, we must regain our control!"

Chad grabbed Frankie and threw him.

"*Our* control? There is no *OUR*." Chad flew over to the visitor.

Smirking, he said to the visitor, "How can you help me?"

The visitor didn't answer so Chad moved closer and closer to him.

"I repeat, and rarely do I repeat myself, how can you help me?"

Frankie flew into a rage. In a matter of seconds, he had pinned Chad to the molten floor.

"Now listen. Listen! He can help! He has a plan! You *will* listen!"

Chad was slightly amused at Frankie's fire. He quickly disposed of the weaker devil's position on him and turned his focus back to the visitor.

"OK, I will do as Frankie suggested." He slowly put a hand up to where his ear used to be. "I'm listening."

The visitor turned to fly away. It took all his effort, but Frankie managed to grab his wing. As Chad had done, the visitor quickly put Frankie in a disadvantaged position.

As he turned to fly away again, he felt another tug on his wing. This time, it was Chad. Chad dragged the old devil to the floor and quickly put him in some sort of wing lock.

"Now, I'm really listening!" Chad hissed.

The old devil had enough. He did a backflip out of the wing lock and threw Chad some ten feet away. Chad thought, *Now we are talking!* He flew hard directly into the visitor and the two of them hit a wall just as hard. Both were semiconscious when Chad rolled over.

"OK, now you've got my attention!"

Chad struggled to one knee and then to his feet. He reached down to the visitor and helped the older devil to an upright position. Frankie, the most surprised of the three, directed them to his weak idea of a table.

Chad and the visitor spent hours planning.

Chapter 44

Lust Stands Down?

Lust didn't enjoy his flight through hell. He knew his destination could not be good. When they were first airborne, he asked the guards for his destination. They ignored his request. He had a quick thought of escape, but unfortunately, he knew escape would not end well for him.

He decided to tolerate his escort. He watched hell below him as he flew. He didn't want to go to the "principal's office."

A fight below caught his eye and diverted his attention. As he watched the fight, he noticed the guards no longer held him. He was descending at a quick rate and he braced for impact.

Lust fell on his head, the impact sending shooting pain through his neck. The pain resembled the anguish he had when he broke his arm falling off a horse in his twenties BH. He tried to move, but his neck felt as though it was in five pieces.

He scanned his landing area. *Yup, I'm in his office*, he thought. At that moment, he sensed the presence of the almighty evil one. He attempted to move his head and pain like one hundred needle jabs, pierced his neck.

"Lust, what are you doing?" Satan demanded.

"Lying here on the floor with a broken neck," he replied.

"WRONG answer," Satan growled as he bolted Lust in the stomach and sent him reeling through the air. Lust hit a rock and wanted to scream. Sadly, he only managed a squeak. He lay there, curled up in a ball.

Satan flew over to him.

"Lust, what are you doing?"

Lust grimaced. "I'm not sure I understand your question."

Satan looked at him with surprise and growled, "WRONG answer," before delivering a bolt to Lust's head.

It was the worst place for Lust to take another hit. With his neck broken from the fall, and now this bolt, Lust was sure his head was missing!

Satan flew over to him again.

"Lust, what are you doing?"

Lust gulped and thought, *what could Satan possibly know?* He decided that continuing to test the evil one would not be a good idea.

"Satan, sir, I always want to serve you," he said in a low voice. "My time at the Innovation Center was one of pure curiosity. I was taken by surprise when Chad was bolted and I find this master plan of Sal's quite intriguing."

Satan delivered another bolt to Lust's head.

"Lust, you will not interfere with Chad, Sal, or any Joint Chief. There will be no further warnings!"

As he left, he roared in anger. All of hell heard him and froze momentarily. Before his exit, he hit Lust with multiple bolts, knocking him unconscious.

Chapter 45

No Answer for Prayers

Barb woke up in her abode again. She rapidly found herself focusing on two memories. She remembered the ground swallowing her and shuddered at the abuse that followed. She pushed that memory aside to focus on what Sal had seen.

She thought of his description, "a white light that sort of begged me to come." She remembered that folks on earth referred to someone known as Jesus as the Light. As she wondered about this light, she decided she had to find it.

Barb knew better than to get excited, so she kept her future goal to herself. She looked around and envisioned a day when she would not be in hell! She found herself spinning around almost joyfully.

Just as she began another spin, she noticed the Guard landing behind her. This time, she decided to resist. Barb kicked and clawed. Though her efforts were valiant, the Guard eventually won and carried her away.

As she entered Satan's room, her pain modifiers began to increase. She let out a request to lower them. Regrettably, her complaint had the opposite effect; her pain modifiers increased.

She cried out and knew that Satan would soon be in the lair.

She could not decide which was worse—time with Satan or the ground swallowing her and the ensuing torture. She decidedly put her hands together and was just about to ask for mercy when she disappeared into the ground.

Chapter 46

Sal's Refusal

After Doug finally dropped Sal to the floor, Sal analyzed his pain levels. To his surprise, his broken leg seemed to have repaired itself. *So, hell must work somewhat similar to earth*, he thought. *Your body can repair itself or even regenerate.*

As he wondered why regeneration would matter after death, it hit him. Ah, this *"feature" must exist such that you can experience the same severe agony repeatedly. Wow!*

Sal looked around the Innovation Center. To his surprise, Doug had been working on the viewing machine idea. Unbelievably, he had made progress with the concept. Doug broke the silence of Sal's awe.

"Sal, as crazy as this idea might be, we will find a way to invent the concept."

Doug tried to engage Sal in a discussion on the notion of a "moving picture." He referenced the discussion he had with Barb specifically about the idea of blowing people up on the viewing machine. Doug then started to introduce his idea to Sal.

"Look, I could tie the sheriff to the railroad tracks and…." he said, trailing off after noticing Sal wasn't listening or engaging in dialogue. He decided Sal was way worse than Slim—by far the most annoying person he had ever had the displeasure of meeting. Still, he began sharing his idea again.

"As the sheriff is tied to the tracks, we can show him being kicked and…."

Still no acknowledgment of my existence, eh? he thought to himself. He looked intently at Sal.

"Listen, I thought you wanted to put this plan in motion. I'm willing to help, and now you are a mute devil?"

"I will do nothing without Barb!" Sal blurted out. The statement immediately caused Sal to double over in pain emanating from the center of his abdomen.

Doug took the opportunity to grab Sal. He knew what to do with him even if Sal had a good idea. He would not stand for his ignorance or defiance. Doug connected Sal to his explosives and started the countdown from sixty.

Sal welcomed the countdown.

"How could anything be worse than hell? I've experienced every possible torture."

Doug glared at him. "Did you change your mind?"

Sal was as belligerent as he had ever been. "No Barb, no help."

Doug continued about his business.

"Forty-five...forty-four...forty-three...."

Chapter 47

Envy's Confusion

Envy landed in the Innovation Center, still clearly rattled by the encounter with that visitor. He was trying to determine whom or what that thing was that visited him. He scanned his memory for every devil he had ever seen. He had never seen anyone like this guy. He seemed familiar, like someone he knew. As much as he tried, he couldn't place him.

As he walked through the center in a daze, he found Sal. Envy had a strange premonition that the visitor and Sal had something in common. He shrugged his shoulders. Most likely, the fact the visitor told Envy to help Sal caused the strange feeling. Then he thought, *Nah, there is something more to that visitor. There is something very different about him!*

Envy walked over to Sal and noticed the countdown.

"Fifteen...fourteen...thirteen...."

He quickly went to work, trying to release Sal from the explosives before it was too late.

"Eight...seven...six...."

Can I get him detached before the countdown ends with my destruction? he wondered.

His mind started to operate in slow motion. He thought, *If I'm caught in the explosion, does that mean I would no longer exist? Would my soul be gone forever?* He was amazed that he still did not want his existence to end. *The desire to live is built into our souls,* he thought. *Survive at all cost—even if you are in hell!*

At this point, Envy would have been sweating if sweat existed in hell.

"Two...one...."

He grabbed Sal and flew straight up. The blast pushed the two of them another fifty feet higher. As they started to spiral down, Envy reversed field and managed to bring the two of them to a soft landing in the Innovation Center. Doug came running up to Envy. "What are you doing? I was about to complete one of my most important tests ever and would have gotten rid of the most annoying and ignorant entity in hell."

"I agree with you," Envy replied. "We should destroy him, but not quite yet. We may need his ideas and inventions."

Doug repelled the idea. "I don't care if he is the greatest inventor since Ben Franklin. He insists on doing everything on his terms. He doesn't have a chance of rising in Satan's hierarchy. In fact, he does not have a chance of even existing very much longer. Chad, me—even Satan—everyone who comes near Sal wants to beat him silly."

Envy wasn't sure how to respond. "Doug, let's not explode him now, OK?"

Doug looked at Envy with dismay. He wanted to respond, *You have got to be kidding me!* Instead, he succumbed to the request and mustered, "Sir Yes Sir!"

Envy turned to Sal and said, "Now that you've been released from the explosives, get to work with Doug on your lunacy!"

Sal got nose-to-nose with Envy. "No. I'm not helping until Barb is free." Sal knew this thought and statement would lead to incredible pain. He no longer cared about his suffering. He had to help her. "Release Barb and I will help!"

Envy glared at him and thought, *I should let Doug have you.* Instead, he decided to reason with the wacky devil. However, the discussion repeatedly led to the same impasse—free Barb. Envy was about to increase the austerity of the options presented to Sal when he realized he was late to Satan's staff meeting. He finally looked at Doug.

"I'm not finished with him. No blowing him up, understood?"

Doug snarled and turned away.

Envy was out of time, so he jumped up and took flight.

Chapter 48

Staff Meeting—Sal?

Lust's eyes popped open. He realized he wasn't in his abode but he was still trying to understand his surroundings. When he attempted to move, he felt pain in his neck and right arm and thought, *Ah, now I remember. I dropped from the sky, was warned by Satan, and then I was bolted.* He was still in Satan's office. He looked around and started to wonder what it would be like to have this office. Although this would never be possible, he thought, *Wow, I've got to have this office! Imagine–I could be the king of all hell!* As if Satan could hear his thoughts, a blast of pain crossed his lower body.

How in the world do I get out of here? he wondered. Lust didn't want to be there when Satan returned. He cried out as he rolled around on the floor. He had to find a way to break out of his pain state. He started to think of Envy. That crafty old devil had taken the bait. Envy actually thought he could become the number one. Lust's plan was working perfectly and he decided to stay away from another pleasurable thought. He rolled over, slowly got to his feet, and decided to return home.

He turned to see the Joint Chiefs entering Satan's office. *Ah, it must be Satan's staff meeting*, he thought. *How could I have forgotten?* He slowly walked over to the meeting table.

Satan turned the beginning of his staff meeting over to Chad, who reported the progress on the theory of evolution plan. He explained his belief that the soul meter would show a surge over the next six months. Chad shared how the concept that God did not create the universe was taking hold with earthly humans.

Satan was about to interrupt him and introduce Sal's plan to the conversation when Envy entered the meeting. Satan did not even look up. He had no tolerance for latecomers. He always bolted them upon arrival to his staff meeting, and Envy was no exception. Envy attempted to explain the reason for his tardiness, but was electrified again.

Satan turned to Chad. "What is your confidence level that Darwin's evolution strategy will actually work? Are you willing to bet your number one status on the plan?"

Lust joined the discussion. "What about Sal's plan?"

Satan winced and glared at Lust. *Didn't I just talk to him about Sal?* he thought to himself. He was enraged.

"Sal is working with Doug at the Innovation Center on the insane idea!" he growled at Lust.

Though still recovering from his bolting, Envy contemplated joining the conversation, although he didn't want to attract Satan's attention again. However, Satan needed to know that Sal had terms and conditions.

"Maybe not." Envy gulped.

Satan turned his glare to Envy. "What did you say?"

"Maybe," Envy hesitated, "Sal is not working with Doug."

"Envy, what are you talking about?" Satan hissed.

Envy gulped again. "Sal is not working with Doug."

Satan stared at him for an uncomfortable amount of time. "How would you know anything about Sal?"

Envy began with his last trip to the Innovation Center. "While I was at the center, Doug was about to blow Sal up because he was insistent on conditions for helping Doug develop the machine."

Satan was amazed that the "Sal thing" had engulfed most of his staff due to intrigue with the plan and situation. Satan screeched uncontrollably. "Sal has a condition? Not possible! Does he understand where he is? Sal has a condition?"

Envy looked at Satan as he ranted, too shaken to respond. Satan was about to bolt him.

"He requires freedom for the female devil, Barb," he squeaked.

Steam was now coming from Satan's head. "What in the world is going on here?" Satan bellowed. He bolted Envy and took off.

The bolts didn't knock Envy unconscious. However, he did find himself fairly dazed.

Chad maneuvered over to Envy.

"Well, look at this. We've found another victim of Sal and his plan. Welcome to the club! Although Satan did not care about your information, I'd like to know how you know what you know!"

Envy looked at him and remained silent. He was still shaking the cobwebs of his stupor. He was alert enough to deflect Chad's query with a "go away" look. However, Chad was obsessed with letting hell know that he was back in charge. He unloaded on Envy with multiple kicks and punches. Envy was barely conscious as Chad repeated his request.

"How do you know anything about Sal?"

Envy wanted to tell Chad to "get lost." Unfortunately, he could not speak! This fact didn't matter to Chad. Before he knew it, Chad knocked him unconscious.

Chad looked around at the other Joint Chiefs watching him. Wrath was about to attack him but abruptly stopped when he remembered Satan's warning to him.

Just then, Chad exclaimed, "I'm back!" before flying quickly into the dark sky.

Chapter 49

Chad Returns

Chad felt the evil power of hell run throughout his body as he flew into the air. He remembered what it was like to know the power of evil. It was a rush for him.

"I'm back!" he bellowed again.

He wondered how in the world one silly devil with a horrible idea could cause so much havoc in hell. He had let his guard down.

He knew where to go next. He needed to go to the Innovation Center to finish this one way or another.

As Chad flew, he felt an odd sensation of excitement. Since excitement was against the ten commandments of hell, Chad knew he would feel pain. He was thinking of the best method for eliminating Sal, the ultimate nuisance in hell.

As the ideas spun in his head, Chad spun in the air. He thought he was dreaming when his left wing was clipped again, causing his spin to accelerate. As Chad tried to figure out what happened, something struck him in the head.

This blow sent Chad spiraling toward the molten floor of hell. In his semiconscious state, he attempted to regain flight. However, just as he started to level off about fifty feet above the floor, another shot hit his back. The blow sent Chad crashing to the floor below with such force that he bounced several times before sliding to his rest. He was barely conscious when another punch hit his left eye socket.

Chad realized he was pinned by an entity. He attempted to discern who was on top of him but his blurry vision from that last punch hindered him. He tried to talk, but was unable because the assailant on top of him had disabled his vocal cords with a knee on his throat.

"Do not go to the Innovation Center; it will be your doom," his assailant growled. "Forget about Sal!"

Chad thought he recognized the voice, though he wasn't sure he recognized anything by this point in their struggle. As Chad opened his mouth to speak, he was interrupted by the visitor. "Do not go to the center!" he said.

Chad shook his head from left to right and right to left to shake the cobwebs loose. He squinted with one eye, although he still couldn't see his assailant. While squinting, he looked around cautiously. He began to sense the attacker had left. He was sure he had heard that voice before, and that he had met his attacker, but he just couldn't connect the two.

He attempted to get up. Unfortunately, he could barely move. He decided to roll over first. As he pushed off with his right leg, he realized that rolling over was much easier than he had anticipated. He tried doing a push-up to get off the hot floor. As he pushed up, his left arm gave out. *How can one of the kings of hell not get up?* he thought before trying another push-up. This time his right arm gave out on him. As he lay there with his face in the molten floor, Chad willed himself to get up and pursue his attacker, but regrettably, he could not. He started to lapse into a semiconscious state.

Chad focused back on the time when he first became the "number one" in hell. He admired his masterful plan of ascension. He turned his focus to Envy. As Envy appeared in his head, his anger intensified. He remembered that Envy also had a plan to get to number one. Envy didn't know that Chad knew this. *How could Envy be so stupid?* he thought. "How could he think I didn't know about his little scheme?" Chad said aloud.

He had discovered it many years ago when he tortured one of the many supporters of the former number one. At that time the poor soul mentioned Envy's plan. Chad decided to let it go since he already ascended and Envy was a useful member of the Joint Chiefs.

"NOT THIS TIME!" Chad yelled. "This time, Envy will SUFFER!"

Chapter 50

Lust Defeated

As Lust departed Satan's staff meeting, he decided to return to his abode, though he was far more interested in seeking Chad out. He wanted to continue provoking Chad. Lust was growing concerned that Chad was starting to look more like the Chad of old rather than the "Sal infected" Chad of new.

Lust flew at a much slower speed than normal due to his wounds. As he descended into his abode, he landed painfully hard on his stomach. Rolling over, Lust looked up at the sky, which was complete blackness. He wondered if he would ever know what it was like up there. It did not have stars or a moon like the skies he remembered from his BH life.

Up there, the darkness was so extreme you couldn't see your hand in front of your face. Lust knew the darkness because two hundred years earlier, he attempted to fly to the top of hell. He thought he would make it to the top. As he flew over two thousand feet high, the air got thinner and thinner. Eventually, Lust couldn't breathe and spiraled out of control until he crashed onto the floor.

Occasionally, he observed devils attempting to make a similar ascent, seeking to escape, but regrettably for them, they all suffered the same demise. One series of ascents by a devil named Harrieta was particularly memorable. Every day, she attempted to soar to the top of hell. Each time, she went higher than her previous attempt. She tried many times but all her efforts were futile.

As Lust slowly sat up, he made his decision. His next destination would be the Innovation Center. Lust rose to his feet. Just then, he thought he noticed an odd aroma and started sniffing the air. He was sure he smelled something. As he spun around, the "something" ran full force into him. Before he passed out, Lust barely heard a voice say, "Stay out of this, or else!"

Chapter 51

Satan Has Had Enough!

Satan and his Guard flew at top speed to the Innovation Center. He was so preoccupied with Sal that he didn't notice several of his guards were under attack by what they perceived to be a gang. In recent years, devils had begun "grouping" and attacking. Satan did not really care for the practice. However, it brought a completely new definition to terror, so he let the practice continue.

As Satan landed in the Innovation Center, Doug immediately met him. "Hello, sir. I will provide you with a quick update, sir."

Satan nodded for Doug to continue. Doug thought, *At last, the end of Sal is near. Satan will never tolerate such total insubordination!*

"Look," Doug began, "we've made some progress on this viewing machine! In fact, I think we just might be able to make it work. To make it happen, you must destroy that mad devil, Sal. He fears no one—not even you." He let the last comment slowly resonate with Satan before continuing. "I tried showing Sal my concept for the machine, but he just ignored me. No matter what I said to him, he just stood there as defiant as a two-year-old fighting with his mother. I tried to get his attention and he just stood there! Finally, I ordered him to listen and help. He said he would not help without Barb. I'm thinking, *Here we go again!* Then I decided to blow him up."

At this, Satan looked at him with rising anger.

"I have to blow him up. He is crazy! I tell you! He's crazy!" Doug said before noticing a cue from Satan to stop ranting and be more reserved in his remarks.

Doug looked up sheepishly. "Well, I would have blown him up. However, about halfway into my countdown, Envy showed up—"

"What was Envy doing here?" Satan scoffed.

Doug took the opportunity to express his irritation with Envy.

"Yes sir. Envy was here and started to argue with me about blowing Sal up. I was like, 'Why do you care?' When I refused to stop the explosion, Envy took matters into his own hands and went to work to free Sal. I saw the two of them shoot up into the sky, so he must have made it out of there." Doug shook his head. "How unfortunate. I could have gotten both of them at one time!"

"What happened next?" Satan growled at him.

"Don't know and don't care," Doug retorted. "I just went back to work."

"Anything else?" Satan queried. "Anyone else on my staff helping Sal?"

Doug thought for a moment. He had seen his share of Joint Chiefs and decided to leave it alone for now. He shook his head in a negative manner.

Satan looked at him. He knew that others had been there and decided to let it go.

"Where is Sal now?"

Doug looked at his master. "Don't know and don't care!"

Satan grabbed Doug and lifted him high above his head. "You will care! I must have this invention!" Satan slammed Doug into the floor.

Doug lay there for a moment, thinking to himself, *Sal caused an attack on me! How do I get rid of him?* He got on his knees in homage to Satan.

"Yes sir," he said, "I will care about this invention. I will do whatever it takes." When Doug saw Satan running toward him, he decided to continue his sentence. "And I will care about...."

"SAL!" Satan shouted, completing Doug's sentence as he ran Doug into a boulder.

Satan turned to his Guard. "Bring Sal to me. Bring him to me now!"

Chapter 52

Sal's Revenge

Sal sat on the ground in the Innovation Center taking in his surroundings. He looked at some of the inventions of the past and got a glimpse of the future. *Humans have no hope,* he thought. *This center has some of the brightest evil minds in all of history working against it. All the pure humans have is their faith. Satan's inventions are real and you can touch them, not at all like that belief in Jesus and invisible God stuff. There is no hope for them.*

Sal walked over to the future area and started to analyze the future weapon ideas. *All of these inventions have one thing in common,* he thought. *Man can kill man without having to be close to him. Man can kill man without seeing the horror of death. Wow, humans have no hope as the dark one wreaks havoc with the future world.*

He walked over to another invention. Just then, out of the corner of his eye, Sal saw the Guard approaching. His natural instinct—running—would not work. He knew he couldn't elude the Guard. Besides, he wanted a piece of Satan.

The Guard surrounded him. Sal recognized the one who kicked him while he was down. He flew full force into that devil, almost knocking him unconscious. His attack had the expected effect. Soon, four guards were pummeling Sal. He did not care. He had just gotten his first revenge in hell!

Chapter 53

Wrath's Next Move

After Satan's staff meeting, Wrath wasn't sure where to go. He thought about going to the Innovation Center, but his master was very clear. Unlike Lust, Wrath had no desire to tangle with Satan. However, he was determined to get revenge on Satan for his attack on him."

He started to fly in the direction of the Warrior's abode. *Should I attack the Warrior?* he wondered. As this thought zoomed through his head, he noticed he was over the solitary refinement area. *Ah good. I will go down there and gather some ideas for revenge!*

As Wrath approached the solitary refinement cells, he marveled at the innovation. Daily existence, as outlined in the Christian scripture, was indeed hell. Amazingly, this solitary environment allowed suffering to rise to completely new levels! The poor souls that landed here ended up cursing their very souls every minute of their most miserable existence.

Wrath began to scan the cells. He noticed some activity around a cell near the top of the honeycomb-like area.

As he peeked into the cell, he was surprised. He saw Sal's female devil. *Why is she here?* he wondered. *I thought Satan had a desire for this female. He must have grown tired of her to allow her to come to this place.*

He watched her cell with uncontrollable lust. *Ah, look, she is being groped. I must participate!* Wrath knew the possible penalty for "jumping" into a solitary cell, so he tried to hold himself back. He even remembered his one trip to solitary early in his career in hell. He shuddered at the memory and tried to control himself. The more he tried, the more he found himself approaching the female devil's cell.

As he drew closer to her cell, his desire for her increased rapidly. He was in a fog, captured by his desire for her. Though he tried, he could not resist.

Wrath couldn't tell what was drawing him to the female. Was it her scent? Was it her spunk? Was it her moves? Whatever it was, there was no resisting.

Soon, he found himself in the cell with her and her voices. He moved toward her scent and was so ready to join in. Fortunately, he caught a quick flicker of light out of the corner of his eye. Someone else was doing the unthinkable and heading into her cell.

Wrath could not risk discovery. He looked for a place to hide but struggled to see through the darkness. His eyes weren't adjusting quickly enough, so he ran in the opposite direction of the light flicker and hit a wall. Then he saw another flicker, and then another. He caught a gasp just in time. He ran again from the light flicker and hit another wall. *What am I to do?* he wondered.

He could smell the visitors as they approached. As a last resort, he dove headfirst onto the floor of the cell. As he hit the floor, someone stepped on his head and moved on. *Oh no, they found me*, he shuddered. Just then, another foot landed on the back of his left leg and moved on. Finally, another foot stepped across his back. *They must be preoccupied with the female devil*, he thought, just before another five feet walked across him almost simultaneously. Wrath held in a scream, putting his left hand over his mouth.

A couple more feet walked on him and then it was quiet.

Chapter 54

Sal is in Charge?

The Guard dropped Sal in front of Satan. He was in a fair amount of agony from the Guard's beating and rolled around on the ground. Satan looked at his Guard with disdain.

"Who did this?"

None of the Guard volunteered to acknowledge their recent work.

Satan got down on one knee and slowly pulled Sal to his feet.

"Now Sal, how could they beat you up again? Who did this?"

Sal attempted to point, but Satan ignored his gesture.

"How could they do this to you? What were they thinking? You are such a great devil and a leader among those in hell. Do you want me to destroy the guards that did this?"

Sal glared at Satan. Though his vision was blurry from the beating, he could tell Satan was serious. Without speaking, Sal started to think he had ascended to the number one slot. He tried to straighten up.

"Yes, you should destroy them all. They work with reckless abandon. Yes, destroy them! Destroy them now!"

Satan looked at Sal with complete astonishment. "Absolutely. Your wish is my command. Which one first?"

The effects of his beating were slowly decreasing. Sal managed to get a strong point at the guard member Satan had punished previously.

Satan looked in the direction he pointed. He recognized the guard as the one he had told to leave Sal alone.

"So, it was him again?" he questioned as he walked over to the singled out guard.

"Didn't I tell you not to attack him anymore? Wasn't that a direct order?"

The guard member didn't know how to respond. Only the Guard leader had conversations with Satan. The guard member began to speak, but the leader gestured for him to shut up. Unfortunately, for the leader of the Guard, Satan noticed the gesture. He flew over to the leader.

"Do you have something to say since you muted him?"

Two guards joined Sal in pointing to the wayward guard. Sal began feeling a new sense of power. He could now point and destroy. That was power.

The leader didn't respond to Satan's first query.

"I repeat, did you authorize this latest attack on poor Sal?"

The leader nodded his head in the affirmative. Satan brought up his hand to bolt the leader of the Guard.

Sal felt another surge of power. "I have been avenged!" He changed from pointing at the Guard to raising both arms in a sign of victory. Then, he realized he didn't actually see the bolting of the guard, so his eyes turned back to Satan.

Unbelievable surprise hit him right before the bolt hit. As Sal flew through the air, his brain attempted to process what happened. *How could Satan miss them and hit me?* he thought. Before he could process another thought, a second bolt hit him right in the mouth.

Sal lay listless on the floor of the Innovation Center. Normally, he would have been knocked unconscious. To his surprise, he maintained complete consciousness.

Satan flew over to him.

"Oh, did I miss the guard and hit you? Oh, poor Sal, I can't believe I missed so badly." At the last comment, one of Satan's fists hit Sal directly in his face.

Satan hit him multiple times. The Guard watched in curiosity. They had never seen Satan so angry.

Satan stopped the punishment because he didn't want Sal to lose consciousness.

"So, you won't help Doug without the female, eh? Well, she is in my lair. Are you sure you want her?" Of course Satan was lying since she was actually in solitary refinement.

Satan continued to talk about Barb within inches of Sal's face. Sal concentrated all his energy to his left leg. He managed to get a knee to Satan's groin.

The kick had no effect on Satan physically. However, it did cause his anger to boil to a totally new level. Out of nowhere, Doug drilled Sal with a punch to his head. Doug was about to pummel Sal when Satan stopped him. "I can handle this devil!"

Satan caught his emotions. He didn't quite know the next best move. He could bolt him again, though that form of punishment seemed to have little effect on this insane devil. He could send him to solitary refinement, although he had survived that, and besides, he was now very close to completing his wacky invention. After weighing these thoughts, an idea finally landed in his head.

He broke away from Sal and turned to the Guard.

"BRING HER TO ME!"

Chapter 55

Barb Wants Solitary?

Barb lay motionless on the floor of her cell. She wasn't sure how long she had been in solitary refinement. All she knew was that after her last prayer attempt and the physical abuse she suffered, she wound up here. The repetitive nature of solitary was destroying her. She would try to run. She would try to pray.

All of a sudden, the voices started again.

"Hi Barb. Oh, you are so beautiful," said the first voice.

Then she heard the second voice. "Wow, you are such a cute lady."

"You must be worshipped," a third one added.

She knew what was next. The voices would continue and then the smell of alcohol would permeate her cell. She remembered the odor from a long night in the saloon BH. It was so strong, she thought it would almost intoxicate her. *Wow. What I would do for a real drink,* was one of her early thoughts. Those thoughts dissipated when she realized the smell was coming from the breath of the taunting voices.

Then the groping would start. It felt as though there were a thousand hands all over her body. The more she would resist, the more hands would join the attack—touching her everywhere. Soon, the voices and their compliments would turn into demands.

"We like you!" and "Ah, come on Barb, we know what you want."

She would run and scream. The hands would follow. The faster she ran, the more groping she would suffer. As her screaming increased, the groping would move from the surface of her body to under her skin. She would bang her head into the wall to stop it, to no avail. The groping would continue, day after miserable day.

During one of the attacks, the groping stopped abruptly. Instead, she felt a lick and then another and another. Within seconds, she knew she was airborne. Barb passed out before she could pray for mercy.

Chapter 56

Wrath Lusts for Barb

Wrath lay motionless for what seemed like a lifetime. *How was I not discovered?* he wondered. Then he pondered, *If I was caught, what would happen?* As he began coming out of this daydream, he rolled over on his back. Noticing his eyes had adjusted, he started to see images. Then he thought he heard a voice.

He felt his adrenaline level begin to rise. Wrath hadn't thought through what would happen to him in this female devil's cell. His concern rose again when he felt something brush against him.

Very few devils in hell actually knew how solitary worked, although everyone knew if you spent time there you never wanted to return.

If you land in another devil's cell, he wondered, *does it convert to your personal nightmare or continue with the previous person's nightmare? Does it just plain shut down? I am pretty sure it just shuts d—.* A voice and someone brushing up against him interrupted his thoughts. Then he heard something that raised his concern further.

"Who goes there?" Wrath shouted. "Who goes there? Show yourself!" he demanded.

The voice ignored Wrath's commands. He decided it was time to exit—and exit fast. Unfortunately, in the confusion surrounding the female devil, he could not remember the way to the exit, so was not sure how to get out.

Wrath sprinted left and hit a wall, which dazed him slightly. Then hands began to grope him. "I'm not your subject!" he blurted out. "Stand down!" However, similar to Barb, the groping moved beneath his skin. Wrath decided there was no negotiation with solitary. He sprinted in what he hoped was the opposite direction, but unfortunately, he hit another wall.

The voice and groping intensified. Wrath decided to ignore the voice and groping. Leaning against the wall, he shimmied himself toward what he thought could be the exit. He quickly recalled his previous experience in solitary, thinking, *I remember that nightmare intensified when I engaged the voice and the physical abuse.* He now noticed that the intensification occurred regardless of one's response, even when the cell "belonged" to another devil.

The groping became so bad that he wanted to brush the sub-skin hands from his body. He had to find a way to stay focused. His mission was to find the exit. The mission would be difficult, even though this was not his cell. *There is no escape and I can barely move,* he began to think.

He focused his anger, but not on the gropers or voice. He found himself chanting: "Hell is efficient. Our goal is souls! Our goal is souls." The more the hands groped him, the louder he chanted! He could barely keep moving. He wanted to give up.

A new series of groping caused him to tremble. He collected himself and resumed chanting, "Hell is efficient. Our goal is souls! Our goal is souls." He decided to make a run for it. Fear caused him to pause momentarily. *I could get totally lost!* He edged forward just a little more, and reached his hand outside. *I think I've found the exit!* He dove to his left, but unfortunately, ran into new trouble. He was in a free fall. *Wow, what a ghastly experience! Oh look, I'm about to*—he thought as he crashed on the floor.

He rolled onto his back and remained motionless, looking up at the solitary refinement structure. He thought he felt groping, although he wasn't sure. He could not move from the crash and soon realized he wasn't in solitary anymore.

"How can anyone survive even a minute in that place?" he said aloud. "Horrible! Horrible!"

Now what? I should go see Satan, he thought.

Oh no! He thought he caught her scent once again. *I must have that female! Our goal is souls! Our goal is souls.* Wrath jumped to his feet and flew off!

Chapter 57

Envy's Confusion Continues

After Satan's staff meeting, Envy returned to his abode. "I can't believe I was bolted by the almighty evil one," he blurted out. "How can that be? What did I do to deserve bolting?"

He lay on his hot molten floor, trying to understand this massive puzzle. *How do all the pieces fit together? What is Chad up to? What is Lust up to? Why does Satan even care about this viewing machine? Who in the world of hell was that mystery guest?* All these questions were spinning in Envy's head.

He lay there for what seemed like hours, using the pain from the floor to try to focus on the answers. *Why is everyone paying attention to this silly concept of a viewing machine? Imagine Satan showing up in everyone's house! It is nothing short of ludicrous. However, it must have some merit if Chad and Satan are so interested in the concept. Why are they so interested? Does Satan really think that Chad's evolution plan won't work? Everything Chad developed in the past has worked. Is Satan really looking for a new way to get souls? Is he really getting desperate?* Envy kept running these thoughts and questions through his head and finally decided the answers were in the Innovation Center. He took flight towards the center.

As he flew through hell, he passed over hell mansion. He noticed a new group of devils was entering the mansion. Envy remembered the grand opening of the mansion. He was sure it would not work. He lobbied that it was a waste of time and a distraction from more important hellish endeavors. New devils are stuck in hell. Nothing more was needed to get new devils acclimated to the rules and environment. The arguments fell on deaf ears. It turned out that Chad was right again. The mansion had a huge impact, quickly making new devils recognize their new world was one of utter futility.

Although Envy was not the smartest devil in the bunch, a lightbulb went on in his head. If Satan was correct before, then Sal's invention—no matter how ridiculous it might be—could actually work. That must be the reason for all the attention on Sal and his stupid idea.

Without realizing it, Envy wound up almost flying past the Innovation Center. He managed to make a smooth and relatively unnoticed landing outside the main entrance. He was about to enter the center when he noticed Satan's Guard surrounding it. *Should I go in or just come back later?* he pondered. *I don't really want to draw Satan's anger again. However, I must know what's going on.* He decided to risk it and go in. As he moved to enter, he saw another Joint Chief come in for a landing out of the corner of his eye. Envy froze.

Chapter 58

Chad's Next Move

After making his point with Lust, Chad pondered his next move. The plan constructed with Frankie and his guest was working. Although there were multiple enemies, he felt in control of the situation. With Lust temporarily out of the way, Chad decided to fly over to Satan's office. He and Satan had not had a nonconfrontational conversation for quite some time. As he reminisced about his longtime connection with Satan, he formed a strategy for getting this recent plan through to him. The conversation would start with the overall status of hell and then quickly move to the viewing machine and Sal.

Chad landed outside Satan's office. He looked inside but couldn't find Satan. The word from devils around the office was that he was at the Innovation Center.

He stood there and debated for quite some time whether he should go to the center. Over the last year, nothing good came from going there. He knocked his head against the wall a few times before he made the decision to go and request an emergency staff meeting. As he took flight, Chad mapped out the discussion he would have with Satan once he arrived.

Chapter 59

Lust's Revenge

As Lust came back from what seemed like the land of the dead, he developed a new sense of anger toward Chad. In fact, he now despised Chad. He vowed he would use all his energy to take Chad out of the number one slot. For Lust, it was no longer just a game of intrigue; it was personal!

Where does Chad get off with, "Stay out of this, or else?" Or else, what? Chad can't hurt me. I'm a Joint Chief!

Lust quickly pulled together several ideas and put his plan into immediate action.

His first stop would be to see Envy. He swiftly took to the air and landed at Envy's abode. Lust quickly scanned Envy's living quarters looking for clues on Envy's next move. His abode had half walls, no ceilings, no bed, no chairs, and no windows. Everything was wide open and easy to scan. Just as he concluded nothing seemed out of the ordinary, Lust noticed a lump in the corner. He went over to the lump and kicked it. Then he slapped it. Nothing happened. He shrugged his shoulders and took off.

His next stop would be the Innovation Center. As he flew, he tried to figure out how he would address Satan if he happened to run into him. *Ah, I want to destroy Chad. Hmmm, maybe not a good idea,* he thought. *I was looking for you, almighty. I would like to give you an update on my progress with new lust ideas.* Lust knew this wouldn't work either. He didn't care.

He landed just outside the center. As he landed, he looked to his left and saw Envy was about to enter the center. Envy froze upon

Lust's landing. The two devils eyed one another cautiously, unsure of each other's goals.

Lust had already decided he was going to help Envy dethrone Chad. He approached Envy.

"What are you doing here?"

"I was about to ask you the same question," Envy retorted.

Seizing the opportunity, Lust said, "I came here looking for you."

"Why were you looking for me?"

"I want to help you," Lust said with an evil smile.

"Help *me*? HOW?"

"I want to help you with the reason you are here."

Lust was a master at this game of cat and mouse. Envy wasn't sure who to trust, but knew Lust was a sneaky devil.

"I'm not sure why I'm here!" Envy replied cautiously.

Lust figured he had a perfect opportunity. "We are here to dethrone Chad!"

Fright engulfed Envy. *How would Lust know I have some desire for Chad's position?* he wondered. *How do I know I can trust him?* He recovered and decided to engage in the intrigue.

"What's your plan?"

"*Our* plan is to...."

After Lust briefly shared the plan, the two entered the center.

Chapter 60

Sal Wins?

After his attack on Satan, Sal found himself in chains. For hours, he pondered what in the world Satan was waiting for. The almighty evil one was either going to blow him up or send him to solitary for his unprecedented assault on him.

Sal looked up with his one working eye and saw several members of Satan's Guard approaching him with a devil. They licked her and threw her at Sal's feet. Barb rolled onto her back, still in a semiconscious state.

Sal felt some elation. *I've beaten Satan!* he thought. Of course, his pain modifiers kicked in, stabbing his left eye and both chained arms with extreme pain. He attempted to move to comfort himself. He tried to roll on the ground or rub the painful areas for relief. Sadly, all he could do was cry out.

The commotion woke Barb. She soon realized she must have escaped solitary refinement, but wondered where she was now. She sensed the new place was even worse than her worst nightmare. She rolled over and saw Sal.

"What have you done now?" she gasped. "I was in solitary and now I'm back in your mess?"

"I've won!" Sal said, attempting to control his elation. "I told Satan I would not help him without you being set free! You are here because I've won."

Barb stared at him, puzzled. *He really believes he can win in hell!* she thought. *He really thinks there is a chance for justice or fairness here.*

They both turned to look at the guards. Barb sprinted toward the gate. Twenty yards or so into her run, she felt the guards' tongues on her body again. "Stop!" she howled.

It didn't matter. The licking would never stop. As they escorted her back to Sal, she caught Satan's landing out of the corner of her eye. For an instant, she wondered whether Sal might be right. Would Satan really allow Sal to lead in hell? Deep in her decaying heart, she knew there was no chance.

She wanted to daydream. She wanted to live without fear. She wanted to exist without pain. She wanted, she wanted, she wanted—to cry, to scream, to run. She was done! Suddenly, searing heat crept up through her extremities. She didn't know what was happening to her. She slowly stretched her arms and felt enormous power rise within her. She grabbed the tongue of the last guard who licked her and threw him a great distance. Then she grabbed the arms of two of her escorting guards and slammed them into one another. They lost consciousness and fell from their flight. She hit the remaining escort hard with a quick elbow and a fist, knocking him from his flight. She escaped!

Barb flew fast and furious toward the top of hell. She briefly wondered about her newfound strength and focused all her energy on escaping hell. She couldn't believe she had thrown those guards around so easily. After all the abuse she had received from them, she was free! She was amazed at how far she had flown away from the prestigious protectors of hell.

She felt intense pain in her back. She tried to continue her flight, but felt a second sharp pain, this time in the back of her head. She thought she could keep flying, but the next bolt clipped her left wing. She started to spiral back to hell. With all her remaining power, she tried to reverse her free fall, but to no avail. She was falling. No escape again!

Sal couldn't bear to watch! He caused another incident for Barb. He wished that he could stop hurting her. Every time he thought he had a win, he lost—and Barb always lost significantly more.

Satan pointed to Doug and then to Barb. Doug grabbed the chains and dynamite. The guards picked Barb up and carried her over to Doug while licking her relentlessly.

Sal looked at her. She appeared to have several broken bones. Sal wasn't sure how Doug would chain her since the devil's body was a train wreck, but somehow he did.

Sal couldn't take it any longer. Though he could not get down on his knees or put his hands together, he decided to pray for Barb. He shouted, "God, please!"

The sirens went off and Sal disappeared.

Chapter 61

The Countdown

Satan turned to see Sal disappear. *I have never seen another devil like Sal. Imagine, attacking Me! What was he thinking?* Satan couldn't remember another time when someone had the gall to attack him. *I will annihilate that devil!* Satan was still thinking to himself while shaking his head in amazement.

On one of the headshakes, he caught a glimpse of two devils. He realized they were Lust and Envy.

"What are you two doing here?" he demanded.

"Yeah, what are you doing here?" another demanding voice joined in.

Satan turned quickly to see Chad.

"What in the—?" He was about to bolt them when Chad interrupted. "Wait, we need an emergency staff meeting."

Satan was furious. He was about to pour out his rage when he was interrupted by Sal's reappearance. The countdown on Barb continued: "Ten…nine…eight…seven…six…five…four…."

When Doug got down to three, Sal blurted out, "I will help! Stop the countdown. I will help!"

Chapter 62

Barb Hangs On

Barb awakened slowly. She quickly realized she could not move. Every bone in her body felt broken. She wanted to screech, but could not. She wanted to cry, but could not. She wanted to pray, but could not.

She kept trying to move, but then remembered that familiar counting. She thought, *Will the dynamite end it all for me*? She wasn't sure.

Barb recounted her massive sufferings in hell. She endured unimaginable torture for prayer. She persevered through the suffering in solitary refinement. The Guard repeatedly abducted her and presented her to Satan. She felt the burn from the almighty evil one's anger and bolts. She struggled to imagine that anything in hell could be worse than these horrific experiences.

What happens when you are blown up with dynamite? She continued to wonder. *Does your soul cease to exist? Do you come back to hell or endure some other horrid existence? Do you cease to exist? Would the end mean the end of hope?* No one was quite sure what "blowing up" the immortal soul meant, although it was clear that everyone seemed to think it led to a drastic end—one to be avoided at all cost.

Barb decided she really did not want to find out. She managed to cry out!

"Five…four…three…." the countdown continued.

She heard Sal say, "I will help! Let her be!" and the counting stopped.

Barb looked up and barely saw Sal. She could not stay conscious and passed out.

Chapter 63

Emergency Staff Meeting

"Ah, now King Sal," Satan sneered, "it's time for you to get to work, if you don't mind. Sir Sal, have we met your royal needs?" Satan bellowed.

He commanded his Joint Chiefs to scatter. All the Joint Chiefs started to move except Envy. Satan noticed Envy's slow state.

Envy was in deep thought about what was happening. He looked around and saw Satan, Chad, Sal, Barb, and Lust. Just then, he saw the bolt approaching him. Satan had decided to assist him in getting moving, and it hit Envy directly in the chest.

Chad just started his flight when he noticed something was about to hit him. He attempted an evasive move. It was too late. The entity slammed into his head at full speed. Chad and the entity hit a small wall in the Innovation Center. The thing that hit Chad landed on top of him. Chad bench pressed it and threw it to the left. He rose to his knees and looked over at the semiconscious devil. *You have to be kidding me!* he thought. *How had this worthless devil hit him? What was he thinking?* Chad got to his feet and pounced on the devil.

"Envy, you must be insane!"

Envy attempted to speak, although he was too groggy from the bolt and subsequent crash into Chad.

Chad looked at him. "No answer, eh?"

Then Chad unloaded on Envy. All the anger of hell and his anger toward Sal boiled through his evil body. After two minutes of pummeling, he was on top of Envy. As he prepared to hit him with several elbows, he felt a thud against his head.

He looked up in time to catch a glimpse of the second blow. It was the foot of a devil. Chad crashed to the floor. He tried to get up and then received another shot to his abdomen. Lust was about to deliver an elbow to Chad's head when Chad reached up, grabbed Lust, and flipped him in the air before throwing him to his right.

Chad and Lust sprang to their feet simultaneously. Lust spoke first.

"Chad, what are you doing? Envy didn't attack you."

"Lust, how is this topic your business?" Chad retorted.

Just as he was about to jump toward Lust, he heard an explosion. The explosion knocked both devils off their feet. As Chad rose to his knees, he realized he had to get to Satan.

Chapter 64

Wrath's Amazement

Once Wrath was airborne, he started to pick up the scent of that female. Before he knew it, he was flying toward the Innovation Center. The closer he got, the more he wanted to head in another direction. He even found himself chanting, "Our goal is souls!" It made no difference. There was no resisting her scent. Just as he began to descend into the Innovation Center, a bolt of lightning flew across the dark sky.

Wrath's red eyes followed the path of light. He realized in amazement that the recipient of the bolt was another Joint Chief. Then he saw what looked like Chad attacking a severely damaged Joint Chief. The victim appeared to be Envy.

He turned to notice that Satan and his Guard were flying directly toward him. Wrath gulped and accelerated quickly to his right. He didn't want Satan to see him anywhere near the Innovation Center, Sal, and most importantly, Barb.

Wrath had never flown as fast as he was flying now! He looked behind him and it looked as though he eluded Satan and his Guard. As he slowed his flight, he heard a large explosion. *What was that?* he wondered. *What in the world of hell?* A fire cloud headed his way. He accelerated his flying again and managed to escape it. When the cloud began to retract, Wrath hovered, waiting for full retraction. Wrath didn't have any answers for his questions.

Where do I go now? he wondered. *Hmm, the scent is returning. Looks like I'm returning to the Innovation Center! Forget the goal. I must have that female. No, I must resist!*

He found himself hovering over the Innovation Center again. *Hmm, what to do? I will go to the female. No, I will go to the viewing machine! Female? Viewing machine? Female? Viewing machine!*

The torment was overwhelming. He grimaced and entered the center.

Chapter 65

Sal's Despair

As Sal returned from his prayer attempt, he immediately saw Barb and heard the countdown. He had to do something fast, so he said, "I will help. You win!" The words poured out of his mouth without thought. The explosion was tremendous. It shook the lava ground all across hell. His eyes fought the fog, trying to see Barb.

Just as Sal thought hell could not get any worse, his post-prayer experience was horrific. Solitary refinement was the most unpleasant experience of his total life. This post-prayer attack was worse in many ways. He had a new appreciation for what rape victims suffered.

Sal shuddered and went back to thinking about winning. For a split second, he felt as though he had ascended to number one, only to realize that deception and trickery continued to reign. *What was I thinking?* he thought. *Satan is impossible. Getting ahead is impossible.* Still, compared with all the devils Sal met in hell, he had made tremendous progress. He was still highly engaged in a game-changing project for the leader—the leader he hated with every part of his miserable being. He caught the remnants of another altercation between the Joint Chiefs. Sal could not understand how these misfits could be in charge of Satan's vast empire.

Barb's screech broke Sal's concentration. He noticed Doug was staring at him. *Not this guy again!* he thought.

Doug had a similar thought. He had no desire to work with Sal. However, he had no choice. *Imagine, this fool actually hit Satan and he still exists,* he thought. Doug shook his head. *I don't get it! He hit the king?!*

Doug picked up Sal. "Let's go work on the idea without the theatrics this time!"

Sal slowly raised his eyes to get a glimpse of Barb, but quickly closed them. He couldn't bear to look at her any longer. He reflected back to when he and the team first created the plan. He remembered trying to convince Barb to remove herself from the team for her protection. Sal wasn't exactly sure what would happen in the future, but he never imagined such a gloomy outcome. Remorse was an emotion that lived in previous days. Now, despair replaced remorse more and more with each passing moment.

Upon arrival at Doug's work area, Sal was surprised to see Doug's progress, though he was still missing a basic piece of the puzzle. Sal remembered reading something about George Carey and his work. Carey used a large array of photocells and wires to transmit a signal to a visual display made of many individual lights. Although in theory this approach should work, each individual pixel required its own photocell and wired circuit.

A lightbulb seemed to go on over Doug's head. He looked around the center for the required materials and yawned, saying, "It could work, but I have other things to do."

He picked up Sal, chained him next to Barb, and departed.

Chapter 66

Chad's Plan to Satan

As Chad flew into the pure darkness of hell, he thought about the events he had just witnessed. Hell was unraveling before his very eyes under *his* reign. *This cannot happen,* he thought. *I will not allow hell to fall apart due to one insane devil! I am the Warrior!*

Chad started to feel the power from his anger and fortitude. It brought an unfortunate smile to his face! The smile caused his pain modifiers to kick in and his normally airy flight turned into a straight nosedive.

He attempted to pull up or change direction. Unfortunately, he was unable to fly since his pain modifiers immobilized both wings. *Look at this. Another example of that menace Sal ruining hell,* Chad thought as he braced for impact.

After his headfirst landing, Chad was surprised he was still conscious. He did a quick inventory of the damage to his body and concluded he had a broken neck, broken ribs, and a badly damaged wing. He tried not to move. He needed his body to regenerate quickly.

Somehow, he felt movement across his body, although he wasn't sure how he was moving. It turned out he received a kick in the stomach that caused him to roll over onto his back. Looking up, Chad quickly recognized his assailant—Satan. Apparently, he had reached his destination prior to his free fall.

Satan got face to face with Chad and demanded, "What do you want?"

"Sir, I've been working on a plan to stop the decay across your leadership team. With your permission, I would like to share the plan with you," Chad responded.

Satan glared at his leader of leaders. "The only thing unraveling in hell is you!"

"The only reason I have issues," Chad said, managing to match Satan's glare, "is that you cannot see the immense stupidity in Sal's ideas, and—"

Before Chad could say another word, Satan bolted him—his number one.

"I have a plan to rid ourselves of this vermin," Chad continued doggedly. The bolt had not even slowed down his speech.

Satan was tired of the lack of respect in hell. *How does Chad get off speaking to me like that?* He fumed. Satan answered his own question with another set of bolts. The answer is, *You do not get away with speaking like that to me!* he thought. Satan followed the bolting with a couple kicks to Chad's head.

Chad decided to lie motionless until the beating was complete. After a couple of minutes that seemed like an eternity, Chad whispered in a defeated voice, "Can you please listen to the plan?"

Satan thought for a moment. "I'm barely listening!"

With every ounce of remaining energy, Chad could only whisper. He attempted to look at the king of evil, but his vision was still blurry from the last set of bolts. Chad slowly and purposefully proposed his plan.

Chapter 67

The Team

Envy left the Innovation Center, confused yet again. Shaking his head, he thought to himself, *Chad attacked me. Lust defended me. What in the world is going on? Hell is messed up or going off the deep end!* It had never been a fun place, yet everyone seemed to respect the chain of command until now. The Joint Chiefs were attacking each other; a devil attacked Satan and somehow remained in hell; the number one devil was attacking everything that moved. *Things are going crazy. What's next?*

Envy's answer came faster than he could imagine. As he entered his abode, he noticed a stranger. When he moved to engage the visitor, he fled. Envy turned and saw the reason.

Chad landed in Envy's domain, flew straight into Envy, and sent him flying. As he attempted to get up, Chad put a knee to his throat. Envy made an unsuccessful attempt to speak. Chad did all the talking.

"I want you to team up with me to destroy Lust and Sal."

Another strange happening! Envy thought to himself. *Chad is requesting help to destroy a Joint Chief! How could this be possible?"*

Chad made his command known again. "Team up or not?" Chad's voice was deeper and more evil than Envy could ever remember. Envy just looked at him. Chad's temper began to rise. One of his claws went straight into Envy's left eye. Envy attempted a scream, but nothing came out.

Chad repeated his command in an even deeper and disturbing voice. "Team up?" Envy knew there wouldn't be another command. Against his better judgment, he decided to agree to the command from Chad.

Chad looked at the pitiful chief and wondered how Envy had ever risen to such a high level in the evil one's organization. *Look at him,* he thought. *He is so helpless and confused.* Still, Chad decided a "weak" Envy could be of some use to him. He slowly released the stranglehold on him. As he released him, Chad noticed that Envy positively acknowledged his command.

Chad gazed at the dazed Envy. Then he told him, "Start with Sal." As these words came out of his mouth, Chad launched into the dark sky of hell.

Envy shook his head several times. He unsuccessfully attempted to see out of his damaged eye. Then, he decided to stop thinking and start acting. After managing to get to his feet, he pumped his fist into the dark air and pointed his flight path toward the Innovation Center. He remembered Chad's parting words, "Start with Sal."

In flight, he attempted to treat his damaged eye. Why am I helping Chad? he wondered. As the thought entered his mind, something hit his left side. Spinning out of control, he cursed his left eye! Before he could finish his thought, another blow hit his right wing, then again on the left side of his head. The last hit sent him into a free fall, and he fell to the lava floor.

Envy used the surge of anguish as a new source of strength. Somehow, he jumped to his feet. He squinted to see his attacker. It was Lust. *Chad was right!* he thought. He flew into Lust at full speed.

"Don't trust Chad!" Lust shouted.

Envy growled and restarted his mission to the Innovation Center!

Chapter 68

Lust and Satan

Lust watched Envy fly away. He knew where he had to go! As Lust hit the murky sky in hell, he decided to fly about twenty feet above the lava floor to savor the agony of hell.

The first thing he noticed was something that looked like gang warfare. Two large groups of devils squared off against each other on opposite sides of a twenty-foot wide hot lava stream. From his vantage point, he could hear obscene language and threats being hurled by both sides. Lust decided to hover and observe the tense situation.

One of the leaders on the left yelled that he would kill someone named Dylan on the other side, adding, "You are lucky this stream stands between us! Wendell, you thought you died when you went to hell? You wait until I get my claws into you! My army and I will destroy you and the sorry-looking idiots with you. I can't believe that you have the nerve to come near our women supply. If I ever see you—"

"We will go anywhere we want, any time we want," said a devil standing next to Wendell, cutting Dylan off. "You can't stop us! And for sure, that group of drunken devils with you cannot stop us."

"We will show you drunk when we pull your eyes out and shove them—," one of Dylan's devils retorted before being cut off by another devil's screech.

Tempers flared, then the lava stream that had been an impenetrable barrier between them slowly disappeared. Both sides flew full force at one another. Lust watched as Dylan and Wendell actually met on the battlefield. At first, Dylan appeared to be winning, though Wendell quickly gained the upper hand. A shriek of pain and one of their hands flew off. At this point in the battle, it was difficult to tell the difference between Wendell and Dylan. Both inflicted a significant amount of damage on the other. Their armies looked similarly maimed and disfigured. It was so perfect. No one ever won. This cycle repeated every day! As Lust passed the battle, he heard Dylan shout, "You will die!" just as he fell forward after receiving a savage blow to the back of his head.

Lust moved on, pondering the battle he just witnessed. He grimaced. *Hell is such a miserable existence. Every day is full of suffering. The constant battles to win something that is unwinnable. The combination of physical and mental pain is the culmination of the ultimate desperate experience. Without love and without God, there is nothing but endless suffering. And Satan set up this existence such that you can get the same pain day after day!"*

Lust's next opportunity to savor hell came a couple minutes later. It looked as though thirty male devils had surrounded five female devils. By the look of the five females, they were relatively new to hell. The thirty devils taunted the females for what probably seemed like several hours to them. Ten of the devils jumped on one of the females. She didn't have a chance. They had their way with her in every unimaginable way. Welcome to hell. All violence. All pain. All the time!

As Lust flew away, he thought, *Every day. Wow! Every Day!*

He eventually landed outside Satan's office. He wanted to encourage the leader of evil to watch Chad and Envy, even though Satan warned him to stay out of it. Lust entered Satan's domain, but Satan was nowhere in sight. Lust glared at the soul meter chart on the wall. It looked like Chad's plan continued to show poor results. *When is this imbecile going to figure out that Chad has lost his ability to lead?* he wondered. Then he tried to determine where the almighty evil one might be hanging out.

Lust took flight and landed outside the Innovation Center, but he didn't see Satan there. However, he did notice that Chad was there. *Now what is Chad up to?* he wondered. Lust hid near the entrance to observe Chad covertly and to see if Envy was with him.

Then, the Guard landed, followed by Satan. Satan was there for about thirty seconds when Chad took flight. Lust meandered into the center. He came up behind Satan.

"Imagine meeting you and Chad here. How can I be of service to you, almighty evil one?"

Satan scanned Lust. Though he nearly said, "Whose side are you on, anyway?" he decided he already had that discussion with Lust. He bolted Lust right between the eyes and departed. Lust lay motionless on the burning floor of hell.

Chapter 69

Barb Hates Sal

Barb began her journey back to a conscious state. She rolled her head side to side. For a brief moment, she thought she was no longer in hell. She waited to hear a countdown. For some reason, it did not start. She slowly opened her eyes, thinking her nightmare might be over. Cautiously, she looked down at her feet. The shackles still constrained her movement. She scanned the rest of her body, from her feet to her chest. Yes, her arms were still handcuffed to a post. She was not free—not at all! Her anger boiled within her. "Not again," she screamed. "Not again!"

At her second scream, Barb heard a moan as she moved her arm. Chains still connected her with Sal. All the anger within her boiled over toward him. She gave him an elbow to the left side of his head.

"If it wasn't for you...." she screeched before kneeing him just below his stomach.

Sal let out a small yelp.

"If it wasn't for you, I wouldn't be in chains again, and I definitely wouldn't be chained to you!" she lamented before elbowing him in the head again.

Sal fell to his knees. "If it wasn't for me?" he shouted back just as she kneed him to the head.

"Yes," Barb said, "if it wasn't for you, my miserable existence would—"

"What do you think?" Sal said, stopping her dead in her tracks. "Your miserable existence wouldn't be miserable? Look around! You are in hell! Yes, H, E, double toothpicks—remember that word? This is not heaven. This is HELL!"

Regrettably, Sal shouldn't have said the word "heaven." He disappeared just as he was saying his last word, "hell."

Barb watched Sal's abrupt departure—swallowed up by the lava floor. Then she looked up.

"Oh no! No, no, no Satan, you lie! You lie! You are all lies!"

She felt the tongue of the Guard on her face and passed out as they grabbed and groped her.

Chapter 70

Chad's First Ascension

As Chad left Envy, he accelerated his flight toward Frankie's domain while collecting his thoughts about the plan. He engaged Envy. Now he just needed the power of Frankie's visitor.

The visitor was an intriguing element of his plan. Although the visitor seemed mysterious to many—even Frankie—Chad had used him in the past. He recalled his ascension to chief of staff. *Wow, without his help, I wonder if I would have become number one.*

Chad knew it required a nontrivial effort to get to the number one slot and keep it. He regularly warded off attempts by others to usurp him. Chad could attest to the importance of the visitor's assistance in taking the number one slot. *Why did he help me the first time?* Chad wondered. There were no rewards for helping in hell. Chad's only guess was that the visitor did not like his predecessor. *So why is he helping me now?* he wondered. As he pondered this, he arrived at Frankie's abode.

As Chad descended, he noticed that Frankie and the visitor were engaged in a heated argument. The fact that Frankie was arguing was troublesome. Frankie was able to survive the opposition of practically anyone in hell. On earth, Frankie was a negotiator. In the world of hell, the devils characterized him as a survivor.

Chad approached the two just as the visitor floored Frankie with a drop kick. The visitor jumped on top of Frankie and elbowed him in the head. Frankie let out a yelp. Chad had a slight urge to jump in and help Frankie. However, he knew that if he did, his pain modifiers would kick in at the highest level. *Besides,* he thought, *I don't need Frankie to make my plan work. I need the visitor.* Eventually, Frankie was no longer resisting and was nearly unconscious, so the visitor retreated.

The visitor pounded his chest and approached Chad. Chad was ready for the battle, but the visitor motioned to the floor. Chad thought, *What? I'm not interested! However, I need help! I must engage this entity in my plan.*

The two sat on the floor and finalized the plan.

Chapter 71

Envy Starts the Plan

After nailing Lust, Envy understood a new sense of purpose and strength. If he had to choose a side, Chad was the best side to choose! *What if Chad fails? Chad will not fail! I will not fail.*

Envy flew into the Innovation Center. As he landed, he scanned his surroundings. He saw Sal and Barb arguing about something and ignored them. He decided to seek Doug out.

He pushed his chest out and walked tall as he scanned the center, even managing to get his infrared eye to work. The amount of activity surrounding innovation in the center surprised him. Eventually, Envy saw Doug darting across innovation stations.

"Hey Doug," he called out. "Come here."

Doug looked up. "I'm busy."

Envy looked at the leader of the center with surprise and disdain. He launched his entire frame into Doug with full force. They hurdled across an invention table, destroying a creation focused on human vanity, which was under development by a junior devil.

As they hit the floor, Doug wound up on top of Envy. This position lasted all of two seconds before Envy grabbed Doug by the chest and flung him ten feet from his prone position.

As Doug attempted to roll over, he received another kick from Envy. Doug curled up in a ball.

"You busy now?" Envy shouted.

Doug shook his head no.

"Good! Now get to your feet and take me to the viewing machine innovation area!" For good measure, Envy kneed Doug in the head as he got to his knees.

Doug lay on the hot floor and looked up at Envy. He thought he could take Envy, but knew that if he attacked, Satan would provide the appropriate punishment. He decided to lay there for a couple minutes.

As he saw Envy approach, Doug quickly rolled over and sprang to his feet. He moved quickly toward the viewing machine area.

As they approached the viewing machine area, Envy stopped and stared. Doug and Sal had made some progress. As Doug talked about their recent work on the machine, Envy could tell Doug was beginning to believe this idea might come to fruition.

Wow, Envy thought. *If this thing works, what will happen to earth?* His thoughts slowed and narrowed. *What will happen in hell?*

Glaring at Doug, Envy asked, "Do you think this could actually work?"

Doug decided not to speak to Envy, so merely nodded affirmatively.

"Where will we get ideas to be displayed on this still crazy invention?" Envy inquired.

Doug looked at him and decided to use "point" language, slowly pointing at every devil in sight in the Innovation Center.

Doug firmly believed that if they made the invention work, there would be no lack of content for the machine. Envy had seen enough. He hovered about ten feet in the air and then delivered a kick to Doug's head before flying straight up. He had to think about this concept.

Chapter 72

Sal Is Back on Top

As Sal regained consciousness after the abuse he suffered from his argument with Barb and subsequent disappearance, he wished for nothing more than to be unchained from her. He did not want to be so close to her. He would attack her if necessary to survive!

Sal shook his head as he fretted about his bondage with Barb and his eyes adjusted to the setting. Just then, Barb screamed.

"Oh no, not her and me again! How can she be so stupid? I did not cause—"

He stopped mid-sentence after looking up to see Satan's Guard approaching. In seconds the Guard was on them, first abusing Barb. She did not resist. Instead, she simply passed out. *That experience with Satan must be totally horrific*, Sal thought. *Before a guard even touches her, she passes out. Wow!*

Sadly, Sal felt a twinge of remorse for her. His reward for this feeling was a tidal wave of pain that shot from his left hand to his brain. He rolled on the floor. He tried to gain his composure. He tried to correlate his attack on the evil one who caused his increased pain state. *I'll bet that fool caused me*—he thought, before being cut off by a pain that felt like nails driven into all of his extremities. He so wanted to attack someone. Unfortunately, he could not move. Even his extremities were shut down. Rolling over was not even possible.

Sal began to reflect on his mess. *I was so close to the top. Now, what have I done? If my viewing machine works, the earth will be doomed to come to this horrific place.* Regrettably, with this thought, he felt remorse again. This time his remorse was for the future of the earth. Just as he had come to expect, pain hit him. However, this time, the pain started in his stomach area and moved quickly to his chest, similar to a massive heart attack. Sal could do nothing to reduce the pain. He screamed for what seemed like thirty minutes before passing out.

Doug watched the Sal and Barb show for some time. Finally, he decided he couldn't stand anymore. "This Sal devil will not get me attacked by anyone anymore!" he muttered.

He found some of his special dynamite. "Sal is expendable," he announced to the Innovation Center. There was no reaction from the devils in the center. He said it again and then began to chant it. "Sal is expendable! Sal is expendable!" The others soon began to join in on the chant. When Doug reached Sal and noticed him coming out of his comatose state, he started a countdown—120 seconds.

Sal heard a noise as he started to regain consciousness. The noise had his name in it. They were chanting about him! *This cannot be good!* he thought.

As his ears adjusted to full wakefulness, he heard Doug counting, "Forty…thirty-nine…thirty-eight…."

Sal looked down. *Oh no,* he thought in shock, *not this dynamite thing again! Well, at least it might be over!* he thought as he prepared for the worst.

"Five…four…three—"

"Stop!"

He raised his eyes. It was Wrath.

"Stop the countdown!"

Just as he heard "one," the countdown stopped.

Wrath flew over to Sal, grabbed him, and dragged him up into the eerie sky.

Chapter 73

Sal Presents Idea #2

Satan's staff meeting started on time. The meeting began with the regular agenda of Chad updating the staff on the state of hell. In his update, he reported that the evolution argument was still transforming earth.

As Chad made his point, Satan's fluorescent red eyes shifted to the soul chart. *What is Chad thinking?* he wondered. *The soul meter continues to show miserable performance. In fact, some on staff believe our year over year soul gathering will drop in the next five years.*

"Earth is prime for the picking," Chad asserted. "We will continue to gain more souls. As we gain more souls, evil will become a stronger force on earth." As Chad finished his last sentence, Satan rose quickly from his seat, bringing an abrupt end to his report. Satan couldn't listen to anything more from Chad.

"Who will give an update on the viewing machine?" he asked impatiently.

Chad glared at the evil one. He wanted to say, "Viewing machine? I will give you an update on that stupid idea." Rather, he cowered and returned to his seat.

Wrath looked up at the evil one. "Why don't we let Sal provide an update?"

The evil one glared at Wrath. "How is Sal here?"

"Well," Wrath responded, "he was about to be blown up and I swooped in, nailed Doug, and lifted the annoying devil away from the dynamite."

Satan eased back in his hard rock chair and stared at the make-shift table. His mind began to boil, thinking, *This lack of respect of power in hell—my power—cannot and will not continue! I will not stand for this concept that everyone is in charge.*

After a long pause, Satan looked up at Wrath, who took this as his cue to start talking. Just then, Envy started talking.

"We must start to build ideas for the viewing machine. It could work!"

At this, Chad was about to jump across the table with a single objective to destroy Envy. However, before he could make his move, a bolt from Satan exploded on Envy.

Satan's anger boiled so intensely within him that he could not speak. He pointed to Wrath and then to the exit of the office. Some-how, Wrath understood the command. He slowly walked out of the staff meeting. Satan and the remaining Joint Chiefs were eerily quiet. Before anyone could react, Wrath returned just as slowly as he had exited, carrying Chad's chief nemesis. He dropped Sal on the table.

Immediately, Satan jumped on his chair and swung his tail, send-ing Sal flying across the conference room. Dazed, Sal rolled over onto his back expecting another shot. He waited for what seemed like an eternity. Without additional punishment, he got to his knees and slowly rose to his feet.

"Sal, how wonderful that you have joined us once again," Satan said in the angriest roar Sal had ever heard from him (*If that was even possible*, he thought).

"How did you like that greeting? Would you like another?"

Now on his feet, Sal slowly shook his head no. Though Sal wanted to be brash as in the old days, he lowered his eyes to the floor.

"No, almighty evil one. How can I be of service?"

Satan did not like the devil's tone. *Who does he think he is, pla-cating me?* he thought.

When Sal didn't hear a response to his question, he slowly raised his head. It was too late to move out of the way. The bolt pierced his left leg and sent him to the floor. Sal waited for the second bolt. *One… two…three…*he counted silently. *What happened?* He wondered why the second bolt didn't come. He stayed on his knees. Though he didn't want to lift his head, he felt his head lifting slowly.

Satan pointed to a chair at the table. *I made it!* Sal thought as he moved slowly to the table and lowered his posterior into one of the rock chairs. Still, he decided to keep a low profile.

All eyes of the Joint Chiefs of sin were upon Sal. Soon Sal heard a voice, although he couldn't tell whether the voice was in his head or streaming through his ears. "Tell us of the progress on the viewing machine!" the voice ordered. "What is the status of the viewing machine?"

It felt like twenty-five voices in his head all at once. Sal screeched. He waited again and fully expected a bolt. Luckily, none came. He was still whole. What had happened? Unfortunately, the voices returned. "What is the status of the—"

"Progress is being made," Sal blurted. "Progress is being made!"

Satan looked at the pitiful devil and thought of bolting him. Instead, he decided to let the questioning continue.

The question, *What's the progress?* filled Sal's head. He struggled to think since the voices in his head were loud and furious.

In torment, he cried out, "The progress is good. Doug has managed to get the first image on the machine, though it is quite blurry."

Satan looked at Sal, who still had his head lowered. Then he looked at Envy, who showed no signs of wanting to speak, though he did try to show a level of concurrence with Sal's update.

Satan was surprised. *How is this possible?* he wondered. *What if it is real?* For years, Satan thought the viewing machine was a pipe dream, but now he could see progress—real progress. *Is it possible this machine will work?*

His mind wandered back to the first time he saw Sal's silly plan. *If this machine is real, then other ideas in the plan may possibly work. No way! What am I thinking? Hmm, what if it works? Well, could it be any worse than the evolution plan, which is clearly not working?*

Satan realized everyone was glaring at him. He wondered how long he had been thinking about the past. Shrugging it off, he decided to have fun with Sal.

"What is another idea from your ridiculous plan?"

Sal wasn't sure how to interpret Satan's request. He never expressed an interest in any of the other ideas. *Was this a trick? How should I answer?* he wondered.

Sal thought about his answer for what seemed like an eternity. The time allowed thoughts of Barb to wander into his head. She was being tortured because of these ideas. She was in a state of complete and utter despair. Satan did not understand business and leadership. These thoughts caused the "old" Sal to return. *So, Satan really needs me*, the thought occurred to him, *yet Satan has not kept his end of the deal with Barb.* Finally, Sal slowly raised his eyes and looked up at Satan.

"Why?"

As Satan released the bolt directed at Sal's midsection, he thought, *Now that's the Sal I remember.*

Sal got what he was expecting and wound up rolling on the floor.

Chad merely watched the latest Sal show. He would have joined in on the destruction of Sal. Instead, he decided to delay action since he did not want to upset the almighty evil one further. Chad glanced at Satan. It did not look like another bolt was forthcoming. *So the idiot is going to get another chance to speak? Come on!* Chad almost blurted out. He decided to wait and see what happened.

They all watched as Sal wound up on his knees. Satan addressed him again. "What is another idea from your plan?"

Sal struggled to speak. "Flying machine," he said quietly.

Chad could not hold back. He punched the makeshift table. "When are we going to stop listening to this disgrace of a devil and these absurd ideas? I have had enough."

He jumped across the table and flew elbow first into Sal's head. He lifted his right arm to punch Sal, but it did not work. Somehow, he had lost power in his arm. Though Chad did not realize what had happened, somehow, a bolt from the king had hit his right elbow. Chad fell over on his back.

"Enough!" Satan snarled.

Chad slowly got up and returned to his seat, maintaining a glare at Sal as he walked.

Satan gave Sal the sign to speak. Sal pondered what to do. *If I speak, I get jumped. If I shut up, I get bolted*, he thought. *Oh well, here goes nothing.*

"The flying machine will break up the family unit and allow destruction to rain from the sky!"

Satan glared at Sal, thinking, *He has another absurd idea. Humans flying like devils or birds?* Satan decided not to respond to the new idea. He needed to process the next steps for the viewing machine.

He pointed to Wrath, and then to Lust. "I want new ideas for display on this viewing machine!"

Satan glared at Chad and flew straight up.

Chapter 74

The Chaos Continues

Lust watched Satan depart. As he turned his head, he caught a glimpse of Chad approaching from the corner of his eye. *Should I attack or see what he wants first?* he wondered. *Hmm.* Before Lust could make a decision, Chad grabbed him by the wing and jerked him around to stand nose-to-nose.

"My place. Now!" Chad commanded before taking flight.

As Chad departed, Lust looked at Wrath. "What does Satan want us to do?" he inquired.

"Make that silly devil's device come alive," Wrath growled back, pointing at Sal.

"How in the world are we supposed to make that happen?" Lust retorted.

Before Sal could open his mouth to answer the question, he was airborne with transportation provided by Wrath.

"What in the hell is going on?" Lust asked, shaking his head as he took off.

As Chad flew, he wondered, *What just happened at the staff meeting? No matter! I am the first lieutenant in hell! I will maintain my power! I will destroy Sal!* Chad noticed that his pain modifiers seemed higher again.

Chapter 75

The Deal—Is It Real?

As they approached the Innovation Center, Wrath mumbled something and dropped Sal into the center. Sal looked down and noticed the drop was around 200 feet. As he braced for impact, he reflected for a second on Satan's last staff meeting.

"I really hate that devil!" He found himself shouting as he fell faster and faster. "I hate him! I hate him!"

With a splat, Sal landed headfirst on the hot lava floor. He wanted to scream, but as hard as he tried, nothing came out. It reminded him of nightmares on earth, BH, in which he would be so petrified with horror that he would try to scream for help and no sound came out of his mouth. No one came to his assistance. *Just like this godforsaken place that I'm in now,* he thought. *I could scream all day to deaf ears! What I would trade to be back on earth, in an imaginary nightmare versus the real deal!"*

He thought he would have been used to the normal misery by now. Sadly, pain was pain. There was no relief. There were no pain management remedies, just pain. After a long while, he did notice that the pain from his broken neck had subsided slightly, such that he could begin to comprehend what had just happened at Satan's staff meeting.

Could it be that I'm going to be number one? Sal wondered. *Satan is now pushing the viewing machine. He even put Wrath and Lust on the team to make it work. In addition, unbelievably, he did not just kill the next idea! I am the future number one!*

Sal managed to get to his feet and started walking to the viewing machine work area. He wanted to strut, but he was still limping from breaking his leg after Wrath's drop. *Imagine, I am going to displace Chad! I have won!* he thought. He pumped his fist in the air just as a pain modifier hit his stomach and knocked him over. Lying on his back, he noticed the pain modifier was actually Doug.

"You're back, eh?" Doug shouted. "Well, get to work or get blown up. I don't much care!"

Sal rolled over and thought, *As the first lieutenant, Doug will be sent to solitary as one of my first actions in my new position.* As he followed Doug, he looked up and saw Satan's Guard descend on the center. He ran toward Barb. Regrettably, he was too late. The licking had already started. He attempted to reach her, but Doug grabbed him!

Sal shook his fist at the dark sky. "Satan, you are a...."

Chapter 76

Chad Gets a Visit

As Chad lowered to sit on his floor, he noticed a devil landing. "About time," he said to the approaching devil he assumed was Lust.

The devil drew closer and Chad was surprised. It was not the conniving Lust.

"What are you doing in my abode?" Chad grumbled.

"How did I get sucked into your nightmare?" Wrath roared. "Now I'm supposed to work with that ludicrous machine? What is your problem? You used to be the Warrior! Now you are weak, feeble st—!"

Chad did not stop to think as the words flew out of Wrath's mouth. He attacked him, flying directly at his head. However, Wrath was ready for the attack. He made a quick move to his left and ducked down. As Chad flew over him, Wrath stood up and sent Chad flying outside his own abode.

Wrath flew and turned in the direction of Chad's last flight path. As he turned, Chad hit his right wing, sending Wrath into a spin. As he spun around, Chad struck him with an elbow to his head, causing Wrath to plummet from the dark sky to the molten floor.

Chad was about to pounce on the fallen joint chief, but Wrath did a backflip and managed to kick Chad while in the air. The kick sent Chad backpedaling. Wrath flew into him, targeting Chad's head with his right shoulder.

Wrath leveled Chad with several punches to his head, roaring, "Are you still the Warrior?" as he pounded his chest. Looking down at Chad, Wrath spit on him and then flew off.

Chapter 77

Envy Still Perplexed

Envy left Satan's staff meeting slightly more befuddled than when he left the Innovation Center just before the meeting. Sal presented a second absurd invention. Imagine a flying machine that could transport people and deliver items to the ground—absurd! *What kind of devil is this Sal?* he wondered. *He comes up with things no one has ever thought of before and challenges the very structure of hell! Could he be a plant from the other side? Have the Christians found a way to infiltrate hell?*

The last thought stretched Envy's imagination. For years, the minions of hell attempted to penetrate heaven. *Could it be that heaven was trying to infiltrate hell using the same tactics that the leaders of hell used against heaven?*

The thought caught him and he stopped. *No way! There is no way heaven would even dream of penetrating hell! If that was the plan and I was one of them, I would send someone like Sal: belligerent, ambitious, evil, and creative. Well, stopping Sal is the number one priority, whether he is brilliant or just plain stupid. He cannot continue to rip apart the leadership in hell. First, he poisoned Chad, the Warrior. Chad, the one who ran hell for years now looks like a five-year-old around this Sal clown! Then, he thought about Lust. Lust loves the opportunity to create dissension, and wow, there has been plenty of opportunity for that. Now, Wrath is sucked into the vortex of this crazy devil!*

Envy decided to head toward the Innovation Center. *Imagine a flying machine and a viewing machine? What will he think of next? Nothing! Sal must go. I will join with Chad to complete the Warrior's plan!* Anger and jealousy began to boil within Envy. He wanted order and Sal was chaos. No more!

As soon as he touched down, he sought out Sal. He quickly found him with Doug. As he listened in on their conversation, it sounded like Doug was actually getting excited. He heard Sal say, "Imagine being able to drop your precious explosives from the sky. You could blow up things and people—and they would be unable to hide!"

Envy had heard enough. He had to stop Sal. He flew directly into him. Envy looked back to see Doug's position in order to guard himself from a rear attack. He noticed Doug rolling on the ground. Envy's deep red eyes scanned the perimeter. There were no signs of other devils. It was unclear what happened to Doug. Nevertheless, he decided to continue with Sal.

He turned back to look at Sal. He could not see him anywhere. He was hiding!

"You can run, but you can't hide!" Envy roared.

Envy looked up and noticed the Guard proceeding toward Barb.

Chapter 78

The Guard Comes for Barb

Barb's last trip to Satan's lair seemed to be the worst. Every time she imagined it couldn't get any worse in hell, somehow it did! She tried to compare her experience to her BH existence. She thought about her addiction to alcohol.

During her alcohol problems, she remembered that the things she did while intoxicated continued to get worse and worse, and her recovery time seemed to follow the same trend. In her early alcoholic stupors, she would say dumb things like, "Did you see so and so and their clothes? You've got to be kidding me." Moreover, the recovery time from her hangovers wasn't too bad.

After a couple years of bondage to alcohol, she remembered that not only did she say things she regretted; she also did things she sincerely regretted. She reflected on one instance, when a young man came to town. Within seconds of setting her eyes upon him, she knew she would have him. After a few drinks, her prediction came true. She tried to recall the day after. Unfortunately, she could only vaguely remember several episodes of vomiting.

She burst into tears, thinking, *If only I could reach my friends on earth, I could warn them!*

Just then, Barb raised her head to see Sal running toward her, yelling at Satan again. Barb screamed at him, "Stay away, Sal. Stay far away!" As she took a breath to scream at him again, she faintly heard him say something about idea number two. *Could it be that this fool really thinks Satan is going to give him a chance?* she thought. *How stupid can he be?*

"Stay away!" she yelped. "Stay a—"

Out of nowhere, a devil who was larger than any he had seen before hit him with unbelievable force. Barb thought of applauding and saying, "Sal, you got what you deserved!"

Sal escaped the devil and started to run toward her again. He looked genuinely concerned. Barb couldn't understand why until she turned to the left and saw a large tongue approaching her face. As the tongue went up and down her face, she could feel the saliva dripping, left behind by each lick. The licks started to spread all over her body! She started to cry hysterically.

Abruptly, the licking stopped, yet she wasn't airborne. *What happened?* she wondered. Slowly opening her eyes, Barb noticed the Guard passed by her. She didn't know which emotion to feel: relief, elation, or fear. Her brain was spinning out of control. *It has to be a trick!* The good news was, the Guard kept moving toward Sal and the giant devil attacking him.

Is Satan really going to keep his deal with Sal? she wondered. *Is he really going to stop my visits to his morbid lair?* Barb's regular thought processes started to kick in. *If the Guard isn't here for me, then why are they here? They must be coming to get Sal.*

As she pieced the puzzle together, two guards apprehended Sal. *I was right*, Barb thought. *They will take Sal first and then come for me!* She started to cry uncontrollably. With her eyes closed tightly, she heard Sal's voice pass by her. Peeking out of one eye, she caught a glimpse of Sal flying by her before landing about thirty feet away. She opened both eyes to see that the Guard had thrown Sal!

Hmmm, they didn't take me and they aren't interested in Sal. What are they doing? she wondered. Looking left, and then right, she could see the Guard starting to circle something else. Barb strained to see the next victim. The devil in the middle of the circle wasn't Doug because he was off to the left. Who was it?

The ensuing struggle was impressive. The massive devil trapped in the Guard's circle put up an amazing fight. He managed to immobilize over eight of the Guard. As she knew firsthand, taking even one of the Guard out was not a trivial task.

Barb found herself rooting for the massive devil to win. She looked away for a moment to see what happened to Sal. When she looked back, the massive devil was airborne with the Guard.

Chapter 79

Chad's Confusion

Chad's wake-up time from the attack by Wrath was much longer than normal. As he came out of his stupor, he touched his face and came away with goo on his hand from Wrath's saliva. He touched his head and pulled his hand away, making a web of stringy goo from his hand to his head.

Chad's anger began to boil. He decided Wrath would have his day! For now, his first mission was to find Lust.

Chad began pacing in his abode, fast and furiously! "What should I do? What should I do? I am the Warrior!" he said aloud. With his last exclamation, he heard a thud to his left.

He turned, thinking Lust had arrived. Chad ignited his wings and flew full speed into the arriving devil. As they hit the ground, Chad realized the devil he was attacking was not Lust.

He jumped off the groaning devil, asking, "What are you doing here?"

Frankie rolled over onto his stomach, moaning. He thought to himself, *What is the point of working with Chad?* In the past, helping Chad had been advantageous for Frankie as it kept his pain modifiers down some. Regrettably, since the Warrior turned to mush, Frankie seemed to be in more distress than ever. It could be that his increased pain emanated from Chad's weakening, or that Chad continued to take his anger out on the wrong devils. Whatever the reason, it was getting quite old.

Frankie was rolling back and forth on the floor of Chad's abode. Chad watched his long-term assistant writhe. He felt no remorse for two reasons. First, his pain modifiers would increase for breaking one of Satan's ten commandments. Second, Frankie should know better than to sneak up on him.

Finally, Frankie crawled to his knees. Looking up at the Warrior, he struggled to speak, "Reports from the Innovation Center have come in." When Chad leaned in to him, Frankie blurted out, "Reports say that Envy has been taken."

"Taken by whom?" Chad replied. "Taken where?"

Frankie collapsed back to the floor. Rolling over, he gasped, "The Guard—and I don't know."

Chad grabbed Frankie's painful shell of a body and took to the air. "Where should we go?"

Without waiting for his response, Chad decided to go see the mystery visitor. *These activities are not in the plan*, he thought. *What happened to Envy? Taken!?*

As he landed at his destination, Chad tossed Frankie to the side and approached the mystery visitor, saying, "Envy has been taken!"

The mystery visitor acknowledged the update.

Chad continued, "Where have they taken him?"

The mystery visitor shrugged his shoulders.

Chad did not have time for games. "The plan did not call for this! Why did I listen to you? You are an idiot!" He gave the visitor an elbow. Then he flew back, grabbed Frankie, and was airborne again.

As he hit the night sky, he saw the Guard fly overhead. He sensed where Envy was being taken. Chad headed toward the Innovation Center. He had to destroy Sal or there would be no more Warrior!

Chapter 80

Sal Could Be #1

After the Guard's departure, it took a few minutes for Sal to gather himself. The Guard must have thrown him over a hundred feet. *How can they be so much stronger?* he wondered. *What is Satan doing to this set of devils?* He shook his head and said, "Never mind. Where is Doug?" and realized he was actually talking to himself.

He rose to his feet, then noticed Doug nearby and started toward him.

"Doug. Doug! What just happened?"

Doug just looked at him and said, "If I could only destroy this devil, I—"

"Doug, what just happened?"

Doug wanted to barrel into Sal. He stopped when he realized that every time he did something to Sal, he wound up paying for it. He shrugged his shoulders.

Sal grabbed Doug's arm. "What just happened?"

Doug grabbed Sal's arm and threw him. "I don't know and I don't care! Leave me alone!"

Wow, what if Envy is out of the picture? Sal thought. *I am going to be number one in hell! My ideas will reign in hell! I am the future Warrior!* With that thought, a shooting pain tore through his head and stomach simultaneously. He continued to think, *I could be number one! I could be number one!* This time, he stopped short of the joy he had felt on his first thought. His mind wandered to deciding his first set of tasks as the new leader. "Fix Barb" would be number one.

He got up, walked over to Doug, and engaged in a discussion about Sal's latest idea—the flying machine. Their discussion was somewhat civil for a change. As the two started to piece together the idea, two landings occurred almost simultaneously.

Sal looked up and followed the Guard's landing to his left. On his right, the current Warrior had landed. Sal's initial focus was on the latter, Chad. *How has this devil ruled in hell so long?* Sal wondered. *He is weak, he is stupid, and most of all, he has no idea how to lead! I will be an amazing replacement for this poor excuse of a leader!*

Sal continued to watch Chad. He did not want to move. He slowly turned his head to the Guard. They were on the move. *Who are they coming for now?* he wondered. *It must be me. They must be my escort to the number one role!*

The Guard were moving all right, but not toward Sal or Chad. "Oh no, we had a deal!" Sal shouted. He started to run to Barb. Sadly, his thought of compassion crippled both legs and he crashed to the floor.

By the time he rolled over, the Guard was airborne. Barb didn't struggle.

Chapter 81

Barb Believes Satan

Barb saw the Guard approach. "Come on, we had a deal," she cried out. Without hesitation, the Guard continued to approach her. Over and over, she screeched, "We had a deal! We had a deal!"

The licking started immediately, and then she was airborne. She decided not to resist because she started to think that resistance was futile.

As she landed in Satan's lair, she realized there was no way to resist Satan's will. As her suffering increased, she found herself in the same degrading situation once again. She worked to produce a message in her head, some kind of deal she could make with the ultimate devil. She had to communicate with him. Every ounce of her wilted soul worked to communicate. *I must get my message to him,* she thought. *I must.*

The harder she thought, the more pain she experienced. She tried to force the pain out, but the more she tried, the more it hit her. Then she felt his presence. She wanted to cry, but pushed the unconstrained motion back to her soul and produced her message. "Listen to me!"

Barb's pain intensified, but she was driven. "I said, listen to me!"

This feisty devil once again surprised the master of evil. After all this time, Barb was still belligerent. The will of this devil seemed unbreakable. *How is she doing this?* he wondered. *It's just not possible!* He looked at the female devil and wasn't sure what to think. *I guess this is why I keep bringing her back. She is unlike the other devils in hell.*

"What do you want feeble female?" Satan finally responded.

Barb felt two emotions to Satan's response. The first was utter surprise. *He is actually responding to me? How can that be?* Unfortunately, the surprise emotion didn't last too long before a missile of pain hit her right between the eyes. She wanted to scream! She wanted to give up! She had to fight!

"Listen to me," she said, managing a much more humble request. A second later, she eked it out again. "Listen to me."

Satan was beyond surprised and now flabbergasted. How can she do this? He looked up at the murky sky and for a second, thought, *maybe she should not be in hell.* He quickly concluded, *Nevertheless, she is here, and she is mine.*

In her mind, Barb heard Satan say, "What?!" Then, just like the first time, multiple pain missiles assaulted her. This time, the intensity of pain became so unbearable Barb couldn't control it at all. She screeched and cried.

Unknown to her, she formed and spoke her message, "I... I will...." The suffering intensified and she screeched again. She was losing consciousness. She had to find a way for her message. It had to get through!

"I...I...will...I will come here freely. Help Sal in exchange for...in exchange for no chains."

Just before she passed out, she heard, "Deal!"

The master of despair produced an evil grin.

Chapter 82

Chad's Last Stand?

Chad's anger rivaled what he felt when he first landed in hell! Over the years, he was better at managing his temper, mostly because he found hell to be a place where one constantly deals with horrible situations. You have no house. You have no money. You have no furniture. You have no roof. You have no privacy. You have no friends. All you have is excruciating pain and turmoil. The more you fight, the more anguish moves in and you realize you have no future.

He was at the point now that there was no controlling his anger. Sal must be neutralized for eternity! *I am the Warrior!*

His beady eyes found Sal. He attempted to burn him with his radiant eyes, but to his shock it didn't work. *No matter, I will destroy him!* he thought, firm in his resolve.

As he moved toward Sal, the Guard landed. As he expected, they took Barb away.

Over the years, Chad never understood Satan's fascination with the female species. If Satan had a weakness, it was for females. He had to have them. He had to toy with them. He would even listen to them sometimes.

Fortunately, most women couldn't handle his overwhelming power and would crumble beneath him. *The female's weakness toward him is probably the only reason there isn't a queen running hell rather than the Warrior!* he thought. *If Satan ever found a strong female, she would be number one, and he would be out of his role.* Chad caught himself in this daydream and shook his head.

He found Sal and drew strength from his anger. Chad attacked and began pummeling the weaker devil. A crowd gathered in the Innovation Center, encircling Sal and Chad.

Doug was in the inner circle and actually found pleasure in watching. *Sal will get his!* He thought. His sense of pleasure sent him to his knees in anguish. Unluckily, he held a stick of dynamite. He managed to toss the explosive away to one side before it exploded.

At the sound of the blast, Chad stopped to look in the direction of the explosion. This gave Sal an opportunity to fight back. From his back, Sal managed to deliver a kick that would have sent most devils to their knees.

Unfortunately, for Sal, the kick only increased Chad's anger and he began hitting Sal with fists, elbows, and feet. Sal was on the brink of unconsciousness when the punishment stopped.

At this point in the battle, only one of Sal's eyes was even barely functional. Through his cracked eyelid, Sal noticed that someone or something engaged Chad in a new battle. Sal wondered who would have the nerve to attack Chad. *Could it be the mystery visitor?* He wondered. Sal had no energy to attempt a look.

Chad was stunned that someone dared to touch him while he was demolishing his prey! The ensuing battle was ferocious!

The Guard formed their circle around Chad and Sal. Chad paid them no attention. He was sure Sal was their target. He continued to wage war on his new foe, his desire burning to get back to Sal.

Suddenly, three guards moved in. They focused on their target, Chad's foe, and quickly removed him.

With Sal immobilized, the Guard seemed to be circling around him! "Satan! Satan! Satan!" he screeched.

On his third screech, three of the Guard attacked him. *How dare they attack the Warrior!* He thought. *Maybe it is time for Satan to go!*

Chad disabled the initial three attackers almost as quickly as they approached him. He felt power beyond any previous encounter!

Chad disabled the next five guard attackers almost as fast. He moved and fought like a machine. There seemed to be no stopping him.

The remaining guard members formed a tight circle. Instead of three or five guards attacking, all the guard members attacked at once.

At first, Chad disabled his foes with the same speed and agility as the first two groups of attackers. He even held the upper hand for most of the battle and his power seemed to increase with every Guard attack. Chad believed he could defeat them.

The battle of all time raged for over five earth hours. In the end, even though twenty-two guards were disabled, Chad was being pulled through the air by the Guard he failed to overwhelm.

Chapter 83

Barb Is Back

Upon falling back to the floor in the Innovation Center, Barb was still reeling from her latest experience with Satan. Due to her great discomfort, Barb struggled to shake the cobwebs out of her mind.

As she stood up, she realized the battle of the century was raging to her left. She thought of rooting for the Guard, but realized she hated the Guard as much as she hated Chad. She finally decided the battle wasn't worth watching because she didn't care about the outcome.

Barb scanned the Innovation Center and noticed Sal was unconscious on the floor. As she hurried toward him, a sound behind her caught her attention. As she turned, one of the guards flew by her head. Barb couldn't believe her eyes. She had never seen one of the elite Guard knocked unconscious. She knew firsthand the unbelievable strength of Satan's elite protectors.

She looked back at Sal, at the unconscious guard, at Chad's battle, and then back at Sal. Barb soon realized she was spinning and spinning.

"I HATE HELL! I HATE IT! I have to save the people of earth!" she shouted.

As the words came out of her mouth, she remembered the light and her feeble attempt at escape. As futile as it seemed, she was resolute. She had to find a way. She could not give up.

These thoughts turned into the worst suffering she felt since landing in hell. Normally, the hellish pain hit one or two parts of a devil's body. This time, the pain traveled across every inch of her body like shattered glass shrapnel from an explosion.

Barb rolled on the floor violently. Though she screamed, no sound came out. She ended up rolling right onto Sal.

Sal's attempts to speak failed due to his broken jaw, courtesy of his wimpy attempt to battle Chad. He felt defeated. As he looked at Barb, he felt sorry for her. This feeling of sorrow caused his pain modifiers to elevate again.

Doug looked at the floor and watched as both Sal and Barb rolled in misery. As he watched Chad depart, he shook his head, thinking, *How stupid are these devils? They are just messed up!* He walked over to Sal and Barb and decided it was a great opportunity to inflict his own brand of suffering on Sal. He delivered several kicks to his stomach. As Sal rolled over, he saw Chad leaving with the Guard. He looked at Barb beside him and saw she was attempting to cry.

Sal wondered, *Now what?*

Chapter 84

Where Is Envy?

The Guard dropped Envy in a place he hadn't seen in all his time in hell. He began to explore the new area. It was dark, although most places in hell were dark. The floor was hot, although the floor was hot everywhere in hell.

As he walked, he noticed something strange. He didn't see any other devils. Just as Envy wondered where everyone had gone, a devil landed ten feet from him.

He turned to the devil and assumed an attack position. After the Guard attack, he was ready for anything. The devil slowly approached him. He squinted and thought he recognized the devil as Wrath. Envy was ready for battle. He was still deciding whether to make a preemptive strike when the approaching devil fell to his knees and chanted, "Hail to the chief. How can I serve you?"

Envy thought it had to be a trick! He decided to attack the head of the kneeling devil as he continued to chant. His wings kicked in and he was about three feet off the floor.

Before he launched his attack, two new devils landed and proceeded to fall upon their knees and chant as well, "Hail to the chief! Hail to Envy! How can we serve you?"

Envy slowed his wings and landed back on the floor. Another fifteen devils landed and proceeded to do the same as the first few and the chants grew louder.

One of the new devils brought a chair that appeared to be a throne. Envy eased into his new chair. *I've made it to number one! I am the new Warrior of hell!* He thought. He started to pound his chest. Another batch of servants landed.

Soon, something started to sound wrong. The chant was changing. Envy stood up, pumping his fists in the air. The servants rose at the same time. They started to transform and began to look like gladiators. The chant changed to, "Attack him! Attack him!"

The servants, now massive gladiators, swarmed over Envy. As he fought valiantly, Satan's Guard landed. Envy directed the Guard to attack the gladiators and they pulled many of them off him. The Guard then formed a circle around Envy, facing outward, awaiting another gladiator attack.

The Guard marched around the circle, chanting, "Hail to the chief!"

Envy jumped onto his mock throne and pumped his fist in the air, shouting, "I'm protected by the Guard! Yes!"

In unison, the Guard then turned to face Envy. They continued their march around the circle. Envy thought he won the chair of the Warrior. As he watched, the circle of guards drew tighter and closer to him.

The chant changed. It sounded like, "Attack him! Attack him!" so the Guard then launched an attack on Envy. The gladiators also joined the attack.

Envy fought with amazing agility. The first five guards and two gladiators were easily disabled. However, after hours of fighting, there were just too many of them. The attackers pinned him and he was barely conscious. They took Envy's throne and placed it over him. Envy did all he could to move, but his entire body was pinned. He looked up at his captors, wondering what had happened.

"Oh no!" He felt something crawling on his left leg and then his right leg. There were at least ten of them that were the size of rats. They moved to his stomach. More appeared and quickly traveled up his arms. He managed to free his right arm to brush them off his left arm. Unfortunately, that turned out to be a big mistake. The crawlies burrowed beneath his skin.

As Envy realized where he was, he let out a bone-chilling shriek!

Chapter 85

Wrath and Lust—Winners?

Now that Wrath "destroyed" the Warrior, it was time to find his next victim. *Oh no, not that scent again?* He thought. *No, I must focus. But I must have her! No, I must focus.*

He picked up her scent and headed toward her location. He wanted her. He had to find her! *Stop! Focus. Focus on…my mission*, he thought. He veered off and decided to destroy another joint chief. He even had one in mind.

Wrath set out for his next victim's abode. In spite of his decision to hunt down another joint chief, his desires kept tempting him back toward the Innovation Center. It took all the anger he could muster to stay on his mission.

After what seemed like an eternity, he landed outside the joint chief's abode.

Lust thought he heard a landing. When he turned, he didn't see anything, so assumed he was mistaken. He began to pace, thinking, *What shall I do? Hmm, maybe I will go attack the Warrior! Or, maybe—*

An explosion to his head interrupted his thought. As Lust reeled and fell to the ground, he thought his head was decapitated. He rolled over just in time to receive the next blast, this time in his groin.

Lust's disorientation and attempts to discern what hit his head were met with another shot to his head.

At least I know my head is still there, he thought just as pain engulfed his upper body. Wrath had found his next target, Lust's chest. He exploded with three kicks to Lust. The third kick sent him flying outside his abode into some hot lavalike lake.

Lust attempted to regain his composure. Shockingly, he soon realized he had much more to regain. The heat from the lava lake was engulfing his body. He felt like he was sitting in the middle of a bonfire. He was so dazed from the attack, he just lay there for what seemed like an eternity. His first attempt to move his legs and arms was futile. He wondered how many bones were broken in his body. His second attempt to move was partially successful. He managed to sit up. Lust knew he needed to get up quickly, for his attacker would certainly be upon him shortly. However, the distress from the attack and the lava were too much. He fell back into the lava lake.

It took Wrath a few minutes to locate Lust. Wrath was amazed at his growing strength. *First, the Warrior, and now Lust. I am the ultimate power.* He scanned the hot lava terrain and finally eyed his prey. He was about to go airborne when another devil landed nearby.

Wrath didn't recognize the little devil and didn't care. However, he heard the devil say something about Envy and Chad, and then the little devil flew away. He processed the new information from the messenger. Then, he shifted his focus back to destroying Lust.

He flew over to where he thought he had last spotted Lust. The dense fog from the lava made it difficult to see. He was flying about two feet above the lava when something grabbed his leg and tossed him into it.

The entity that grabbed him, quickly landed on top of him.

Although the heat from the lava was disturbing and somewhat distracting, it lasted just a second before Lust was airborne. This time, Wrath watched the trajectory of flight and quickly pounced on him. Lust managed to use his remaining strength to roll to Wrath and found himself on top of him again. Wrath was about to initiate a new maneuver when he was interrupted by another landing.

"What are you two doing?" Satan bellowed. "Staff meeting in ten minutes!"

Wrath and Lust looked at each other, baffled!

Chapter 86

Barb in Chains?

Meanwhile, Barb was still rolling in agony. She knew she had to pull herself together. She had to block her escape thoughts and her disdain for hell from her mind. If not, she wouldn't be able to think for even a second. She rolled to her knees.

She attempted to focus her mind. *Envy taken. Where? Chad taken. Where? Doug carried Sal. Could it be Sal is the new number one? Not possible! There is no winning in hell, but could it be?* She soon decided she really didn't care. It was time to focus on Barb.

She remembered the deal she made with Satan—another deal with the devil. Would it work? She knew better, though for some reason, she continued to hope. Now that her pain was down to a more tolerable level, she had to find a way to warn her family and friends of the future. The doom that hell would unleash on earth was going to be monumental, and worse, the people there would not know Satan was the mastermind behind the plan. They would be like sheep with an invisible shepherd and be bound for the existence she now suffered. *If only I had known*, she thought to herself.

Barb was dying for a second chance. Perhaps if I warn them, God will show me mercy. This thought broke the boundary of her pain tolerance and she was back on the floor, rolling in agony again.

On one of the rolls, she saw the Guard approaching. She was desperate to escape. She wanted to pray. Dejectedly, she found her hands and arms locked to the floor. She couldn't even roll to gain some relief.

The Guard was drawing closer. "No! Not Satan already! No! No! No! Leave me alone! I have to get out of here! No! No! No!" she ranted hysterically. Unmoved, the Guard reached down, picked her up, and commenced licking.

Barb fought for only a couple seconds. However, she was surprised that as the Guard lifted her, she did not go airborne herself—they were carrying her. *What could they possibly be up to?* she wondered as she tried to ignore the licking. *How can I escape?*

They passed right by Doug and the latest rendition of the viewing machine and Barb wondered where they were going.

"Put me down!" she yelled at the Guard. "I have a deal with your boss! Put me down!"

She quickly realized her mistake as the licking and groping only intensified. She tried wiggling away, but to no avail. *Note to self: Do not talk to the Guard!*

The Guard dropped her about twenty feet from Doug and Sal. That's when she saw the dynamite. Barb tried to utter curses toward Satan. Sadly, she found her mouth was somehow sealed completely shut. It was as if someone had sewn her lips together!

Sal watched as an Innovation Center devil chained Barb to the dynamite. He ran toward her. Doug saw him moving toward her. *Ah, now is my opportunity!* he thought. *Satan can't fault me for stopping Sal's interference with the Guard.* He flew into Sal's back and began to pummel the back of his head.

Barb saw Sal's failed attempt to save her.

All she could do was feel the tears stream down her face!

Chapter 87

Chad Taken?

As the Guard flew with him, Chad worried about his destiny. This was the reason for the intense battle. Chad knew this could be his last stand. If he did not win, he could be done.

The Guard dropped him into a room and Chad attempted to find an exit. He found himself banging into walls at full speed and suffering intense pain. *I must escape*, he thought. *There's got to be a way out!*

After hours of futile attempts to escape, it grew eerily quiet. *Hmm, maybe I'm just outside his office in a holding area. Maybe he wants to consult the Warrior on his next move?* Chad calmed his anger with this new expectation. He sat quietly for what seemed like hours.

A door opened and a large devil entered the room. "Chad, I've decided you are most valuable to hell," Satan said. "We must destroy Sal and his idiotic ideas."

"Yes, most evil one, you have my complete support!" Chad responded with a dash of joy.

"How should we eliminate this nemesis to hell?" Satan asked.

Chad awaited this question for years. As he started to answer, an image appeared on the wall above Satan's head. Chad stared at it. He could not make it out. The image bounced between blurry and clear. Finally, Chad recognized the image.

"Satan, what is Sal doing on the wall behind you?"

Satan turned and saw nothing. "Chad, you OK? I see nothing. Now let's talk about Sal's destruction!"

Chad shook his head several times and looked up again. The image was gone!

"Satan, I think we should dynamite the nemesis!" Chad said slowly as he looked up at Satan.

"Hmm, interesting idea, but what about—"

"Why are there two images of Sal above your head on the wall?" Chad interrupted.

Once again, Satan turned and saw nothing. "Chad, I don't see any images. What do you see?"

"It looks like Sal with a number one below his image," Chad shouted.

"Chad, Chad, dear old Chad. I don't see these images."

Chad glared at Satan and then at the wall. There were now ten images of Sal.

"You lie! You see them!" Chad complained. "I know you see them! In fact, you probably put them there!" Chad closed his eyes and counted to three, waiting for a lightning bolt to hit him. *Hmm, no bolt! That's not right!* he thought.

"Chad, my dear Warrior," Satan said, "there are no images. Relax. Let's get back to the plan!"

By now, there were over fifty images of Sal on the wall. Chad gave Satan a look that could have cut him in two.

The images began to chant, "Sal is number one. Sal is the Warrior!"

Chad looked at Satan. "I'm guessing you don't hear the chant either?"

Satan grinned broadly. "Chad, I'm worried about you. Now you hear a chant too? What does it say?"

Chad could not take it any longer. He flew into the wall and destroyed twenty of the one hundred or more images. Then, he flew into Satan. Unbelievably, Chad went right through the almighty evil one.

Satan grinned at Chad and joined the chant. "Sal is number one! Sal is the Warrior!"

Chad felt something on his arm. As he attempted to brush it off, the thing burrowed under his skin.

Chad now knew his new location. "NOOOOOOOO!" He ran into every wall at full speed for hours until he lost consciousness.

Chapter 88

Lust and Wrath

After Satan left, Lust and Wrath continued to stare at each other. Finally, Lust snarled, "Staff meeting? For what?"

Lust kicked Wrath off him and was quickly airborne. As he calibrated the direction to Satan's office, something clipped his left wing. As he turned to look, he received a kick in his head and started to spiral down. It was Wrath. He was really starting to hate him more than Chad, and he never thought he would hate anyone more than Chad!

Lust yelped as he face-planted on the ground. Severely dazed, he gathered himself to resume his flight. Lust's determination to make it to staff meeting on time enticed him to hold his head to steady his broken neck. He managed to get airborne, though he maintained flight only a few feet above the floor.

He decided to land about a mile from Satan's office. He was in no shape to tangle with Wrath again. As he landed, he noticed Frankie passing by. Frankie looked at him and shook his head.

"What?" Lust asked.

Frankie didn't speak, and Lust had no time for games. He had to tend to his broken neck. He confidently deduced that Frankie had not noticed his physical condition. Lust flew toward Frankie at full speed. As Frankie started to speak, Lust slowed down.

"Chad and Envy have been taken!"

Lust looked at Frankie. "Taken? What do you mean, taken? Taken where?" As Lust attempted to comprehend Frankie's message, a sharp, intense pain hit him in his knees. That was the moment Frankie noticed Lust had some sort of issue with his neck. Sensing his weakness, he pushed his wheelbarrow into Lust.

Lust hit the lavalike floor as Frankie sped away with his wheelbarrow. *That was a different use for my wheelbarrow*, he thought. He typically used it to remove bolted devils from Satan's office.

Lust did not have time for pain or to strike back at Frankie. He crawled to his knees and slowly stood up. Although he wanted to fly, he couldn't due to the wheelbarrow attack and his broken neck. He decided to run. Unhappily, he could only manage walking at a slow pace.

As he approached the office, he noticed several devils huddled outside. Wrath and Lust locked eyes. Wrath approached him.

"You weak devil! What are you doing here?"

"Wrath, someday I will destroy you!" Lust snarled.

Wrath took the snarl as an attack. He looked for just the right place on Lust to attack. He thought that hitting Lust right below his shoulder might displace his head, since he noticed Lust was still holding it. A grin formed on his face as he thought, *A headless Lust would be so perfect*. He let out an evil set of groans.

Wrath looked at the floor and made his decision. Attack!

When he looked up, he didn't see Lust. Rather, he noticed Satan staring him in the eye. Wrath looked down again just as Satan hit him with an elbow and proceeded into his office without saying a word. Wrath and Lust followed.

Chapter 89

Sal Is #1

Sal lay face down in the Innovation Center, waiting for Doug to stop. There was a time when he would have engaged in a battle with Doug, but he was too busy trying to figure out what in hell was going on.

The Guard had taken Envy. The Guard escorted Chad away. Barb was in chains again. *Are there openings at the top?* he wondered. *Might I be the new number one?*

Doug grabbed Sal by the back of the neck and dragged him to the viewing machine. Sal had only one thought, *One day my invention will rule earth and hell!* They had made tremendous progress on his viewing machine. It would be ready in an earth time year. After that it would permeate the very fabric of Earth's culture. It would work. It would be successful. *This invention will allow Satan unlimited communication power. He will be able to unleash his staff. Lust will show skin in every home, every day. Wrath will produce anger in every home, every day. Envy will cause unbridled jealousy. In the end, I, Sal, the new Warrior, will rule hell. Satan has to know the power of this invention and future inventions.*

Doug looked at Sal. He could tell he was daydreaming, probably about his future. *Poor devil. He will never learn,* he thought. *There is no winning in hell.*

Doug learned this lesson the hard way. Even with all of his accomplishments, Doug thought of himself as worthless. He was just Doug—fully expendable and useless. If he didn't find a way to meet Satan's expectations, someone else would step in. There were tons of souls in hell, all dying for a chance to slave at the Innovation Center.

Doug kicked Sal as a signal for him to get back to work. Sal groaned and grabbed some tools. They were both working in the same area of the machine when an image appeared. Before they could converse about what they saw, Sal was airborne.

Sal was going to protest, but knew the Guard would take him, regardless of his concerns. As the Guard flew Sal over hell, he watched one of the many daily battles below. *Soon I will reign over all of this!* he thought. *The first thing I will do when I become the number one is replace this Guard and release Barb.*

The thought of releasing Barb caused his pain modifiers to sky-rocket. As he squirmed, the Guard took his movements as an escape attempt and immediately hit him with several kicks and punches. Sal was barely conscious when he arrived at Satan's office.

Satan instructed the Guard to place Sal in an empty seat.

Chapter 90

The New Staff Meeting

As the Joint Chiefs gathered in Satan's office, each one expressed their astonishment that Chad and Envy were both missing, although many thought Envy was just late again. They were even more stunned about Sal sitting in Chad's seat.

Chad held that seat for such a long time. He was the cornerstone as the Warrior of hell. They thought it would take an act of Satan to displace Chad. The fact that an upstart devil with a wild and crazy idea had Chad off his game and had all the Joint Chiefs bewildered was unfathomable.

Lust listened to the chatter before asking, "Where is Envy?"

One of the Joint Chiefs shouted, "Forget Envy! Where is the Warrior? How will hell function without the Warrior?"

Another responded, "All I know is that if I were that devil Sal, I would not sit in his chair! Chad will rip him to pieces when he finds out!"

Yet another shouted, "What in the hell is going on? There is no order in hell! Chad is missing. Envy is missing. Some crazy devil is in Chad's chair. Where is the order?"

Satan began to speak, looking at Wrath. "Sal, as the new number one, what is your first order of business?"

The mood was surreal. Sal had a thousand thoughts all at once. He would first eliminate the Joint Chiefs. He would free Barb. He would push his inventions. He cleared his throat and began to speak.

"Satan and distinguished Joint Chiefs, my first order of business would be to...."

As soon as "to" rolled off his tongue, a lightning bolt rolled in, sending Sal reeling from his prized seat. Many in the staff meeting thought Chad had attacked Sal as a repercussion for Sal's occupation of the Warrior's chair.

Satan stood up, looking much larger than normal. A sense of omnipotence filled the office. He felt somewhat relieved that he created a new order, although, at the same time, he was concerned this change could rip hell apart. Over the last few years, hell seemed to be falling apart. The decay accelerated when Sal's invention began to develop as a potential reality.

Looking over his staff, he still wondered if he should continue to depend upon Chad's evolution idea or move forward with the viewing machine. The intrigue around the viewing machine grew by the day as the team drew closer to a working prototype! *What is the king of hell to do?* he wondered.

He continued to scan his leadership team. It felt strange to preside over a staff meeting without Chad seated at his right hand. Chad had served him well. For many years, Chad had kept order in hell. Satan didn't need to focus on order, which allowed him to focus on getting souls to hell. To Satan's disappointment, Chad lost his edge over the last couple of years. He was no longer dependable. He consumed his being with the destruction of Sal.

"Wrath!" Satan shouted.

Wrath slowly looked up. He did not meet Satan's eye before saying, "Yes, your majesty?"

"Wrath!"

"Yes, your majesty!"

Satan pointed to the chair.

Lust jumped out of his chair.

Satan turned and stared at him. "Can I help you, Lust?"

Though he had intended to speak his mind, Lust simply said, "No sir."

"Then sit!" After a long pause and giving the entire room an intimidating glare, Satan issued his orders. "Lust, your job is to generate ideas for the viewing machine. Wrath, find the mystery visitor." Finally, he pointed at Sal and told Wrath, "Then take that back to the Innovation Center.

Satan flew away quickly.

Chapter 91

Barb Redeems Herself

Barb attempted to take in everything that was happening. She kept repeating in her head a summary of the most recent events. *Envy gone, Chad gone, but where? Doug destroyed Sal. The Guard took Sal, but where? Satan keeps telling me that I have a deal, and yet my world continues to get worse and worse, like now somehow my lips are sealed.*

She attempted to move, but then came to the dark realization that she was unable because she was chained again. If she truly had a deal with Satan…she tried to shout, "Why the chains?" Gloomily, the harder she tried, the tighter the seal on her lips grew. Her mind raced a million miles a second. *The leaders are gone,* she thought. *The Guard took Sal—probably to solitary refinement. I'm in chains. What is going on? I must warn the people of earth.* As she looked up to pray, she saw members of the Guard circling the Innovation Center.

In her mind, she shouted, *Go away, Guard! Go away!*

She looked around for any escape. She wanted to run. She *so* wanted to run! In all her existence, she could never have imagined the utter sense of helplessness she now felt.

The pain was intolerable. Even worse, for Barb, was that hell had total control of her actions, her desires, and even her thoughts. This made her feel even crazier. She began to cry uncontrollably.

I hate hell! I hate Satan! she silently fumed. Somehow, she sensed these thoughts were more than thoughts. Somehow, she knew her thoughts were being heard—like real communication.

As she thought, *I hate Satan,* two things happened. As expected, shooting pain consumed her entire being.

She also discovered she seemed to be able to communicate telepathically.

She managed to look up. To her dismay, she saw the Guard descending! *Go away Guard! Go away!* she screamed silently.

Her wish did not come true. The Guard landed and circled her. They grabbed, groped, and licked her as they dragged her through the air.

I have a deal! I have a deal! she screamed silently. Though futile, it focused her anger.

At one point during the flight, she noticed another large devil flying parallel to them. Somehow, she sensed it could be Wrath.

They dropped her into Satan's lair. She immediately dropped to her knees, desperately wanting to pray. Sadly, his approaching presence disabled her desire. With every ounce of remaining strength, she thought to Satan, *We had a deal you no good, piece of....* She wanted to curse him, but could not. *I know that you can hear me! For once in your miserable existence, keep your word. You are not even worthy of the title of—*She stopped again.

Satan drew closer to her. She could even smell him, though for some reason, she couldn't see him. Still, she knew he would be with her soon. *Stop! Stop! Stop!* she thought. *I know why God banished you!*

For a second, she believed her last thought would get him to stop, or at least make him communicate with her.

Neither occurred.

Instead, he pounced on her. She tried to pass out, but the more she tried, the more he kept her awake. The feeling she had with him was worse than ever. Her only choice was to be submissive.

When he left, the Guard returned her to the Innovation Center, where they chained her up again. Barb wanted to die. Exhausted, she passed out.

Chapter 92

Wrath Feeling HIS Number One Status

After Satan left the staff meeting, Wrath remained in the Warrior's chair. He knew better than to experience joy, so he decided to experience the power of being the number one in hell, for clearly he was the new lord in hell!

He stood up and pumped his fists in the air, thinking, *I am the Warrior!*

Wrath's eyes moved over the staff he would command. Suddenly, a quick burst of pain shot through his abdomen, sending him flying across the room.

After he landed, he shook his head from side to side and tried to determine who would dare touch the Warrior. As he shook his head again, the knee of his assailant met his chin, followed by a blow to the top of his head. He found himself face down on the hot lava floor. *How could this be happening?* he wondered. *I am the Warrior!* As he attempted to roll over, a foot shot into his abdomen and sent him flying again!

In the air, he caught a glimpse of his attacker.

"Lust!" Wrath gasped. "When I catch you, you will be the first victim of my new—"

"How could you be the Warrior?" Lust smirked before flying off.

Wrath's attempt to fly after him failed due to the damage inflicted on his left wing from the last battle. He was forced to lay there contemplating his next move.

OK, I must destroy Lust! However, my first task is to get to work on the tasks that Satan gave me. OK, I need to get Sal working.

Wrath rolled over onto his stomach, pushed himself up, and leaned back on his knees. Slowly, he managed to stand. He scanned the table. Most of the Joint Chiefs had left the room. Only Sal and Gluttony remained. Wrath motioned to Gluttony, who took flight. As he departed, Gluttony shouted, "Attack, new Warrior, attack!"

Wrath approached Sal and said, "You have destroyed one Warrior." He moved such that he was nose-to-nose with Sal and said, "You will not destroy another!" Wrath's voice seemed to carry through all of hell. "Do you understand, you pitiful excuse for a devil?"

Sal thought about when he first arrived in hell. He would have laughed at Wrath and told him to—

Simultaneous blows to Sal's stomach and head knocked him to the floor. Sal's first instinct was to charge Wrath, until he played out the future in his head. He was sure the battle would be over quickly. He kept his head down and took another blow to his head from Wrath's foot. He fell back and his head snapped as he hit the floor.

"Enough!" Somehow, he quickly rose to his feet. "You would not be the Warrior if not for me!" Sal shouted. "You better stand down or you will need to find another devil to help you!"

Wrath looked at Sal with disgust. "I am Warrior because I am Wrath," he roared just as he realized his left wing was functioning again. He flew into Sal at top speed. "And don't you forget it. You will be around for as long as I need you. If you resist me, you will see hell like you have never seen hell."

Wrath grabbed dazed Sal's back and took flight toward the Innovation Center. Semiconscious, Sal was no longer a threat to him. As he thought of threats, he smelled that distinctive scent again. He knew Barb was near his current location. Wrath scanned hell's murky sky. He found her! The Guard was escorting her again.

How does Satan get everything? I must have her! Wrath said to himself. *I must have her!* With that, he found himself changing his course toward her flight path. *No, I am the WARRIOR! I must focus on the mission.* Still, he couldn't stop his desire to follow her.

With his free hand, he slapped his face, saying, "I am the Warrior!" His flight stopped and he began to free fall, quickly approaching the ground. Within a few feet of the surface, Wrath regained his thoughts and swooped back into flight!

As Wrath rose, he could no longer sense her. His thoughts of thankfulness caused him agony in his back. He grabbed his back with both hands, losing his hold on Sal and dropping him. *Should I let that disgusting, annoying devil crash?* he pondered. Wrath swooped down and grabbed Sal just five feet from the ground. He resumed his flight path to the Innovation Center and soon arrived there.

As he landed, Wrath had a new air about him. He was in charge and hell needed to know it was worship time!

Doug watched the two of them land and rolled his red eyes. *Not these two again,* he thought, *the proud and the prouder.* As Wrath approached, Doug bowed before him.

"How can I be of service to you?"

"You can be of service through true worship and by getting this piece of junk working!" Wrath bellowed. "I am the Warrior!"

In response, all devils in the Innovation Center bowed. As Wrath strutted around the Innovation Center, he delivered random shots to some of his worshippers. Restraining himself from being pleased, he decided to grow his anger. He strutted toward Sal. As he walked, he wondered, *If I were to remove one leg from him, what would he be able to do? Would it grow back? Either way, he will know who's the boss!*

Wrath picked up Sal, held him over his head, and prepared to sever his leg. Just then, a familiar scent encircled him. "She is here," he whispered. "I must have her." Then he shook his head multiple times and blurted out, "I am the Warrior!"

The scent encircled his head again. This time, he almost dropped Sal. *I have to have her,* he thought. Yet once again, he knew he must stay the course.

Wrath threw Sal as far as he could and bolted into the air.

Chapter 93

Chad Does Not Give Up

As Chad slowly rolled over, he thought he was back in his abode as his eyes adjusted to the environment. He rolled over until he was face down on the floor. He let the heat from the floor fuel his strength. He was glad he managed to escape from solitary refinement.

As the concept of solitary formed, the goal was to develop the hell of hell. Satan realized that the reason souls wound up in hell was that God could not tame them. Even Satan understood that God was the ultimate power in the universe. If these souls wound up in hell because of greed, lust, murder, etc., he was going to need many methods to keep them in line with his commandments.

As they designed solitary, they combed hell for souls most experienced in the ways of torture and death. They found the inventor of the guillotine, the inventor of crucifixion, and others. Chad cursed them all. His thoughts focused on, *I will destroy Sal. I will destroy Wrath, and I will destroy Satan! I am the Warrior!*

Satan appeared. "Chad, I'm so pleased that you are my number one. Let's talk about how to destroy Sal."

Chad did not respond.

"Chad, old buddy, come on, let's talk!"

Chad still didn't respond. Just then, images of Sal appeared again. Chad attacked them for what seemed like a couple hours. In reality, it had only been a couple minutes. He realized that he didn't escape from Solitary after all!

As Chad attacked, he heard a new voice.

"You used to be the Warrior, eh?'

Chad stopped and listened.

"To think that I feared you! You are so weak!"

Chad looked around. The images of Sal were multiplying and Satan was laughing. He could not figure out the new voice. It spoke again and Chad triangulated the location and flew full power toward it. He hit something hard. It felt like a fist. As he tried to get back to his knees, he shook his head and said aloud, "It can't be!"

"How does it feel to be reduced to this?" the voice asked. "You were the Warrior? Good thing Satan has me!"

"Wrath!" Chad snarled. He flew in the direction of the sound again. This time, it felt like a foot hitting his head.

The chanting started. "Sal is number one! Sal is number one!"

Wrath joined in on the chant with an evil smirk.

Chad attacked every sound.

Satan appeared. "What is going on?"

Chad heard his voice and attacked. However, before Chad could reach Satan, the Guard slammed into him. Chad began attacking the Guard. From his last battle with them, he had learned their attack formations. Chad quickly eliminated ten of the Guard. He was winning.

As he zoomed in on his next target, he felt something hot cut across his wings. As he turned to look at them, he saw a flash of light hit his abdomen. The second bolt sent him to his back.

Wrath let out a hearty roar as he watched bolts rain down upon poor Chad. As the roar echoed through the room, it was returned with a flash of light that quickly sent Wrath flying to where he had entered solitary refinement. The next five streams of light sent Wrath spiraling out of solitary refinement.

Chad watched the new number one receive his just reward! Though the bolts he received would have disabled most devils, they didn't disable Chad. He shook the cobwebs from his head and soon realized the real Satan might be there. The hope caused him to blurt out, "Satan, get me out of here! How stupid can you—"

Three streams of light burned into his chest before he could finish.

Chad wanted to speak. He wanted to fly. Tears rolled from his eyes as he rubbed his skin.

Satan stomped over to where Chad lay. He shook his head, spat on him, and flew away. There was nothing to say to his former number one.

Chapter 94

Wrath—"Can I Do It?"

Wrath's multiple bolts from the almighty evil one and his subsequent fall out of solitary refinement left him unconscious for many hours.

As he awoke and began to assess the damage to his massive body, he realized he could not move his head. He guessed that he had broken his neck, probably during his fall out of solitary.

The damage to his being was extensive, which in his mind might not be such a bad thing. Had Wrath simply been injured and conscious, the almighty evil one likely would have interrogated him to gain some answers to questions like, "What are you doing here?" "Why are you toying with Chad?" and, "Isn't it enough that you replaced him?" It would have been nonstop.

As he lay there, Wrath took the opportunity to ponder his future. *I must stay number one, but how?* What could he do to avoid winding up like his predecessor?

He thought for hours and finally decided that the key strategy needed two ingredients. He couldn't trust anyone and he needed a plan to increase the number of souls in hell. Whatever his plan, whether the lunacy of Sal's plan or some other plan, it had to work.

Satan wouldn't tolerate failure. Now that Satan had replaced Chad after such a long tenure, he could replace Wrath in seconds. Wrath didn't have a track record of successes as number one. Rather, he had just angered the almighty evil one with his visit to Chad's solitary cell.

Fear and worry began to grip him. It felt like the hands of Satan were choking him. He managed to get to his knees, and then to his feet. He took flight. After a few seconds, the grip kept tightening on him. He managed to rise to a hundred feet before spiraling downward.

Wrath managed to get his feet pointed to the ground to land feet first. Still, the grip drew tighter and tighter. It seemed to feed on his fear of failure. He fell to his knees and looked up.

Wrath was unsure what to do. He saw Frankie gazing at him.

"How can I serve you?" Frankie asked.

Wrath did not respond, mostly due to the chokehold that kept his vocal cords from functioning.

"Wrath, sir, I am here to serve you!"

Wrath managed to get to his feet and whispered, "I don't need you to serve me!"

Even at half strength, Wrath was still one of the most powerful devils. He grabbed Frankie, looked him in the eyes, and tossed him aside. Frankie landed somewhere in the murky swamp of hell.

Frankie's first thought was to get up and go back at Wrath. Instead, he just lay there in the hot lava. It was probably less painful than confronting Wrath, at least for now.

Wrath looked toward where Frankie might have landed. He didn't see any movement. His anger and disposal of Frankie seemed to loosen the chokehold on his neck. He attempted to roar like a lion, "I am the Warrior," but he sounded like a small cub.

He thought of his future and felt another jolt of anger. "I am the Warrior!" he said, sounding significantly louder this time. "I am! I am!"

Chapter 95

Sal Back at Work

Sal rose up from the floor of the Innovation Center. He watched Wrath fly into the murky sky. He was really starting to hate him. *How could he think he could be the number one without me?* he wondered. *How could he think that I can't take him down? Where does Satan get off with his stupid joke? They have to understand that I am the king of hell!*

"I hate this place!" he groaned.

Doug looked over at him and plotted his attack on Sal as he waited for his pain levels to drop.

"Wrath, I will have my revenge!" Sal screeched again.

Sal reflected back on his few moments in the chair of the number one. *I must have that chair! I will dethrone even Satan! I will be the leader of all hell. I will be the Warrior!* He pumped his fist in the air!

Sal felt a sharp pain in his abdomen. As he looked down, he saw a fist headed for his head. He attempted to avoid the punch—too late. The uppercut knocked him on his back. He was still shaking the cobwebs from his head when he saw Doug ready his kick to his abdomen. This time, he managed to roll over and avoid the kick.

The missed kick caused his assailant to lose his balance and fall backwards. This gave Sal an opportunity to get to one knee. He looked over at the attacker. To his surprise, it wasn't Wrath.

Sal managed to stand and regain his senses. He decided to attack. He flew into Doug just as he was standing to his feet. Doug hit the lava floor with such force that it seemed to shake the entire Innovation Center.

Sal was on top of Doug and whaling on him with multiple blows to his head. Doug's attempts to fight back were futile. Somehow, Sal was overwhelming him.

Sal was feeling the strength of his anger. It fueled his relentless punishment of Doug.

"You will obey Sal!" he bellowed.

He looked at Doug and noticed he was cowering and no longer offering resistance. Sal decided to stop the punishment so he and Doug could get back to work. With Doug pinned, Sal made sure he was close enough that Doug could feel his breath while talking to him.

"You will not strike me again, understand?"

Doug nodded agreement to Sal's command.

Sal head-butted him anyway.

Sal got off Doug and grabbed him by his back. He tossed him in the direction of an invention table.

"Now give me an update!"

"Wh—What would you like to know?" Doug whimpered.

Sal glared at Doug and delivered an elbow to his head.

Doug recoiled and cried out, "OK, OK, the most impressive news is that the ideas for the viewing machine are surging in from all over hell. It is unbelievable. The number of images and the potential could surely have an impact on soul collection from earth."

Sal smirked at him. "How is the machine coming?"

Doug turned to two devils and pointed to Sal. The two devils gestured for Sal to follow them. As Sal looked at Doug and the devils, he sensed newfound respect from them. Perhaps this was due to his pummeling of Doug, or because his ideas were actually working. *What would Satan do if my ideas actually worked?* Sal pondered quietly. *He would have to admit that I am the true number one! I am the leader of this Godforsaken place!*

Sal started to look at the ideas that were coming in from all parts of hell. He saw the devils' suggestions: show Satan giving lectures on the lack of God in the world, show Satan in a documentary about problems with the Christian churches, show Satan with the Joint Chiefs, analyzing the basis for hell, etc.

Sal looked at the devils and then at Doug. He knew the ideas were all wrong. The idea of the viewing machine was not to actually show Satan. Hopelessly, no matter how many times he tried to explain it, they just didn't seem to get it! Still, he decided not to correct them since they were at least thinking of ideas!

Sal turned to see the actual machine. *Wow, the machine is working!* he thought. Though difficult to see, faint images appeared on it.

He turned to Doug. "How about the flying machine?"

Doug signaled to two other devils. They led Sal to an area of the Innovation Center that looked like an airplane hangar.

Sal entered just as they conducted a takeoff test. The devil in the plane started running on the hot lava floor. He managed to rise to twenty feet in the air before crashing into one of the walls in the center. The crash split the rudimentary flying machine in half, and unfortunately, cut the test pilot into three pieces. As the pieces of the test pilot hit the floor, the devils in the Innovation Center pumped their fists in the air, shouting, "The machine worked!" There wasn't a hint of concern for the poor sliced up test pilot.

Sal began to daydream. *Wow, my plan lives! I can be the Warrior! Too bad Satan is not smart enough to see the brilliance. What an idiot! Why is he running hell? He seems incapable of running anything! To think, he chose Wrath over Chad or me. How could he pick Wrath? That devil is a bowl of emotion and no thought. At least with Chad, there was an intellectual challenge versus pure anger and bullying.* Sal concluded that he must destroy Wrath.

He returned to the viewing machine and began to work on the design with Doug.

Without warning, Sal noticed that he was airborne. He looked up and saw he was approaching a wall. "Doug, I thought I taught you a lesson!"

Sal hit the wall hard, though he managed to turn his body so his head didn't hit first. Rising quickly to his feet, he looked for his assailant. Out of the corner of his eye, he caught a glimpse of an incoming fist. Too late! The punch caused Sal to stumble and fall to his knees. A knee to his head nearly knocked him unconscious.

The attacker grabbed him by the back of the neck and flew him back by the viewing machine.

"You will focus on the machine!" the voice boomed, resounding throughout the Innovation Center. "I have spoken!"

As Wrath dropped Sal on the floor and was about to drop kick him in the head, Sal caught his foot and delivered a blow to Wrath's groin. As he doubled over, Sal delivered a solid uppercut. The attack caught Wrath by surprise and he went down hard on the lava floor, headfirst. Sal seized the opportunity and pounced on the downed number one. He delivered multiple jabs to Wrath's head and roared at him, "You think that you are number one? You are nothing without me. You should bow down to me!"

Several minutes into Sal's attack, Doug came to Wrath's aid, pulling Sal off him. Sal pumped his fist in the air. He managed to destroy Doug and stop Wrath. He wondered what would come of his triumphs. *There is winning in hell!*

Chapter 96

Barb and the Light

The first thing Barb noticed as she came out of her sleep state was that she was awake and she couldn't open her eyes. She replayed the last horrific visit with Satan. She could see him and he was coming closer. His image grew larger and larger. She shuddered. Her eyes were now wide open. She felt relief that it was only a sleep state and Satan was not back. Oh, how she despised him.

Barb looked to her left and barely caught the end of the battle between Wrath and Sal. She watched with amazement. Wrath was unconscious. Sal could win battles. *No way!*

Barb thought to herself, *What is up with that devil? He is a lunatic! Imagine trying to beat Satan!* She knew it too well. All Barb's attempts to make a deal with the king of devils had been in vain! Satan would reel her in and she would believe, only to be disappointed later. It was worse than the donkey and the carrot.

She tried to shout to the world of hell, "There is no carrot!"

Barb had to get to earth to warn the poor souls destined to join her. She looked up and thought she saw a flicker from the light. She made the light her destination.

As Barb searched for the light in the dark sky of hell, both her eyes began to burn. She fell to her knees and tried to move her hands to her eyes, but they would not move as they remained locked at her sides. Her eyes began to throb and burn in sequence. She felt as though they were about to explode.

For a brief second, she thought, *What would happen if anyone that was looking at pornography experienced a similar burning? There would be no more porn.*

Just then, she fell face-first onto the lava surface and chirped, "If only I could get out of here!" To her surprise, her lips seemed to be working again. As she rolled around, she noticed she had rolled farther from the stake than she thought possible. She kept rolling. Could it be she was free?

Sal flew overhead.

Barb rolled to her back, kicked her legs in the air, and sprang to her feet! It was true! It was true. She was free! She began to run, thinking, *I must find the light!*

She took flight. Looking down, she noticed Wrath moving slowly. She flew faster. *I have to find the light. I've got to!*

Something nicked her foot. "Fly faster! Fly faster!" she grimaced.

Something nicked her wing. "Fly, Fly, Fly!"

Something grabbed her foot. Barb kicked at the something. She looked left and right.

The Guard had discovered her. She kicked and kicked and finally broke free! *Wow, I'm stronger than I thought!* She glanced down. *Hurray!* Both feet were free. Someone had attacked the Guard. *Wow, I need to keep going! I can make it! I can escape!*

Barb sensed that the Guard was gaining on her. No matter what, she had to try. There had to be a way! She saw the light. It was real. She could sense the goodness coming from it. Warmth emanated from it. Barb was accustomed to the heat of hell, but this warmth was different, something she hadn't experienced in a long time. It was like love. "Oh, do I miss love," she said aloud.

She reached for the light and....

Chapter 97

Lust Lusts for the Viewing Machine

Lust looked across hell from his lowly abode. *How could Satan pick the imbecile Wrath to be the new number one?* he wondered. *At least Chad had a brain to go with his brawn. Wrath is a dope with no ability to think. What was Satan thinking?*

He began to pace. *What in the world of hell is going on? Chad gone! Envy gone! Wrath is number one? I must be dreaming!* He was unaware that his pacing had picked up from light movement to light running. He found that running alleviated some of the pain from the lava floor. *I must be number one! But how?*

After more pacing, an idea appeared in Lust's head. It was the viewing machine. *I will be ruler of this viewing machine! It will please Satan and my reward will be the Warrior seat.*

His pacing picked up significantly. "But how? How?" he screeched continually. All of this must have helped Lust's thought process. *I've got it!*

If Sal's theory is correct, then I must fulfill the promise of Lust. I will be king of the machine. Sex, greed, and the thirst for power will rule. I will redefine the feeble Christian message of sharing and caring to "Thou shalt have more stuff than your neighbor" instead of "Love your neighbor" and "Take care of the poor." I will replace it with, "You must have more and more stuff. You can't live without stuff." Stuff will become more important than feeding the hungry! The people of earth will lust for lust and they will not even realize it.

He kept planning. *Sex will reign. The drive for sex that I will create will be an unparalleled peril for earth! Sex will go from secret bedroom intimacy to "Everyone can and will do it all the time—forget about marriage!"*

What could get in the way of my plan? Certainly not Sal's master plan. My plan will reign!

An image began to form in his head. *Wrath? Ah, I should be worried about the new Warrior,* he thought, with delighted sarcasm. *I will handle him with annoyance. I will annoy Wrath hour by hour.* He will hate me, but Satan will need me for the machine. Lust pumped his fist in the air and took flight. His first destination would be the Innovation Center.

As he flew, he began to realize the success of this plan relied on Sal. *Well,* he thought, *there's a hole in that plan. Sal is a wild card. I need to strengthen the plan. I can't lose number one because Sal is an idiot, but oh, such a smart idiot. Imagine a real live viewing machine!*

As Lust drew closer to the Innovation Center, he saw the Guard in hot pursuit of two devils. He recognized one of them as the female that Satan could not resist. He decided to watch the show.

Wait! What in the world of hell is that? Lust watched in amazement as Barb flew upward toward the ceiling of hell. *Wow! She is attempting an escape!*

It looked like the Guard was gaining on her, though.

What was that? Lust's eyes had to adjust. He thought he could see more flickers of light.

As he watched in sheer disbelief, an alarming thought came to him, *Wait, Wait, Wait! She can't escape. She keeps Sal going!*

Lust took flight in the direction of Barb at his fastest possible speed. *If she escapes, what will motivate Sal? She cannot escape!*

He flew with a vengeance!

Chapter 98

Chad Escapes?

Chad lay on the floor of solitary refinement. He looked up to see his personal nightmare begin to play out before his eyes. As one of the inventors of solitary, he knew all the tricks of the intense, personalized hell experience. Few in hell's dark history had ever escaped the grasp of special punishment in solitary.

As he lay there in physical and emotional torment, he directed his focus toward escape. *I must escape. This is not real!* Deep down, Chad feared he could not escape, but he also knew he must try. He knew if it was possible for a devil to do it, of all the devils, he was the one who could do it.

By now, images of Sal were everywhere. "This is not real!" he blurted out. He felt a twinge of the crawlies on his extremities. It took all his concentration to resist rubbing his arms. The persistent rodents and insects proceeded to his back, followed by a slow migration to his groin area. Still, he resisted. He had to believe the torture wasn't real. He needed this belief to muster the energy and focus for an escape attempt. By now, the crawlies were beginning to nip and grind across his entire body.

Chad focused on the solitary refinement invention. The only way out of this misery was to resist reality and control the brain. The brain's fear was at the root of the nightmare experience. The experience was not real, although any poor devil stuck in solitary would never know this.

Chad focused hard on the invention. As he did, the crawlies began to leave. The images of Sal began to disappear. He saw the exit and ran toward it, hitting a wall. *Can I make it?* he wondered.

His despair caused the crawlies and images of Sal to return. "This is not real! I will escape!" he screeched and began to lose focus. "I must escape! I must!"

The crawlies intensified their chewing on the most sensitive parts of his evil body. Chad raised his left hand to rub them and find relief, but managed to grab it with his right and forced himself to focus again. *This is not real. This is not real!* As he moved reality into his mind, the crawlies began to slow. Sal's images began to dissipate.

The exit appeared in front of him again. He ran full steam toward it. Unfortunately, he tripped and fell and began rolling uncontrollably. He tried to focus on escape while the crawlies intensified again. "I must escape! I will escape!" he roared.

To his surprise, the last roll left him near where he projected the exit to be. As much as Chad had resisted, he couldn't hold back. He started to rub and hit at the crawlies. Anger engulfed him. "Satan, I hate you!" he growled.

Chad moved to bang his head on the wall in despair. As he moved his head, he did not hit it. *Hmmm.* He was sure the wall was there.

He had to find a way to stop the crawlies. He had to find a way to stop the suffering. He had to stop it all!

Chad swung his head harder and braced for impact, but rather than hit a wall, he did a flip in the air. He was flying?

"What's happening?" he shouted, alarmed.

Chad flipped a few more times before his eyes started to focus. *This does not look like solitary.* He tried his wings. He was able to fly. *I must have broken free. I have escaped from solitary! I AM the Warrior!* Pride filled Chad from his head to his toes.

Mistake! The pain modifiers kicked in, disabling his wings. This caused him to spiral downward toward the molten floor at full speed.

The force of the fall broke both his legs. He didn't have time for broken legs. He knew that he had to get moving—and fast. The longer he stayed on the floor, the sooner he risked discovery. He had to gather his strength.

Chad rolled onto his back. He started to see devils circling. He sensed it was probably the Guard. He rolled over onto his stomach. The molten floor began to consume his face. Chad wanted to cry out.

Instead, he informed his body that he was in charge! The agony continued to grow as the lava slowly entered his eyes.

He couldn't take it much longer. He wanted to escape. He wished his legs would heal faster. "I can't hold it!" he groaned.

Chad rolled onto his back.

Between his red beady eyes and the lava on his face, the devils in the air above could not miss Chad. The Guard began to descend, encircling Chad. He rolled back onto his stomach and managed to push himself up and rise. He was ready for the battle.

Chapter 99

Sal Struts

After defeating Wrath, Sal realized he had started to make his mark in hell. He could easily be the number one. There was no doubt that when his inventions started to cause more souls to migrate to the eternal world of suffering, Satan would have to make him the Warrior!

The thought caused more amazing thoughts of freedom to fill his mind. He glanced at Barb. Flying at full speed, he managed to free her from her chains, although she didn't acknowledge him. She just started flying straight up into the black sky. She flew at speeds Sal had never seen before. He gazed into the sky, watching her attempt to free herself from the confines of hell.

Out of the corner of his eye, he caught Doug watching him. Sal glared at him, silently conveying the message, "Get back to work, or else."

Doug wanted to destroy Sal with all his being. Sadly, he would have to wait for another day for revenge. Now was not the time. *It's probably better to get back to work than to engage Sal in another battle,* he thought to himself.

Sal began to realize he was becoming a center of power. *Look at that! Now Doug is listening to me! I am all-powerful!* Sal pumped his fist in the air and shouted, "I am the champion!"

As he pivoted, his face was destroyed. The blow that hit him felt like a speeding locomotive smashing into his head. The force of it sent Sal flying through the Innovation Center.

Quickly assessing his situation, he rolled onto his back and thought about his assailant for a second. He knew it had to be Wrath! No one else had such force and power.

He attempted to look up at the sky to track Barb, though he had difficulty adjusting his sight. At least one of his eyes was not working because of the latest attack on him. He squinted several times until finally, he thought he saw images in the sky. *Images? Why do I see images?* He figured the damage to his head was causing multiple problems.

As he continued to scan the sky, he counted well over twenty images. He was not suffering from double vision. *It must be the Guard,* he thought. "Go for the light, Barb!" he shouted so everyone in the center could hear him.

Sal rolled back over onto his stomach and managed to get up on his knees. He slowly rose to his feet. Regrettably, he wasn't ready to get back up and he fell backwards to the floor.

Sal knew he had to get up. He rolled back over to his stomach. With the warmth of the floor motivating him to get up quicker, he pushed himself to get up on his knees again. With a mighty screech, Sal managed to rise to his feet again. Though wobbly, he started walking.

He moved toward Doug and the viewing machine area. After taking about ten steps, he stopped and looked up. He wanted to watch the sky and find Barb, but he could not see even one image. Sal figured that either Barb traveled beyond his sight, or his eyes suffered more damage than he originally imagined. Looking up, he saw Doug again and approached him.

A mighty wind swept over Sal's head, causing him to duck. He turned around to see multiple devils heading his way.

He forced himself to a facedown position in the lava, and then rolled over. He saw multiple devils flying overhead and heard a woman screaming. *Oh no, they caught her!* he thought.

Sal flipped over and got to his knees just in time to see chains being reattached to Barb. He shrieked in horror. After they chained her, they abused her repeatedly.

Sal assessed the possibility of overcoming the Guard. He decided not to attack, especially since he was in no shape for a battle after fights with Wrath and Doug. He watched in shame. He knew he had to either stop caring for Barb or find a way to help her escape. He had no idea how to do either.

He looked at Doug and moved toward the viewing machine. He felt the mighty wind again. As he turned to face the approaching devil, he found himself airborne.

Chapter 100

Chad and Mercy

Chad observed the approaching Guard. He was unable to remember the number of times he had led missions with the Guard to capture noncompliant devils. *I have flown well over five thousand missions with that group. I never would have imagined I would be their prey!*

The Guard landed in force and assumed their normal circling pattern. The first group of four attacked in pairs. Chad designed the Guard's attack formations, creating many of their attack patterns and moves. As the first two guards attacked, Chad simply ducked and they slammed into each other. The next two came at him from different directions. As they approached, he counted *One...two... three,* and fell on his back before kicking straight up. He managed to connect with the head of one of the assailants. He missed the other one entirely. Chad sprang to his feet and mused, *Three out of four! That's not too bad!* The one he missed was on his feet and approaching fast. Chad glared at him and braced for impact. At the last second, he stepped to the left and clotheslined the unsuspecting devil.

Chad looked at the ground and then the Guard. "Fellows, we have flown together so many times! Let's call a truce before you all end up like your buddies on the ground." Each of the four was either unconscious or close to it. "Fellows, just give up. We can work together!"

Chad was surprised to see that over half the Guard left when he made his last point. *Wow!* he thought. *Maybe they are ready to form an alliance. I will be number one again!*

Chad's sense of victory did not last long. Another four guards began their attack. *I wonder why half the Guard left?* he wondered.

There must be another emergency in hell. That's what you get when you have Wrath running the show!

This time the attack did not come through the air. The guards simply walked toward him.

"Bring it on boys, bring it on! Just remember, I AM the Warrior!" Chad shouted.

With that, Chad flew fast at two of the four guards. He knew these two would attack first and try to hit him low. Chad surprised them, slamming into both of them. Once they were down, Chad delivered kicks to both their heads.

He turned, ready for the other pair of the foursome to attack. When they hesitated, he decided to perform another preemptive attack, starting with the guards on the left. However, as he reached his target, something hit him in the back, then in the back of his head, and finally in his legs. He rolled on the floor.

"This is not your attack formation!"

Four other guards broke formation and attacked. The surprising strategy left Chad writhing on the floor, looking up at over ten attacking devils, five on the ground and five in the air. As Chad struggled to his feet, two of the ground assailants kicked out his knees. Two in the air flew directly into him, one hitting his chest, the other striking his foot.

Chad managed to roll on the floor and get to his knees. He tried to stand. Sadly, it was too late. Three flying guards hit him in quick succession. Chad was down.

Three more guards pounced on him.

"I am the Warrior!" Chad yelled unceasingly.

Chapter 101

Sal's Mission

Sal kept turning, trying to see who had grabbed him. Unfortunately, every time he looked up, his captor clawed his head. He tried to flip out of the hold. To his frustration, every attempt failed. Eventually, he gave up and decided to save his strength for the impending battle.

Sal turned his focus to the captor. He thought, *this devil is unusually strong. I can only remember this kind of strength in a couple of devils—Chad and Wrath. What pitiful examples of leadership and number ones. Chad was fixated. Wrath is just plain stupid. By all rights, I should be the number one. How come Satan doesn't get that? Maybe he does and he doesn't care. I should be the number one!* He thought back to his time BH. The similarities between earth and hell were amazing. In both places, everyone tried to win or get ahead, but even the people on top end up reporting to someone. Unfortunately, everyone spent way more time losing than winning without understanding his or her infinite loop of despair.

Satan tried to manage earth like he managed hell, with pure deception. When the viewing machine succeeded, he would have unparalleled control of earth. Satan would be unstoppable. *What will I get from the success of the plan?* he thought.

Sal snapped out of his daydream. *Yes, the plan will work and I am the father of the plan! I will be number one even if I have to take Satan himself out. I will win!*

Sal's confidence reminded him of his early days in hell. He began to feel power and strength drive through him. He was ready for the battle.

Thud. Sal hit the floor, rolled several times, and sprang to his feet. They must have been flying low!

Sal quickly scanned the area. It was darker than usual. He slowly looked around. Unable to see much, his other senses began to kick in. *I have been here before*, he sensed. *There is something familiar about this place.*

He scanned his perimeter. As his eyes adjusted, he began to see images of items around him. *Ah, this is extremely familiar!* he thought. He set his body in an attack position and pivoted on his back foot to see all around him. *Why doesn't he show himself? Why doesn't he attack? Could I be in solitary refinement? Hmm, I doubt it.*

Sal was becoming concerned! He thought he heard a noise, but could not identify it. Spinning around, he saw a chair he recognized. *Did Chad escape?* he wondered. *If so, how? No one escapes from solitary.*

Sal heard another noise, this time behind him. He spun around again. He discerned his location. It was time to do battle with Chad.

I relish the opportunity to complete the destruction of Chad, the Warrior. Hah! Since Sal had won battles against Wrath and Doug, he was confident he could destroy Chad. He decided to entice his attacker.

"Chad, you coward. Show yourself! I have been waiting for this moment since our first meeting in Satan's office. You will regret that you ever met this devil!"

Sal heard laughter. He attempted to triangulate the source. As he pivoted, the laughter seemed to be coming from everywhere. A quick fear traveled up his spine. *Could I be back in solitary?*

His captor spoke in a deep and disguised voice, "You will destroy me? Sal, when will you learn?"

Sal pondered his next move. The voice almost sounded female. Barb? No way. If it was Chad and he was in his chamber, there was no escape. He didn't know his way to anywhere from this place. "Chad, I'm ready when you are. Let's do it!"

Sal did not need to provoke his captor further. He never saw the first blow coming. It took out his knees and put him on his back. The next shot was to his head and he started to lose consciousness. Two more blows hit him in the stomach and head, the force sending him through the air.

In his semiconscious state, his captor flipped him over and strapped him to the chair. Sal wanted to escape but couldn't move.

His attempts to see his captor were unsuccessful since his vision was still too blurry. He was, indeed, in Chad's chamber. The million-dollar question remained, who was the captor?

His captor began talking with a loud, though still disguised voice. "Sal, you have been a menace in hell too long! You will conform! You will never be the Warrior, for I will always be the Warrior!"

"You are nothing without me!" Sal retorted. "I recommend you release me and stand down or I—"

"You will what? You have no bargaining power. You are a puny little devil with unproven ideas."

"Hell cannot be successful without me. Satan knows—"

"Satan knows what? He can't even keep a number one lately—and he is playing you like the fool that you are." The captor got in Sal's face. "You slithering lowlife. Do not try to make a deal with me!" He delivered punches to Sal's stomach and head.

"Sure, hit me while I'm strapped in!" Sal erupted. "You know you won't win if we go one-on-one."

The last comment earned Sal multiple kicks to his abdomen.

"I knew it," Sal gasped. "Once a coward, always a coward."

He suffered another strike. This time it was a blow to his head. He began losing his vision and consciousness.

"Did you think your feeble attempts at getting to me would actually work?" his captor quizzed. "Sal, Sal, Sal. When will you learn?"

The captor took a moment to assess Sal. *What makes this fool tick? Of all the lost souls I've seen or met in all my time in hell, Sal is one of the most interesting specimens. No matter what happens, this devil continues to be an idiot!* He reviewed Sal's current injuries and selected a part of his body for his next target.

Just as he was about to strike, a voice shouted, "Wrath!"

The captor looked at Sal. Wrath wondered who shouted his name. He looked around.

"Yes, I'm talking to you!"

Sal's captor grew concerned and hoped it wasn't Satan! "Stand down. This isn't your concern!" he said.

"Wrath," the voice said with authority, "you need to stand down. Now!"

Wrath continued his assault on Sal.

The voice drew closer to the captor, and he recognized the devil. "Lust!" he said. "Get lost. I will deal with you later!"

Lust watched the captor and thought, *What an idiot! How can he be the number one? Satan is just not that bright!* He ducked instinctively in anticipation of a lightning bolt if the almighty evil one heard his thought.

Lust planned his attack. He would hit Wrath in the knees, knocking him off balance. Then he would swoop straight up and straight down and land an elbow on Wrath's head. Just as he was set to launch his attack, he saw something from the sky hit Wrath, nearly blowing him to pieces. The blast was so strong it knocked Lust off balance. Lying on his back, he observed a new foe capture Sal. Lust shook his head. *What in the world? How in the world? What was that beast? What did it just do to the number one? Where is Sal going?* Lust decided to follow the new captor. As he started his pursuit, Lust flew over what looked like Wrath. *What a mess!* He thought shaking his head.

Sal struggled to see his latest captor. There was something vaguely familiar about him. He felt as though he knew this devil, although he couldn't place the memory.

They traveled together for what seemed like hours, although it was only around twenty seconds. The captor slowed his speed and came to a halt. Sal was about to attack. Surprisingly, he decided to hold back because somehow he knew this devil was not a threat.

Sal decided to communicate. "Who are you? What do you want?"

The captor just looked at him.

Sal broke free and said, "I don't know who you are, and I don't care. Later!"

As Sal turned to depart, his captor grabbed one of his wings, spun him around, and placed him in a headlock. Sal was stunned at the speed and agility of this new potential foe.

The captor whispered specific instructions to him. He stressed that the instructions must remain a secret.

As the captor finished whispering, Sal had many questions. "What is the meaning of your comment on the Light?"

Sal's captor quickly released him and flew due north.

"Wait! Wait!" Sal shouted. "I have questions."

Sal quickly understood the reason for his captor's quick departure as several of the Guard zipped by at high speed. *Ah, so that devil must know something,* he thought. *Otherwise, the Guard would not be so interested in him.*

Sal realized he was free and decided to take off. Regrettably, he waited just a little too long. As he started to fly, his wing wouldn't move. Looking back, he realized Lust had grabbed hold of him.

"What did that devil tell you?" Lust inquired.

"Who was that devil?" Sal retorted.

Lust delivered an uppercut to Sal's chin.

"I will ask the questions! Now, what did he tell you?"

Sal looked at Lust and thought, *Is he kidding me? Why would I even bother talking to him? He is so unimportant in the grand scheme of hell.*

"Get lost, Lust!"

Lust was not in any mood to put up with Sal. He tightened his grip on him and said, "Tell me what he said!"

At this point, Sal was unable to speak or move, so he could not respond, causing Lust's anger to grow.

"Tell me, you miserable piece of garbage!"

Sal reflected on what the captor told him. If it was true, there was hope. Telling Lust or anyone would surely mean the end of Sal's existence. Sal managed a quick gesture for Lust to release him.

Lust loosened his grip on Sal just a little. "OK. Speak!"

"Release me and I will tell you!" he whispered.

Lust was surprised at the stupidity of the request. "Why would I release you? You have no bargaining power!"

"OK, then release me before you get hurt!" Sal said.

Lust almost smiled. "Talking to you is like talking to a child. How could I possibly get hurt?"

"I don't know, Lust," another voice said. "Let me count the ways!"

"Who are you?" Lust protested. "Get out of my business!"

The voice appeared and the being was immediately eye to eye with Lust.

"Almighty one," Lust said, "how can I serve you?" Five lightning bolts exploded on him. He fell toward the bowels of hell.

Satan flew closer to Sal. "Now what have you done? I can't leave you alone for a second, can I?"

Sal's attempts to speak all failed as his vocal cords refused to work.

Satan's Guard grabbed Sal and transported him to the Innovation Center. Upon Sal's arrival, Satan struck him with three lightning bolts before departing.

Sal was surprised that Satan hadn't interrogated, abused, or insulted him, though the bolts were as painful as ever.

He crawled over to Barb.

Barb saw Sal coming toward her.

"Go away! Go away!" she screeched.

Sal got close enough to whisper to her before he passed out.

Chapter 102

Satan's Office—CNN Update 2016

Satan shut off his viewing machine. He snarled several hearty belly growls. As he pondered what Julie Ratelle actually had in that folder, he reflected back on the master plan. Over the past couple years, Satan didn't think much about Sal's old plan. It was clear—and the Joint Chiefs all agreed—that the plan was working. Over time, the viewing machine, now known as television or TV, helped deliver on the promise of more souls to hell! With the help of TV, Satan was more in control of the earth and humans than even Sal could have imagined.

One of his favorite aspects of TV was the "talking head." Satan didn't really need to control too much of the TV news media. He only needed to concentrate on a handful of special personalities and his message reached all of humanity. The talking heads didn't just report the news. They had to make it interesting and always added their personal bias to every story. *How perfect!* Satan thought.

He also reflected on Lust's accomplishments. As Sal predicted, sex and lust ran rampant across the TV, 24/7. The tolerance for sex on TV was unbelievable.

On TV fifty years earlier, the regulators wouldn't allow the showing of a married couple merely sleeping together in the same bed. *Now, sex rules!!! Humans are even willing to pay to watch other humans sin,* he mused silently. *What a concept!*

To think, I almost banished Lust from the Joint Chiefs after one of his encounters with Sal, Satan thought. *Ah, I should have banished the troublesome devil anyway!* The trait Satan hated the most about Lust was that he really knew how to push others' buttons! However, that was the very trait that made Lust so effective in his goal of increasing the number of souls coming to hell.

Satan reminisced on the skillful injection of the master plan ideas on humans. *It was astounding to watch Wrath and Lust team up to get humans on board with the inventions and their subsequent usage. It was nothing short of pure brilliance. Their initial thoughts to the humans were that the inventions would be fun, entertaining, and drive togetherness. As some speculate, devils cannot really invent items on Earth, but they can influence the ideas. Once an invention was established, they unleashed evil ideas on the Earth at an unbelievable pace. They would target leaders in entertainment, news, and government. Once these subjects embraced the idea, they sold it across their domains!*

Satan's thoughts continued. *I have to hand it to Sal, most of his ideas worked over time.* Now Satan could show up in anyone's home at any time. The flying machine caused family dispersion except in one small community known as the Amish, and the Internet thing had become yet another playground for Lust! Just a few years ago, pornography was limited to finding a "girlie" magazine and now porn was omnipresent. With mobile devices, one can find pornography anytime and anywhere.

A noise in his office disrupted his daydream. He turned to see Sal and Chad II. Satan wasn't sure why Wrath changed his name. He guessed he was mocking either the popes or Chad. Satan couldn't care less for the reason.

"What do you two want?" he grumbled. "Also, what does this Julie Ratelle have?" Satan demanded.

Chad II threw Sal to the floor. Sal immediately shot back up and attacked his longtime nemesis. Over the years, both Chad II and Sal's strength had grown to the point that they were two of the strongest in hell. Their battles were more fascinating than any heavyweight title bout.

Satan looked at the two of them and wondered, *How are these imbeciles helping me lead hell? They can't even exist in the same space for more than ten seconds.*

He had to admit, he was quite impressed with Chad II. Over nearly one hundred years, Chad II's ability to incite fear in the hearts of other devils in hell was unparalleled. Over time, his stewardship of

Sal's insane ideas had also been amazing. At every critical juncture, Chad II would eliminate all objections to any of the plan's ideas, and then he would press Sal until the idea materialized. He knew how to manipulate Sal. However, Chad II was much sloppier than Chad I. Chad I had always performed his manipulations behind the scenes. Chad II used total "in your face" violence.

Satan spent a moment reflecting on his old number one. Chad I broke out of solitary refinement on several occasions. Once, he even had a set of twelve devils assist him in his mutiny. Chad I's raids and attacks were moderately successful. In fact, Chad I even managed to capture Chad II, then Wrath, on two occasions. Sadly, for Chad I, his efforts were ultimately in vain. They caused Chad II to tighten his grip on solitary, and specifically Chad I, by stationing guards outside his area in solitary refinement and Chad's clandestine torture area.

Satan broke from his daydream to absorb the battle a little longer. He saw it was a brutal stalemate, and both combatants were barely conscious. The office was illuminated in bright lights with both Chad II and Sal barely moving on the floor.

"OK," Satan bellowed. "Now that I have your attention. What does Julie Ratelle have?"

Chad II spoke first. "She is a lunatic. She has nothing!"

Sal laughed aloud. Chad II rolled twice to his right and gained position on top of Sal. Then he began pummeling him in the head.

Satan allowed the hammering to continue for several minutes. Then he signaled the Guard to get Chad II off Sal. Satan hoped this latest beating would knock some sense into Sal. Even after all Sal's years in hell, Satan doubted the turbulent devil would ever understand his role.

After the Guard removed Chad II from Sal, Satan strolled over to him and placed a foot on his throat.

"What was so funny, Sal? Did Chad II create a new joke?"

"He's an idiot!" Chad II interjected. One of the guards kicked Chad II in the lower abdomen, quieting him.

Satan returned his focus to Sal. "Now let us all in on the joke. What was so funny? You know we all enjoy a good joke!" Satan snarled, nodding toward the Guard.

Sal pointed to Satan's foot on his throat.

"Oh, you are having a little trouble talking? Tsk, tsk," Satan growled and removed just a bit of the pressure.

"Now, what was so funny?"

Sal stared at the almighty evil one with disdain. *I could run hell much better than that idiot could,* he thought. *No wonder God hit the eject button and threw him out of heaven!*

He decided to speak softly. "Chad II is delusional. You should get the old Chad back. At least he knew how to run hell!"

Chad II broke free from the Guard, pushed Satan away, and attempted to tear Sal apart. Satan sprang to his feet, thinking, *No way! No way! Did he really push me?*

The bolts flew at Chad II! Satan targeted his legs, arms, and chest. He wanted everyone conscious for at least a little bit longer. Satan lay down next to him.

"If you ever touch me again!" he hissed.

Chad II attempted to nod his head in acknowledgment, but was unsuccessful because the Guard was pummeling him with multiple punches to the head. After some time, Satan signaled for the Guard to stand down. When one of the Guard decided to give Chad II one final kick, Satan was displeased with his insubordination. Without a thought, he bolted the defiant guard to the point of unconsciousness.

Satan strolled back over to Sal. "Now, where were we before we were rudely—"

Just then, Lust landed in the middle of the office. Satan did not even bother to ask. He was tired of this cat and mouse game. Within seconds, multiple bolts lit into Lust.

Satan glared at him. "What are you doing here again?"

Lust pointed at Chad II. "Just doing his job."

Chad II flew into Lust. There was no controlling Chad II. He attacked everything in sight. After several kicks to Lust's head, he set his sights on Sal. His moves were amazingly quick. As he flew through the air to disable Sal, he managed to nick Satan's left shoulder.

"Who dare hit me again?" Satan's patience ended. Smoke emanated from the openings in his head. He bolted everything that was moving. He even hit a couple of the Guard accidentally as they attempted to restrain Chad II.

Satan pounced on Lust. "What do you mean, doing his job?"

One of the bolts hit Lust in the throat, so he had trouble responding. Satan delivered an elbow to his head. Then he asked the question again. "What did you mean?"

Lust pointed to his throat. Satan took the clue and delivered a knee to Lust's throat. "What's the matter, Lust? Cat got your tongue?" Satan squawked as he stood up and kicked Lust in the abdomen before motioning for the Guard to remove him.

Lust was tired of Chad II. *Chad II? Huh?* he thought. *Wrath is no Chad! I'm getting tired of Satan's inability to recognize talent. In fact, I'm tired of hell. I'm tired of the suffering and the endless game of trying to win only to lose again.* He had a theory about how the master plan escaped from hell. It involved Sal, the female devil, and a time traveler. He wasn't about to share the lunacy of the concept with Satan. *No matter what, I cannot let Chad II get away with this!*

With his last ounce of strength, Lust dug deep down and got two words out. "Plan escaped!" Then he passed out.

Satan flew to Lust and saw he was unconscious. He shook him for a second and then threw him in the direction of the Guard. Then he strolled over to Chad II.

"The woman on the Empire State Building is a nut case, correct?" Satan said with authority.

Chapter 103

Chad II Will Live?

Satan motioned to the Guard. Several guards swept in and removed Sal. Then Satan glared at Chad II, who had managed to rise to a standing position. *Has the master plan actually escaped from hell?* he wondered. He looked at Chad II long and hard. *Maybe it is time for a new number one,* he thought, shaking his head from side to side. *How unfortunate. This one had made such great progress! However, we cannot have chaotic leadership in hell!*

"What happened?" Satan bellowed.

Chad II looked Satan in the eye. He had no fear. He was the Warrior! He was the ruler of evil! He couldn't figure out how to tell Satan the plan had escaped. He had spent the last year trying to figure out how it happened. He still didn't have any concrete leads. He couldn't fathom losing HIS number one status due to this incident. *If it weren't for me, the number of souls coming to hell wouldn't have increased by 1 percent per year!*

Unfortunately, for Chad II, he felt a twinge of pleasure that quickly turned into an avalanche of agony. Chad II's attempts to hold firm in his stance failed as his knees buckled and soon he was face down in the lava.

Three of the Guard jumped on Chad II's back. One of them grabbed him by the back of his head and pulled it out of the molten lava. *What caused him pain?* Satan wondered. *I wonder what Chad II's weak point might be.*

"Feeling good about you, eh?" Satan growled. "I always knew you were the stupid one!"

As the words traveled to Chad II's ears, his level of anger grew significantly. He twitched and two of the guards that were restraining him flew off his back. Unfortunately, on his next attempt to move, at least six guards pounced upon him. Chad II couldn't move due to the restraining guards. The guard holding his head off the molten floor decided to dip it in and out of the lava several times until Satan bellowed, "Enough!"

Satan pointed at Chad II. "Now, stupid one. What happened to the plan?"

Chad II's first attempt to speak resulted in two dips of his face into the lava floor. Chad II's anger burned stronger and stronger while any attempt to move resulted in another dip of his face into the molten lava.

He attempted to speak but could only muster a whisper. "Satan! Satan, my Lord!"

Satan had to lean in to hear, Chad II's voice was so weak. He scanned Chad II's head. "You pitiful excuse for a leader. I thought you were the Warrior! Now look at you! You are no different from Sal—no different than Chad I. Now, what happened to the plan?"

Chad II's anger was at full boil. *How could Satan compare the Warrior to those inferior beings?* He thought about an attack. Sadly, there were no weak spots in the hold the Guard had on him.

He waited and finally whispered, "Satan, my Lord, for the last one hundred years I have served you well!" It took all his remaining energy to push these words across his lips. If not for a guard holding his head, the lava would have engulfed his face.

Satan's anger was now at an all-time high. He crawled to Chad II's left and unleashed several flashes of light into his side. The force of this attack sent at least three of the guards restraining Chad II flying.

Chad II grimaced as he slowly rolled over to his back. He looked up to see Satan just inches from his face. "Chad II, what happened?"

"How dare you address me like that?" Chad II whispered defiantly. He was still the Warrior. "Who do you think you are?"

As he was explaining how he increased the number of souls coming to Satan's world of eternal damnation, he was stopped short by several hits to his abdomen and groin.

"Did the plan escape?" Satan demanded.

Chad II couldn't take it anymore. "Yes, Yes, Yes!"

Satan glared at him with utter surprise. *Nothing escapes from hell,* he thought. *Never has and never will. How is this possible?*

Satan's anger was uncontrollable. Lightning bolts flew in all directions. At least seven of the Guard went down.

Satan drew to within inches of Chad II's nose. "What are you talking about? Nothing—Nothing has ever escaped from hell!" Devils would travel to earth. None ever escaped and no item ever went to earth without Satan's permission.

Chad II wasn't sure what to say. As he thought of an answer, his face met the lava again. When the guard pulled his head up again, he glared at Satan. Apparently, Satan did not care for his disrespect so the guards delivered several shots to all areas of Chad II's body. With each hit, he toughened. His glare could not be broken.

Eventually, Satan motioned for the Guard to stand down. Wrath's stare was unchanged.

Satan got nose-to-nose with him again. "What happened?" he bellowed so loudly Chad II was sure that even people on earth could hear him.

Chad II decided to speak, whispering, "The master plan did escape."

The words were unfathomable to Satan. "Chad II, mighty Warrior, clearly you are mistaken! Nothing escapes my domain!"

Chad II continued his glare and thought to himself, *How could someone be so stupid and be the everlasting king of evil?*

"How?" Satan screeched again.

Chad II continued to glare. He was unable to move and unable to speak. Regardless, he had no answer to the question.

Satan was back on his knees, nose-to-nose with Chad II again. "How did the plan escape?" he snarled.

Chad II did not respond. The Guard slowly lowered his face into the floor. As Chad II's eyes appeared again, he locked his glare back on Satan.

Satan waited for a response. He motioned to the Guard and they pulled Chad II up from the floor and stood him up with much support.

"Chad II, I can't believe you are number one! You have two sleep cycles to find out how the plan escaped." Hell lit up with multiple flashes of light and Chad II received numerous kicks and punches. He looked dead. The Guard grabbed Chad II's beaten body and flew away.

Satan sat back in his office. He looked at his soul meter and sank deep into thought. *Did the plan actually escape from his domain? Who or what could have pulled that off? What would Earth think?* He glared at the soul meter. *Even if the plan did escape, it doesn't matter. I will send my leaders to the newscasters. The talking heads will ridicule the woman and the plan! Besides, who will believe or care about a one hundred-year-old plan? Those humans don't believe in hell anyway, let alone a silly plan that led to the creation of their beloved TV and other coveted inventions. Actually, it will be entertaining to watch the humans "play" with the plan.* He turned his head from the soul meter to his desk. An evil grin formed on his face. *Humans! So weak! So inferior! So stupid. They have no idea how much influence I have over them.* He pounded his desk in victory and the glare in his bright red eyes returned to the soul meter.

Chapter 104

Lust Is Number One?

Chad II's red eyes slowly flickered and opened. He looked up at the black sky, attempting to determine his location. He slowly scanned from left to right. Nothing was familiar. "Where am I?" he whispered.

He cringed, expecting a voice to respond to him, because if a voice responded, he knew he was in solitary. He waited and didn't get a response.

He managed the strength to speak louder. "Where am I?" He heard a slight sound to his left and shifted his eyes in that direction. He wanted to move his head to the left, but he was unable to move. In fact, as he scanned his body, the only thing that even partially worked was his left foot. Satan and his thugs had almost destroyed him.

He spoke again. "Who goes there?" No response. Now there was a noise to his right. He shivered. *Why would Satan put me in solitary if he wanted me to find out what happened to the plan?* he thought. *Well, Satan is not the brightest devil in the bunch. Imagine, he almost destroyed his most productive leader of all time. Under my domain, more souls have made it to hell than ever before, and they continue to come in droves.*

He shifted his eyes left to right and right to left. He heard sounds at the five o'clock and ten o'clock positions. *I must be in solitary.* He prepped himself for major irritation and the crawlies. *They are coming!*

He found he could now move his neck. He looked left. Somehow, the sound was now on his right. "Show yourself!" he screeched.

The sound began traveling around him in a circle. He managed to sit up. "Coward!" he chirped. "If you want me, show yourself!"

As the sound stopped, he managed to rise to his knees. On all fours, he peered out, trying to see the source of the sound. He looked left and then right. The sound felt closer to him—now directly in front of him. He turned his head again.

Slam! A foot hit his head. As his head snapped back, he landed on his stomach, face down on the hot floor. He managed to get back to his knees just in time for an uppercut to knock him backwards. He lay on his back on the ground, looking up. He felt himself drifting into unconsciousness.

His attacker wound up on top of him. It licked his face and managed to move its forearm under his neck.

"How can you be the number one?" his attacker hissed. "The Warrior? Chad I dwarfed you!"

Chad II wanted to attack. Woefully, he found he could not. He still hadn't recovered enough from Satan's wrath. He attempted to identify his attacker as he spoke again.

"The answer to the plan leak is Sal." Chad II's attacker was Lust.

Lust delivered multiple elbows and punches to Chad II's head and flew away. Chad II was down again, struggling to remain conscious.

Lust headed to a new destination. As he flew away from the downed Warrior, he wondered how he had not ascended to number one. After all, he had come close to number one on multiple occasions. His closest brush had come fifty-five years before. He had come up with the idea of showing suggestive dancing on the viewing machine. The Joint Chiefs were surprised at the rebellion that developed over dancing within Christianity. Lust looked unstoppable with that new idea. He embellished it and could do no wrong. Though he had Satan's ear, just as he was about to launch his coup to gain the number one role, Chad II came in with a new set of violent themes and another new idea from Sal's plan.

Back then, Lust gave an impassioned appeal to Satan, urging him to accelerate the programming for the viewing machine. "The humans are already hooked," he argued. Lust could see a world of hundreds of millions of television sets. "We don't need to wait one hundred years!" Lust yelled at them. Ultimately, Chad II and Sal convinced Satan to stick with the long-term deception plan, insisting it would work better.

With Lust's contempt for the leadership team, Chad II and Satan had been tempted to eliminate him, but he was too valuable. Many of his ideas for the viewing machine were off the charts. Lust dominated TV and the Internet. In fact, pornography had become more addictive than the drug cocaine. There was sex and pornography everywhere you turned in electronic media.

However, for his attempts to take over the number one slot, he had been rewarded with a few years in solitary—in spite of his ideas being proven over time. After all, at present time, the number of TVs in homes number well over 200 million.

Breaking from his reflection, Lust shouted, "Not this time! I will be number one. Chad II will not recover! How could he let the plan escape?" Power emanated from all points of his evil body.

Chapter 105

The Father of Hell's Success

The Guard threw Sal into the Innovation Center. As he regained a conscious state, he lay on the floor of the center, looking up. He thought back to his "fun" in Satan's office. *Even though it would have practically killed Chad II to confess, Satan must now know that the plan has escaped,* he thought. *This should cause at least two things to occur. Chad II will go on a rampage, and Satan will become very upset that Chad II is in danger of losing his number one status again. This could give me another opportunity!*

As Sal pondered his next run at number one status, he wondered aloud, "Why would I try again? The morons running this place obviously don't understand talent even when it's right in front of their noses!" As he looked around the Innovation Center, he smirked and said, "Doesn't matter. I am the king of this center!"

As the pride bubbled up within the now senior devil, the familiar pain began to increase. First, it traveled up his spine. Then it went down to his stomach and shot back to his head. The next thing he knew, he was rolling on the floor of the Innovation Center, shouting, "I hate hell! I hate hell!" He screeched and rolled uncontrollably.

As his pain modifier level decreased, his anger level increased. "I have made this place a success and I get no credit. I get no comfort. I get no acknowledgment. Chad II—Wrath—is the Warrior? Yeah, right!" Sal attempted to spit on the ground.

He scanned the center from left to right. He saw Doug was in some sort of rest state. He located Barb and crawled over to her. Sal studied her body. There was something irresistible about her. She was still naturally attractive even after many years of abuse from Satan. Sal despised Satan for his abuse of Barb.

She was still in chains and attached to dynamite. Over the years, she managed to escape at least twice. Try as she did, each escape ended with her apprehension, extreme abuse, and a return to chains. No matter how many deals Sal made with the master devil, nothing changed for Barb.

He wanted to feel pity. It was good that this emotion eroded from him many years previous. He studied her more intensely. *Revenge will be sweet!* he thought. Another round of agony greeted Sal's excitement over his potential revenge. Sal rolled around on the floor, eventually bumping into Barb.

"Sal, stop!" she said. She pushed him away.

She couldn't curl up in a fetal position due to her chains. She frantically shook them for what seemed like hours. She had enough of hell, Chad II, the Guard, Sal, and most of all, Satan! It was time for revenge!

Sal rose to his knees and looked up at Barb. He was about to speak when the sky opened up. Chad II landed between Barb and Sal. Although Chad II was not yet back to top form, he began attacking everyone in the center. He zipped right and hit Barb. He zipped left and hit two assistants. Then he bounced back, delivered several blows to Sal, and wound up on top of him.

Chad II maneuvered his forearm under Sal's chin and ground his teeth, growling, "The master plan escaped. I know you know how. Tell me!"

Sal looked at Chad II and wanted to destroy him. Unfortunately, he was fairly immobile.

"Get lost! I don't know anything about my glorious plan escaping!"

Chad II unleashed his fury. He stopped just before Sal lost consciousness.

"How did it escape?" he demanded.

Sal stayed silent.

Chad II had enough. He went over to Barb and started the countdown.

"Twenty...nineteen...eighteen...."

Sal rolled to his stomach and yelled, "Stop! Stop it now!"

Doug was now wide awake. As he surveyed the situation, he heard the countdown. *I must stop the countdown,* he thought. Though he loathed Sal, he needed his next set of ideas. The effectiveness of his original ideas surpassed everyone's wildest and highest expectations, something he wouldn't have believed had he not seen it himself. The humans were not only watching and thinking that what Christians had long identified as sin was the new normal for behavior, but they were actually paying to watch others sin.

Humans seemed to believe that sin wasn't real. TV had desensitized them to the reality of murder, violence, and illicit sex. It was unbelievable. As a result, more and more souls were joining him in the world of continuous torment. As he reflected on the increase in souls coming to hell, he could see the effect of all Sal's ideas was unfathomable and unprecedented. Sal's inventions managed to deliver on all their promises.

Doug flew over and stopped the countdown. Just then, Chad II flew into him, full force. As Doug attempted to speak to Chad II, he discovered his voice was not working. With a wave of his hand, Chad II disabled Doug's vocal cords. Chad II leveled Doug with additional punishment until he was unconscious.

Chad II resumed the countdown, "Ten...nine...eight...."

Sal slowly crawled over to Barb. Chad II kicked him and Sal landed on top of her.

"I got the plan out!" Barb sneered.

"Seven...six...five...." Chad II screeched, "Tell me how or you will be blown up!"

Sal looked up at his longtime nemesis.

"Four...three...."

Sal grabbed Barb and screeched back, "Go ahead and blow us up! By the way, that woman on the Empire State building did not have our original master plan from the 1800s!"

Chad II looked at Sal, stunned. He flew to stop the countdown as Barb shouted, "She has the master plan we just completed for the next one hundred years, for the year 2100!"

"Two...one...."

To Be Continued

Luke 16:19

'There was a rich man who used to dress in purple and fine linen and feast magnificently every day. And at his gate there used to lie a poor man called Lazarus, covered with sores, who longed to fill himself with what fell from the rich man's table. Even dogs came and licked his sores. Now it happened that the poor man died and was carried away by the angels into Abraham's embrace. The rich man also died and was buried. 'In his torment in Hades he looked up and saw Abraham a long way off with Lazarus in his embrace. So he cried out, "Father Abraham, pity me and send Lazarus to dip the tip of his finger in water and cool my tongue, for I am in agony in these flames." Abraham said, "My son, remember that during your life you had your fill of good things, just as Lazarus his fill of bad. Now he is being comforted here while you are in agony. But that is not all: between us and you a great gulf has been fixed, to prevent those who want to cross from our side to yours or from your side to ours." 'So he said, "Father, I beg you then to send Lazarus to my father's house, since I have five brothers, to give them warning so that they do not come to this place of torment too." Abraham said, "They have Moses and the prophets, let them listen to them." The rich man replied, "Ah no, father Abraham, but if someone comes to them from the dead, they will repent." Then Abraham said to him, "If they will not listen either to Moses or to the prophets, they will not be convinced even if someone should rise from the dead."

Hell – a place where humans still hope and sadly have no hope...

About the Author

As a messenger from God, Robert hopes that *Hell Can't Wait* will help you every day of your life. Robert came from a poor background and his parents divorced when he was a teenager. In spite of living with his alcoholic dad and being separated from his brother and two sisters, he managed to make it to college. He graduated with degrees in computer science and economics, completing his MBA at the University of Delaware. He enjoys a wonderful career in information technology leadership, serving Fortune 500 companies. He has also been blessed with five amazing children and has the most wonderful and patient wife in the world. In his spare time, he serves in his calling, helping teens and providing them with religious education. His life experience and work in teaching youth for over ten years were both motivating factors in writing this book. More and more, we see Satan's influence growing, especially among our youth. It is time—"No Soul Left Behind!"

CPSIA information can be obtained
at www.ICGtesting.com
Printed in the USA
BVOW09s0508130817
491899BV00001B/3/P